BEHOLD THE NIGHT WIND

Borgo Press Books by VARICK VANARDY & CHRISTOPHER R. YATES

THE NIGHT WIND SAGA

1. *Alias The Night Wind* (by Varick Vanardy)
2. *The Return of The Night Wind* (by Varick Vanardy)
3. *The Night Wind's Promise* (by Varick Vanardy)
4. *The Lady of The Night Wind* (by Varick Vanardy)
5. *Behold The Night Wind* (by Christopher R. Yates)

BEHOLD THE NIGHT WIND

THE NIGHT WIND SAGA, VOLUME FIVE

CHRISTOPHER R. YATES

Foreword by Win Scott Eckert

Cover Art & Interior Illustrations by Mark Maddox

THE BORGO PRESS

MMXIII

BEHOLD THE NIGHT WIND

FIRST EDITION

Published by Wildside Press LLC

www.wildsidebooks.com

BEHOLD THE NIGHT WIND

CONTENTS

Behold The Night Wind is dedicated to my Grandpa, Elmer Pfleager, 8/8/08—10/16/97. Grandpa was an avid reader of the fiction magazines *The All-Story and Argosy* and a fan of Douglas Fairbanks, Sr., who, in his opinion was the best and only Zorro. Photograph circa 1915, courtesy of Jean Pfleager. Elmer is seated at the lower right, surrounded by his siblings.

ACKNOWLEDGMENTS

I wish to thank Robert Reginald of Borgo Press for rolling the dice on this, as yet, untested author. Also, "Thanks" to John Gregory Betancourt, Publisher of Wildside Press, for making the same bet. My gratitude and apologies to my dearest wife, Nancy, lovely sister, Susan Yates-Brown, and friend Holly Wallinger for suffering through reading and editing my first, second, and third drafts of this novel.

I would also like to thank the following persons and institutions for their generous assistance in making this book possible: My sincere thanks go to Beth Berning Weinhardt, Local History Coordinator and Curator of The Anti-Saloon League Museum at the Westerville Public Library, who created the Anti-Saloon League website at www.wpl.lib.oh.us/AntiSaloon. "Thank you" to the Archives/Library's Manuscript and Audiovisuals Department of the Ohio Historical Society and their online OhioPix image database for providing me access to their fantastic photograph collection of the Presidential campaign of Warren G. Harding in Marion, Ohio and the Ohio activities of the Ku Klux Klan. (www.ohiohistory.org) and especially to Teresa Carstensen, Photoduplication/Library Acquisitions Coordinator, for permission to use the Warren Harding presidential campaign poster, "America First!" displayed in the "Foreword" to this book.

Also, my gratitude goes to the persons—friends and family— who permitted me to add their fictionalized portrayals to this novel. In order of appearance, they are: Dr. Michael Conaway,

Glenn Redick, Dan Drake, Fred Hanshaw, Jon Hanshaw, and Joe Hanshaw.

Acknowledgment is made to include the following material:

We need another Lincoln / To do the country's thinkin' / Mist-ter Harding / You're the man for us! —A verse from the song written for the 1920 Republican Presidential campaign, "Harding, You're the Man for Us!" by Al Jolson.

We must keep this a White Man's country... ...When it comes to the point that they cannot and will not recognize and respect those rights, they must be reminded that this is a White Man's country! —From a 1920 pamphlet, "Ideals of the Ku Klux Klan."

America's present need is not heroics but healing, not nostrums but normalcy... ...If we can prove a representative popular government under which the citizenship speaks what it may do for the government and country rather than what the country may do for individuals, we shall do more to make democracy safe for the world than all armed conflict ever recorded. — Warren G. Harding's 1920 Presidential campaign speech entitled "Readjustment."

...ask not what your country can do for you—ask what you can do for your country. —John Fitzgerald Kennedy's Inaugural Address, January 20, 1961.

I am merely a bulldog running along at the feet of Jesus, barking at what he doesn't like. —Quote from Carry Amelia Nation, member of the American temperance movement, description of herself.

FOREWORD

Bingham Harvard is an enigma.

But then, readers of the four original volumes of the "Night Wind Saga," so meticulously compiled for publication by Christopher R. Yates, almost a century after they first appeared in print, already know that.

The two mysteries surrounding Harvard are those of his parentage (he is an orphan) and the source of his extra-human strength and speed. Without going into specifics, one of these mysteries is solved in the pages that follow, the first new Night Wind novel since 1919. The other, that of Harvard's strength and speed, is not.

In his Foreword to the Borgo Press edition of *The Return of "The Night Wind,"* Peter Coogan provides a cogent literary analysis of how Harvard fits—or rather, doesn't fit—into the normal conventions of pulp supermen. Conversely, my approach is to treat Harvard's status as a superman as a reality—something which we accept as true, and thus can explain.

This is not a new approach, nor is it original to me. It follows in the Sherlockian tradition in which the object of study is treated as a real person. Sherlockian biographical scholarship (frequently referred to as the "Game") arose in response to the discrepancies in Watson's writings of the master detective Sherlock Holmes. In the Sherlockian Game, Holmes' amanuensis, Dr. Watson, is also treated as a real person. As Dr. Watson narrates the cases, Arthur Conan Doyle is relegated to the status of Watson's "editor." In the Game, theories are proposed which solve the mysteries of the discrepancies, or which fill the gaps in the information Watson provided.

Stepping outside of the Sherlockian Canon and into the wider pulp fiction universe, the mystery of Bing Harvard's super-strength is one such gap.

The late science fiction author Philip José Farmer took this type of Sherlockian scholarship a giant leap forward when, in his "fictional biographies" *Tarzan Alive: A Definitive Biography of Lord Greystoke* and *Doc Savage: His Apocalyptic Life*, he proposed a cosmic explanation for the almost superhuman nature of many popular characters' adventures and abilities: the ionized radiation of the Wold Newton meteorite, resulting in the Wold Newton Family.

Briefly:

On December 13, 1795, at 3:00 p.m., a meteorite came plunging to the earth, landing near the English village of Wold Newton. The impact site became part of the local folklore in the countryside of the Yorkshire Wolds in the East Riding of Yorkshire. Pieces of the Wold Cottage meteorite[1] are held at the London Natural History Museum, and in 1799, Edward Topham built a brick monument to commemorate the event:

On this Spot, Dec. 13th 1795
fell from the Atmosphere
AN EXTRAORDINARY STONE
In Breadth 28 inches
In Length 30 inches
and
Whose Weight was 56 Pounds

---

1. The meteorite is named after The Wold Cottage, the house owned by Edward Topham, who was a poet, playwright, landowner, and local magistrate. Apparently Magistrate Topham was instrumental in the Wold Cottage meteorite's role in promoting worldwide acceptance of the fact that some stones are not of this Earth. The Wold Cottage is still privately owned, and is currently the site of a micro-brewery, the Wold Top Brewery, where one can procure the local brew, Falling Stone Bitter.

THIS COLUMN
In Memory of it
was erected by
EDWARD TOPHAM
1799

Monument to the Wold Cottage Meteorite

History also records that several people observed the object in the sky. "Topham's shepherd was within 150 yards of the impact and a farmhand named John Shipley was so near that he was forcibly struck by mud and earth as the falling meteorite burrowed into the ground." (*Wold Cottage*, fernlea.tripod.com). A contemporaneous account observes that:

> Several persons at Wold Cottage, in Yorkshire, Dec. 13, 1795, heard various noises in the air, like pistols, or distant guns at sea, felt two distinct concussions of the earth, and heard a hissing noise passing through the air; and a labouring man plainly saw (as we are told) that something was so passing, and beheld a stone, as it seemed at last, (about 10 yards, or 30 feet, distant from the ground), descending, and striking into the ground, which flew up all about him, and, in falling, sparks of fire seemed to fly from it. Afterwards he went to the place, in common with others who had witnessed part of the phaenomenon, and dug the stone up from the place where it was buried about 21 inches deep. It smelled, as is said, very strongly of sulphur when it was dug up, and was even warm, and smoked. It was said to be 30 inches in length, and 28 ½ in breadth, and it weighed 56 lb. ("Remarks concerning Stones said to have fallen from the Clouds, Both in these Days and in ancient Times" by Edward King, Esq. F.R.S. and F.A.S, *The Gentleman's Magazine*, 1796, p. 845.)

What many historians fail to adequately record is the presence of eighteen other persons in the immediate vicinity at the time of the Wold Newton meteor strike. We know about these eighteen people through the extraordinary and singular work of one historian.

Wold Cottage (page 17)

The historian to whom I refer, of course, is Philip José Farmer. In the course of his researches into the life of Lord Greystoke, Farmer extensively traced the Jungle Lord's ancestry, and came to discover that the Ape-Man was closely related to several other august historical personages. The nexus of this relationship was the Wold Cottage meteor strike in 1795.

As Farmer uncovered, seven couples and their coachmen "were riding in two coaches past Wold Newton, Yorkshire.... A meteorite struck only twenty yards from the two coaches.... The bright light and heat and thunderous roar of the meteorite blinded and terrorized the passengers, coachmen, and horses.... They never guessed, being ignorant of ionization, that the fallen star had affected them and their unborn." (*Tarzan Alive*, Addendum 2, pp. 247-248.)

The eighteen present were:[2]

Coach Passengers (14)

John Clayton, 3rd Duke of Greystoke, and his wife, Alicia Rutherford—Tarzan

Sir Percy Blakeney and his (second) wife, Alice Clarke Raffles—The Scarlet Pimpernel

Fitzwilliam Darcy and his wife, Elizabeth Bennet—*Pride and Prejudice*

George Edward Rutherford (the 11th Baron Tennington) and his wife, Elizabeth Cavendish—*The Lost World*

Honoré Delagardie and his wife, Philippa Drummond—Hugh "Bulldog" Drummond

Dr. Siger Holmes and his wife, Violet Clarke—Sherlock Holmes

Sir Hugh Drummond and his wife, Lady Georgia Dewhurst—Hugh "Bulldog" Drummond

Coachmen (4)

Louis Lupin—Arsène Lupin
Albert Lecoq—Monsieur Lecoq
Arthur Blake—Sexton Blake
1 unidentified by Farmer

The meteor's ionized radiation caused a genetic mutation in those present, endowing many of their descendants with extremely high intelligence and strength. As Farmer stated, the meteor strike was "the single cause of this nova of genetic splendor, this outburst of great detectives, scientists, and explorers of exotic worlds, this last efflorescence of true heroes

---

2. It has since been revealed, by researchers inspired by Farmer's original discoveries, that there were several more persons present that fateful day, not named by Farmer. I restrict myself herein to Farmer's original findings.

in an otherwise degenerate age."[3] (*Tarzan Alive*, Addendum 2, pp. 230-231.)

In addition to Tarzan and Doc Savage, Farmer concluded that influential people whose lives were chronicled in popular literature were part of the "Wold Newton Family," including Solomon Kane (a pre-meteor strike ancestor); Captain Blood (a pre-meteor strike ancestor); The Scarlet Pimpernel (present at meteor strike); Harry Flashman; Sherlock Holmes and his nemesis Professor Moriarty (aka Captain Nemo); Phileas Fogg; The Time Traveler; Allan Quatermain; A.J. Raffles; Professor Challenger; Arsène Lupin; Richard Hannay; Bulldog Drummond; the evil Fu Manchu and his adversary, Sir Denis Nayland Smith; G-8; The Shadow; Sam Spade; The Spider; Nero Wolfe; Mr. Moto; The Avenger; Philip Marlowe; James Bond; Lew Archer; Travis McGee; and many more.

It is distinctly probable that Bingham Harvard—absent any other explanation for his super-enhanced strength and speed—is a member of this great and adventurous family. He is certainly a worthy addition, especially given that in *Behold "The Night Wind"* Bing finally embraces his super-human abilities; he puts them to use in an all-out assault on crime, becoming involved in a war between an ultra-militant sect of the KKK and Al Capone's mafia, against the backdrop of the newly-enacted Prohibition and Senator Warren G. Harding's 1920 campaign for President of the United States.

Yes, The Night Wind is indeed a fitting candidate for membership in the Wold Newton Family. In the time since Mr. Farmer conducted his groundbreaking genealogical research, many other researchers have followed in his footsteps. I leave the tracing of The Night Wind's precise genealogical connections to others—or perhaps will take it up myself at another time. To pursue the exact family relationships herein would ruin

---

3. Of course, not all the Wold Newton Family members were heroes. Some turned the genetic advantages with which they had been blessed toward decidedly nefarious pursuits.

the solution in *Behold "The Night Wind"* to the other Harvard conundrum, that of his parentage.

And to those who have difficulty accepting a larger "pulp fiction universe" in which all our favorite heroes and villains mingle and interact, I leave you with this. In *Behold "The Night Wind,"* Lady Kate's devoted protector, Julius, reveals that he has a daughter, Rosabel, who is getting ready to graduate from Tuskegee, with honors.

That Julius' daughter Rosabel later married Joshua Elijah Newton, also a Tuskegee honors graduate, cannot be doubted— especially in light of the fact that in The Avenger short story "Death and the Countess" (*The Avenger Chronicles*, Moonstone Books, 2008), Josh and Rosabel are planning a trip to visit her father.

Her father's name?

Julius.

I rest my case.

—Win Scott Eckert
Denver, Colorado
June 2009

(page 21) *The Black Mask* magazine, June 1, 1923, cover by Lowell L. Balcom. The mild incarnation of the KKK as contrasted from the ultra-militant sect portrayed in the pages that follow.

(page 22) One of the backdrops of Bingham Harvard's all-out assault on crime: Warren Harding's campaign for President of the United States. Howard Chandler Christy, artist.

AMERICA FIRST!

Additional Sources:

Coogan, Dr. Peter M., Win Scott Eckert, Chuck Loridans, Brad Mengel, and John Small. "Myths for the Modern Age," *Comics Arts Conference, San Diego Comic-Con International*, July 20, 2006.

Eckert, Win Scott. An Expansion of Philip José Farmer's Wold Newton Universe, aka The Wold Newton Universe, www. pjfarmer.com/woldnewton/Pulp2.htm

Farmer, Philip José. *Tarzan Alive: A Definitive Biography of Lord Greystoke*, Doubleday, 1972; Popular Library, 1976; Playboy Paperbacks, 1981; Bison Books, 2006.

—*Doc Savage: His Apocalyptic Life*, Doubleday, 1973; Bantam Books, 1975; Playboy Paperbacks, 1981.

UK & Ireland Meteorite Page, http://atschool.eduweb.co.uk/ bookman/meteorites/-C18.HTM

Win Scott Eckert holds a B.A. in Anthropology and a Juris Doctorate. In 1997, he posted the first site on the Internet devoted to expanding Philip José Farmer's concept of the Wold Newton Family, *An Expansion of Philip José Farmer's Wold Newton Universe*.

He is the editor of and contributor to *Myths for the Modern Age: Philip José Farmer's Wold Newton Universe* (MonkeyBrain Books, 2005), a 2007 Locus Award Finalist for Best Non-Fiction book. For Moonstone Books, he has contributed stories to *The Avenger Chronicles, The Captain Midnight Chronicles, The Phantom Chronicles 2, The Green Hornet Chronicles* (which he also co-edited) and the forthcoming *More Tales of Zorro*.

He was honored to provide the Foreword to the new 2006 edition of Farmer's seminal "fictional biography," *Tarzan Alive: A Definitive Biography of Lord Greystoke* (Bison Books, 2006).

His short fiction has appeared in all eight volumes of the annual anthology *Tales of the Shadowmen* (Black Coat Press) for which he has written about such adventurous characters as the

Scarlet Pimpernel, Hareton Ironcastle, and Doc Ardan. Win's latest books are the encyclopedic two-volume *Crossovers: A Secret Chronology of the World* (Black Coat Press, 2010), and the Wold Newton novel *The Evil in Pemberley House*, about Patricia Wildman, the daughter of a certain bronze-skinned pulp hero (co-authored with Philip José Farmer, Subterranean Press, 2009).

He is currently writing a series of inter-connected "regency-punk" tales covering the secret history of the origin of the Wold Newton Family, the first of which appeared in the just-released *The Worlds of Philip José Farmer 1: Protean Dimensions* (Meteor House, 2010). Find Win on the web at *www.winscott-teckert.com* and *www.pjfarmer.com*.

CHAPTER ONE
FIGHTING BLOOD IS ROUSED

Two explosions racked his body. The first was a blast of sound; the *THWACK* of at least two solid objects coming together, startling for anyone typically fast asleep at this predawn hour. Bingham Harvard wasn't "anyone," and sleep had failed him entirely. To him, the noise was near physical. It came to him at the speed of sound, but split through his physiology faster than light. Indeed, the blare was merely a fuse for the second, uniquely personal explosion. His body was the bomb.

At a pace no timepiece could track, Harvard's gray matter transmitted the auditory signal through a nervous system unusually blunted at the top layers of his skin—thereby sparing him pain of at least a flesh wound—but oddly more concentrated elsewhere and therefore capable of reaction infinitely faster than would be the norm. This spark plug engaged the critical parts of an engine at the highest threshold of efficiency whilst still just narrowly being "human." Cellular power plants, called mitochondria, two-hundred times the number found in a profoundly physically fit person, flashed to full capacity. These cells were aided and abetted by a heart with the strength of a race horse, yet compacted to human size, and lungs, both giving the appearance of a "barrel chest" and having the volume or capacity of a barrel.

From these organs, oxygen and energy were sped to a musculature unseen in even the most advanced course of anatomy at any institution of higher learning. By appearance, muscle "volume" was normal—betraying nothing unusual from the exterior view. Bingham's muscle "mass" however, defied classification. While remaining flexible at the joints—Bingham's various "Achilles' heels"—his muscle was as dense as steel, and had the appearance of being finely corrugated, like the craftsmanship of the inner layer of a cardboard box. The only thing keeping Mr. Harvard from looking like so much polished, piled rock was a skeletal system of porous bone, having the appearance of sea corral, and the strength of iron.

Knowing of Bingham Harvard's unique physiological characteristics—although, no one, other than his family physician knew—one might exclaim "Inhuman!" or "Unnatural!" Of course, they would be mistaken. Bingham Harvard was proof that there was a God...and that He played favorites.

A primal growl escaped his mouth, building in volume as he grabbed his hood and robe from the headboard of his bed, yanking them on as he raced the few steps from bed to doorway to staircase.

The clock on the bedstand read 4:20 a.m., but even with the early sunrise of August, not a ray of light yet lit the outdoors. "All the better," Bing thought as he clasped the hood to matching robe, covering his entire body, from head to toe. "Stray cats won't be able to see me in this pitch-black outfit, let alone the coward that took a shot at my front door."

One-hundred and ninety pounds of infuriated, super-powered midnight leaped down the steps from the second to the first floor, skipping two and three at a time. A black-leather gloved hand shot out and grasped the doorknob of the front door. The vice grip would have pulped a wooden knob, but merely left adult finger-sized impressions in the brass door handle.

The force exerted in pulling open the oak door would have detached knob from wood but for the hardy craftsmanship of both; not so with the upper door hinge that could not resist the tempest and yielded all but one nail from its connection to the doorframe. Next, the wood-framed screen door, loose from the day of its installment and rackety in even a light wind, ejected from the door frame entirely, with the help of a black-booted foot.

It was dark as pitch outside. The moon and stars shuddered from Bing's wrath behind the last dark clouds from an unusually rainy summer.

The dearth of illumination and the narrow, restricted vision from the eye holes in his hood kept Bing from noticing the scrolled newspaper on his porch, just a foot away from where the noisy wood-framed screen door used to be.

The banner, *The Ohio State Journal*, with the date August 11, 1920, was face-up, but dwarfed by the three-inch headline:

SEVENTH SPEAKEASY ARSON!
MAFIA & KKK BATTLELINES
DRAWN IN WESTERVILLE!

Bingham was oblivious to anything but the seizure of whoever assaulted his residence. Breath violently exhaled in his black, pointed hood created an uncomfortable moisture. Its multilayered silk construction was engineered to stop at least low velocity bullets. Proper ventilation was a secondary consideration at best.

Bingham was a blur as he raced across his front lawn to the curb of Plum Street. Skeletal leaves and dusty earth took to the air marking Bing's path. The violence of his passing created a backdraft of flying lawn debris that overcame him as he came to a sudden stop on the brick-paved road.

Bingham's already significant size (6 feet) and girth (large-boned and full-chested) were only amplified by the loose fitting, full-length black robe and pointed hood. He stood akimbo, to keep his balance from the abrupt stop. He was silhouetted in the street by the electric streetlight from a post at the sidewalk. The whites of his eyes were the more apparent from his excited expression and their contrast to the black hood. They were two bullet holes letting piercing sunlight through a mourning veil.

Lacking only the long-handled, double-edged axe, Bingham Harvard was the spitting image of the executioner at the chopping block in sixteenth-century Europe.

This gruesome similarity was not lost on the young newspaper carrier astride his bicycle just twenty yards uphill from Bingham. A quick look over his shoulder, after hearing the crash of Bingham's screen door, caused the young boy to lose his balance and fall over, pinning him to the brick road under his own seventy pound bike. Undelivered newspapers cascaded from his canvas bag.

Bingham, not once suspecting the news carrier, guessed that the perpetrator would flee for the more concealing terrain of Otterbein College campus, just beyond the boy. With barely a second's hesitation, Harvard sprinted up Plum Street bound for Towers Hall, the center, and the entirety of the small liberal arts college.

The newsboy's name was Elmer Pfleager. Up until this moment, Elmer had thought himself a grown man, despite his age of twelve years. He had a means of transportation. So what if it was only a bicycle; he could move faster than any of the motorized buggies if he peddled hard enough. He had his own business. He wasn't Henry Ford, but you had to start somewhere. A paper route was as good a place to start as any.

Now, however, Elmer felt *barely* twelve. He was not a man, he was a scared little boy. He wanted his mom. In all fairness, even a grown man standing in the path of the awesome, oncoming rush of the black-robed Bingham Harvard, would consider his end nigh. For young Elmer, sprawled on the cobbles and staring up at an eerily silent steam locomotive dressed up as the grim reaper, his twelve years of life raced before his eyes all too quickly.

Elmer screamed. The cry was high, piercing and distinctively soprano—more akin to something from the mouth of a classically trained seven-year-old girl, not a boy just on the brink of manhood. Tears came to his eyes as self-pity and sheer terror raced to overwhelm him.

His single-minded pursuit temporarily side-tracked by the repeated, falsetto screams, Bingham finally observed the fallen newspaper boy, nearly losing his balance in the effort to break his rapid pace.

"Oh my!" Bingham managed.

Elmer lay on his side, twisting his neck and head upward from the ground, eyes bugged, gasping sobs robbing him of the ability to speak. The black-clad messenger of death towered immediately above him. An incomprehensible mumble came from under his pointed hood. Elmer looked at the figure. He did not want to die, but he had the courage to want to see it coming.

It took a second or two for Bingham to realize that a) this child was crying because of him, and b) his proximity and regalia were only making things worse. Bing pulled the hood from his head.

"Oh, son, I'm truly sorry!" Bingham took hold of the bicycle with his left hand and effortlessly lifted it clear from Elmer and the ground. He stood it up, swatted the kick-stand with his boot and bent down to help the child up.

Elmer, only slightly comforted by the fact that his assailant was at least human under the hood, quickly rolled himself to Bingham's right and sprang upward. He crouched, anticipating the sweep of the scythe known to be the grim reaper's weapon of choice. Human face or not, this fellow moved like nothing Elmer had ever known.

Strangely, the wraith didn't move in for a killing blow, and there wasn't a scythe in sight in any case. Elmer quickly swept his hand across his face, wiping away tears and sweat.

With his hood limp on the ground, both palms up, Harvard said "I didn't mean to scare you. I apologize. Are you hurt?"

Even in the darkness of early dawn, Bingham's rich pleasant voice and soft gray eyes soothed the "fight-or-flight" tension of the terrified newsboy. His thick, bushy brows matched the color of his wavy dark blonde hair, and together with the classic Roman nose, Bing had the appearance of a film star, certainly a hero. One of the good guys.

Elmer straightened his back, attempting lamely to restore some tiny shred of dignity after having screamed and cried—neither of which seemed to have roused even one resident along the sparsely populated street.

"Mister, I don't feel so good right now, and I gotta finish my route. Maybe you could go on to your meeting and we'll just say our 'good-byes.'"

"It's probably just a nervous stomach young man but—Hey! What makes you think I'm going to a meeting?"

"Look, I don't want no trouble. You shoulda left your hood on so's I didn't see your face. I don't recall ever seeing you before in any case, and I can be real fergetful, or so's my mom says. I'm guessing in the morning I couldn't pick you outa a small crowd." Keeping a cautious eye on the grim reaper, Elmer bent to gather his papers, brushing them indiscriminately into his bag.

Bing knelt to help him out. "Look...I didn't get your name."

His courage and wit restored now that he knew his demise wasn't imminent, Elmer thought fast, "Name's Charlie...Charlie Russell."

"Look, Charlie. Just answer one question for me? Did you see anyone, on foot, horse or buggy, race by here just a couple minutes or so ago?"

"No sir. Not a soul." Elmer finished re-bagging his papers, glanced at a weathered piece of paper from his pants pocket, grabbed a paper, cocked his right arm back and let fly to a stoop roughly twenty feet away.

THWACK

"Gotta go now, mister. Any more questions?"

"No son. I think that mystery is solved."

CHAPTER TWO
FROM THERE TO HERE...

November 13, 1918; Greendale, Long Island, New York:

"Mr. Chester has symptoms of the flu, Mr. and Mrs. Harvard; the cough, the aching head, general weakness, a fever, all the usual symptoms of garden-variety influenza. I cannot be certain at this early stage that we are dealing with the Spanish Flu. Sterling tells me that you called me, Mrs. Harvard, at the onset of symptoms, so he could be playing golf next week...or not."

"'Or not'? asked Mrs. Harvard. "What are we to make of the fact, Dr. Conaway, that you have worn a gauze face mask from the moment Julius drove you to Myquest...and that you are still wearing it in the company of otherwise healthy persons? Is there some other fact we should know?"

"I do not mean to put your considerable powers of deduction to the test Mrs. Harvard," replied Dr. Conaway. "I have treated every member of this household for as long as you have resided here at Myquest, and before." The physician took a nervous glance at Bingham Harvard. "In that time you have disclosed to me your experiences as a New York City police detective. It seems that you would not have hastened to contact me on the basis of a single cough if you too did not suspect that the Spanish Flu pandemic had finally struck your wonderful estate here on Long Island.

"You are aware of all of the facts that seem to point to Sterling Chester's diagnosis. He has just returned from an extended tour of the globe—from Egypt to the African sub-continent and back through the principle port here in New York. His vessel docked alongside many boats returning from the European war front with hundreds of thousands of our doughboys on board—many of whom were already infected with the Spanish Flu. Add to that Mr. Chester's advanced years; he is within reaching distance of seventy-two. He would tell you that he's no spring chicken."

Dr. Conaway continued, "Flu is also highly contagious. It is transmitted by inhaling a respiratory droplet from an infected person or by indirect contact, such as drinking from a contaminated glass. I guess that explains clearly enough why I am wearing a mask. Consequently, I strongly encourage you to take advantage of the New York public health department's mask distribution program."

The doctor sighed. "I have had the unfortunate experience of having signed death certificates for entire households...and their immediate neighbors just days apart over these last few months. This is a fact I wish I did not have to convey, let alone experience, but I hope you understand."

Bingham Harvard had remained quiet and contemplative up to this point, but interjected, causing the M.D. to visibly tense-up, "I appreciate your candor, Doctor. Centropolis Bank, of which you know I am president, is operating on a skeleton staff—with as many transactions conducted by telephone and mail service as is possible. What should we and Mr. Chester look for in these coming days as far as threatening symptoms?"

The family doctor recovered his nerves and turned to look at the master of Myquest. His skittishness in the presence of Bingham Harvard was not a reflection of his opinion of the man...but a byproduct of the medical anomalies that comprised this gentleman to which only he, the trusted family doctor, was privy. His years of medical training and many more of varied medical practice dictated to Michael Conaway that Bingham Harvard could not be a living, breathing human. And yet there he was. The chair Mr. Harvard sat in should be a splintered heap. But it wasn't. His slippered feet should have left noticeable impressions in the oak flooring. But they didn't. Dr. Conaway respected and admired Bingham Harvard for his fiscal acumen and impeccable manners. But as a medical specimen he was terrifying.

"Please call me Michael, Bingham, we are friends here. The disease starts off as any other flu. Sterling has those symptoms. My experience with the Spanish Flu indicates that the body temperature, breathing and heart rate will increase rapidly. Pneumonia comes next. The lungs will fill with liquid, drowning the patient and turning him blue from lack of air. Patients bleed from every orifice: mouths, noses, ears, eyes. Most who are infected are dead by the fifth day. Those who do survive often suffer temporary or permanent brain damage— Oh! Mrs. Harvard, please forgive me...."

Lady Kate bowed under the weight of the graphic prognosis, clasping her hands to her tear-streaked face. She excused herself and hurriedly began to leave the room. With her back to Bingham and Dr. Conaway, she gasped, "I fear my womanly sensitivities have come to the fore, dear Doctor. I do not mean to 'kill the messenger,' no apology necessary. Practically, however, in light of your information, I do have many pressing arrangements to make."

On Katherine's departure, Dr. Conaway turned back to Bingham, "I fear that my experiences at the front line of this battle against the plague has numbed me to its horrors. Just last month, in one day, New York tallied up over eight hundred and fifty dead...too many of those were my patients. Please forgive me, Bingham."

"Say nothing more, Doctor...Michael. There is something sadly comforting in the knowledge that we are by no means alone in our tragedy. Is there anything we can do for Mr. Chester?"

"Sterling will need bed rest and extra fluids—at least one full glass of water or juice every hour. Without a cure, or even a known cause, this is all I can advise by way of treatment."

"Thank you. May I visit with him now?"

"With the proper precautions, I see no reason why you cannot spend a few minutes in calm discourse. Here," said Dr. Conaway, as he handed Bingham an inch-thick stack of layered gauze with dangling strings, "Please let me tie this mask on you, and take a few extra until Kate can secure a more considerable supply."

* * * * * * *

"Bingham, is that you?"

"Yes, gov'nor, I am here."

"Dr. Conaway certainly comes prepared; he had this circus-tent-sized netting on his person somewhere and tossed it over the canopy of my bed. It reminds of my sleeping quarters along the Nile, except I doubt a sand flea could squeeze through the mesh on this."

"Dr. Conaway is very efficient." Harvard said, disinterestedly. Although stoic during his conversation with Dr. Conaway, his resolve began to melt in the presence of this man, Sterling Chester, who raised him and loved him as a son. The fact that they did not share a drop of blood made Sterling's sacrifices all the more praiseworthy.

"He is also very, very good at what he does, Bing."

"What do you mean by that?"

"Please, Bingham. I am old, but my mind is still sharp. My number is up."

Sterling slapped around the gossamer netting until he found an opening and grasped at Bingham's hand. Bing responded by clasping his foster father's hand in both of his. His chest tightened and his throat hitched. He fought a losing battle against deep-felt emotion and tears began to flow.

He managed to say between sobs, "It should not have to come to this, for you, gov'nor. You are too good a man."

"I am flattered that you entertain the idea that I am too good to die, Bing. But, we all pass on, son. It is neither good nor evil. There isn't shame in death; the shame comes when you realize, at death's door, that you have not lived to your potential. Like the banker I have been for a lifetime, I have made a good accounting. Alone, I have raised an extraordinary child and I have had the supreme pleasure to see him grow into an honorable, decent man." Aching muscles notwithstanding, Sterling doubled his grip on his son's hands.

"I succeeded my own father as president of a sound institution of personal and business finance in the largest city in the world. When my term had run its natural course, I was blessed to have the very capable, competent hands of my own boy to take the helm. Providence endowed me with the skills and temperament to be a banker and I believe that I have made good, and more."

"You have indeed provided to me a trim ship to sail, gov'nor. The Centropolis Bank exists only from yours and your father's labors. These last few years there has been little for me to accomplish as the president, short of the day-to-day transactions, because of the remarkable foundation and reputation you have established."

"Bing, running a bank, even the Centropolis Bank, is a task wasted on you."

"Huh?" responded Bingham, the word muffled through the gauze mask, now saturated with tears. He had lowered his head in embarrassment over his freely flowing emotion, but now it involuntarily snapped to attention in response to Sterling's odd declaration.

"Fate, God, or some biological inheritance from my parents predisposed me to be a banker...and a damned good one. But, Bingham you were cut from entirely different cloth.

"I sent you to Harvard University and groomed you as a banker because that is exactly what my father did for me. It was all that I knew. How could I have known...how would anyone have known precisely how to foster an übermensch?"

Concern for his foster father and self-pity for his feared loss of a loved one began to ebb ever so slightly to make room for confusion and frustration. "Are you telling me, sir, that it is *I* who will have regret upon my deathbed, that *I* have not 'lived to my potential?'"

"That is precisely what I am saying, Bing. Please, do not feel angry at me. It is not your fault. You had but one parent, one role model, and you have done the best under those restraints. You have made yourself equal to me...but you can go so much farther." Sterling inched his back further up on the headboard and leaned with his head forward, staring at his foster son with intensity.

Even through the fine netting that warped his image, Bingham was taken by Sterling's sincerity and passion. "Do not misunderstand. Your life and experiences have not been wasted. It is simply that, in your mid-thirties, it is time to move on...to graduate, if you will, and I am ill-equipped to take you there.

"What better training for a man who has the voice to command legions than to condition it to speak in the hushed tones requisite for the conduct of business in the columned chamber of a bank? How better to acclimate Herculean muscle and the strength capable of rending the limbs from a man like husk from corn than by counting and sorting delicate paper currency, or stacking coins? You could have been the proverbial 'bull in the china shop,' Bingham—a threat not only to others, but to yourself—but for your experiences to date.

Sterling continued; "And the lessons you have learned from your run-ins with the law and unscrupulous villains!? You have been robbed of your reputation and my fatherly love by a corrupt New York City police department, and earned an alias, the Night Wind. Your own beautiful wife has been abducted from under your nose in a plot financed by money stolen from your bank. And a notorious, murderous counterfeiter, hunted for years by federal authorities infiltrated *your* home, blackmailed your wife and attempted to rob your houseguests."

Sterling paused for breath and swallowed. "It would seem that despite your wish to remain discreet, to stifle your God-given, God-like strength, the universal battle of good versus evil has repeatedly sought you out and forced you to engage, albeit subtly thus far. I take no stock in this growing fad of occultism and fortune-telling, but I am certain that providence has called you to battle, Bingham, and it is high time you took that battle to the villain instead of awaiting fate to drop yet another scoundrel on your doorstep."

The elder banker coughed thickly and leaned his head against the headboard again.

"What would you have me do, sir?" asked Bingham, shocked. "Romp around the globe, righting wrongs like some modern day Sir Galahad? I have a wife, a household to maintain, and a grand banking institution to guide."

"Horse-feathers, Bing! Ward Cheever has been cashier under you and I both, and knows Centropolis from the bottom up. You could do much worse than to nominate him to the board of directors. As for maintenance of your household, what of it?! From your youth you have squirreled away your allowance, invested your salary as a young adult and sold your stock as president to invest in enormous swaths of real estate in the most lucrative holdings conceivable—Manhattan Island. It is advisable that you do the same with the significant wealth and holdings from my estate. That wealth will sustain you, and endless generations of Harvards to come."

Sterling's voice was beginning to fade from the exertion, but still he continued. "Do not discredit your dear wife by suggesting that she would hesitate even a moment to give her all to your new-found destiny. It is, in fact, a destiny she shares with you, even before either of you realized it. She has been for a time an undercover police detective for the New York police department. Before that she had already commissioned the construction of a super-charged, imitation taxicab and brought along her loyal servitor, Julius, to act as driver and protector. Her thirst for adventure was not stifled upon your marriage, if the construction and use of her trap-infested chalet, the 'Nest' is any evidence. It was she who captured and taunted the villain who invaded your home, Myquest, inside her personal 'funhouse.'"

Sterling hesitated for a moment, then continued with restored determination, "There is one thing more I must tell you Bing, and then I must rest. It is fitting to disclose this information now, as it must put to rest even fleeting reservations you may have as to fulfilling your potential. It is about your heritage."

Harvard's left brow arched, as did his upper lip, a subconscious, physical manifestation of his rapt attention. So attentive was he that he forgot the circumstances of Sterling's condition and swept the annoying face mask to his neck. "You have repeatedly informed me, sir, that there was nothing to tell on that subject. I was a foundling, without name or pedigree."

"And that is no less true today, Bing" agreed Sterling. "The circumstances leading to my custody do not reveal anything of your bloodline, but even the few, seemingly inconsequential facts I know may prove useful to you in your psychological exodus from banker to bane of villainy."

He began, "It was a brutally cold January day, over three decades ago. I was the cashier at Centropolis Bank with the duty to unlock and light up each morning. I noticed a woman huddled in the foyer between the interior and exterior doors. She was out of the merciless wind, but still exposed to twenty below zero temperatures. I did not see you at all at first. You were thickly swaddled and hidden under her threadbare coat. She might have been twenty years old, but appeared much older. Her skin was raw from extreme cold and her blond, matted hair long and in need of combing. But a small fire sparked in her eyes when I approached. 'You are a good man,' she said, as if she had any basis whatsoever to know me. I knelt down and gave her my attention. I could see then your little nubbin' head, just peaking beneath your mother's chin.

"'He is all that I have, all that I am,' she gasped. 'But he is for this world, not for me. He is my gift to you first, and then from you to humanity.' She said this between coughs that seemed to tear at her fragile frame. At the time her declaration seemed a normal thing for a mother to think; to say. What matron would not think her child a blessed gift? Little did I know at the time how literal she meant her brief expression. How could I have known that a babe just a month or less in age would have the strength of ten men, the forgiving soul of a saint?

"As she raised her head to talk I saw that her coughs were not without consequence. Blood, some dried, most fresh, clung to her shriveled lower lip and chin. Droplets spattered your bald head.

"'What is his name?' was all I could think to say in my shock and pity.

"'His name is Bingham...,' and another torrent of coughing interrupted, this time seeming to rob her of her final breath. I heard what sounded like an incomplete name, 'Har...,' and that was it. She rolled over on her back leaving you to wriggle on her chest."

With a deep sigh, Sterling went on: "I picked you up, unlocked the interior door to the bank and hit the alarm bell, as the telephone was not invented yet and I needed to summon the authorities.

"The experience overcame me and it seemed then, as I maintain now, the only thing to do was to provide for you and raise you as my own. Nothing on your mother's person indicated hers or a father's identity. The formal foster care process required I provide *a* full name for you, so I took my best guess, along with some thought to my alma mater, and dubbed you 'Bingham Harvard.'

"Let this be my last comment on the matter, Bing, because I am tiring: Wrapped in your swaddling was a poem by John Greenleaf Whittier. It was handwritten on the back of a Nick Carter, nickel-detective magazine cover. The words were faded, but a line was underlined. I'll never forget what it said, and neither should you: 'The hope of all who suffer, The dread of all who wrong.'" Coughs wracked Sterling's body.

After a long moment he continued, hoarsely, "It is not an exaggeration, Bing, that your mother thought you were justice personified and she had evidence of your strength. There was a small, solid lead toy soldier in your infant hands, and *your fingerprints were deeply embedded in the body*. She harbored very high hopes for you.

"Those hopes could have had nothing to do with banking. You were born an original, Bing. Don't die a copy."

And with those words, Sterling commenced another fit of coughing and waved a dazed and confused Bingham from the room.

CHAPTER THREE
...AND BACK AGAIN

"Charlie. Charlie!" Bingham raised his voice to the departing newsboy. Every exuberant fling of a paper threatened to topple the inexpert bike rider. At least three rolled and rubber-banded papers had been left behind after Elmer's, aka Charlie's, fall from his bike. Bingham knew, by route's end, that those three papers would be missed.

Despite Bingham's clear, resounding voice, Elmer didn't acknowledge him. Forgetting that he had used an alias on the black-robed and hooded fellow, Elmer could be forgiven for not immediately responding to a name other than his own.

He continued to pedal furiously and nearly toppled again in shock when Bing loped up beside him, easily keeping pace with the bicycle. "Look, stop a moment and let me say something." Bing said.

Elmer continued to push the bike forward, striving to escape the frightening man. "Please, son," Bing added politely.

Something about his gentle tone caused Elmer to slow his pedaling, and he finally braked, touching both feet to the brick road. "You have dropped three newspapers, and I have no doubt stalled your delivery. Please let me come along with you, and help. If you smack any more doors with your papers you are liable to get yelled at, or worse. I can teach you how to hit your target, without property damage. What do you say?"

"I appreciate the offer, mister. Really. But given the choice between being a few minutes late with someone's morning news and being seen with a member of the Black Guard, I'll suffer a couple complaining telephone calls. Okay?"

"Look, Elmer. I'm not a member of the Black Guard—appearances aside. As for being seen with me, if no one sounded the alarm after your screaming, I doubt anyone will report seeing me. Unless I miss my guess, this neighborhood has been pretty cowed of late."

"Hey, where do you get off calling me Elmer? It's Charlie."

"Suit yourself. But you don't respond to that name and it seems strange that the name 'Elmer' would be etched onto the back fender of your bike." With a wry smile, Bingham pointed at the neat inscription. "I will take a guess that Charlie Russell is a not-so-good friend of yours?"

"Gee-whillikins! I give up. Look, I just wanted to make sure when you go talking to others about the kid that cries and screams like a little girl, Charlie would get the rap. That's all, mister."

"Okay. Fine. Let us make a deal. For my silence on the topic of your effeminate scream, you will tell me what you know about the Black Guard—and while you are doing that, I can help you with your route."

"Seems my options are a bit limited, so I'll accept. But could you do something for me?"

"What is that?"

"Assuming you're decent underneath that get-up, could you take that creepy robe and hood off? You can stuff it in my bag here."

Bing considered for a moment then reached up and pulled the robe over his head, revealing tousled slacks and shirt underneath. "It so happens that I have slept in my clothes, so you have a deal. Shake?" They shook hands. The black garments easily fit in Elmer's delivery bag.

"My offer to show you how to pitch still stands, Elmer. What is the next address?"

Elmer told him and Bingham spied the house number a few feet away.

"How about something a few doors down? That address is little more than a horseshoe's toss away."

"Uh...whatever suits you. How about this one." Elmer pointed to another house fifty yards away.

In one fluid motion Bingham reached into the boy's bag and launched a paper. Giving the appearance of rushed, brute strength, the pitch was anything but. An imperceptible twitch at the wrist gave the tightly rolled and banded projectile a remarkable back-spin. It *whizzed* like a saw blade, hovered, feet from the target, then dropped to earth onto the single, concrete step just below the door with a soft *thud*.

"Elmer, that slack-jaw is singularly unbecoming," Bingham said, smiling.

Elmer quickly shrugged off his daze and snapped his mouth shut. A whistle of awe escaped his lips. "By all that's sizzlin'! You are a wonder! The best baseball player around couldn't match that throw, let alone me. How's about I just rattle off the addresses and you do the slingin'?"

"Okay, as long as you can manage to answer a few questions in between addresses?"

"Fine."

Thereafter, the pair proceeded along the paper route. The angry cicada *whizz* of spinning newsprint preceded them along their course.

"So you have seen people dressed like me before, have you?" Bingham inquired between throws.

"Sure. Who hasn't? Just last week the Klan had a parade up State Street."

"But those Klan members were dressed in white hoods and robes, right?" Bingham added.

"Yeah."

"I was wearing a black version of the costume. You've seen folks dressed that way too, right?"

"Yes, I've seen them. But just once or twice, during my route. Every other week or so. Usually they are walking in twos or threes along the street heading to the same spot."

"And what 'spot' is that, Elmer?"

"Just there, that building" he pointed south along State Street at a sprawling, saw-tooth roofed, single-storied factory. A three-story, red brick residence brooded just in front and to the left.

"That's the printing plant for the American Issue Publishing Company, right?"

"Yes, sir. It's four-thirty or five in the a.m. 'bout the time I've noticed them. It's hard to miss pairs of black ghosts anytime, let alone this early in the morning when no one else is movin' about. Gives me the wil-" The squeal of tires drowned out Elmer's words. Then the clatter of horse hooves suddenly erupted on the hard brick road, followed by the staccato patter of gun fire.

Bingham and Elmer ran and pedaled to the source of the ruckus. An enclosed delivery truck roared into view and continued at a speed not intended for delivery trucks. The driver had a death-grip on the wheel, but his passenger lurched wildly out of his window squeezing bullets from his gun at something behind.

The truck sped by Bingham and Elmer like a pilotless freight train, passing out of sight just as its pursuers came into view. Four black wraiths on horseback stormed along the grass and sidewalk hot on the truck's tail. Their jet-black robes—dupli-cates of Bingham's—flowed behind them from the breakneck pace. One rider held aloft a flaming crucifix. At least one other mounted rider leveled a pistol and returned fire at the fleeing truck. It wasn't a wonder that the driver of the truck appeared so terrified. Bingham froze in awe. Elmer's lower jaw unhinged.

Gently lifting Elmer's jaw closed, Bingham announced, "You should get home Elmer; we will talk later."

Although he attempted to give voice to his objection, Elmer barely verbalized a "What!!?" before Bingham had yanked his black robe from the now empty newspaper bag and sprinted off in the direction of the chase.

For the second time during the wee hours of the morning, Bingham Harvard hurtled along at lightning speed, quickly catching sight of the four horsemen.

Unbeknownst to Bing, Elmer had mounted his own "steed," and taken off, not homeward but in Bingham's wake.

Both heard the lengthy squeal of brakes and the jarring crunch of metal on rock. For the span of a heartbeat thereafter the air was free of the sound of popping gunfire and the clatter of racing tires and horseshoes on brick road. Then the explosions redoubled.

The scene revealed itself to Bingham upon his rapid approach. Failing to make a left-hand turn from the dead-end road, the enclosed delivery truck had plowed into the limestone gates of Otterbein Cemetery. The impact had popped open the back doors of the truck, launching at least two wooden barrels and a heavy, wooden crate. The crate lay crumpled and oozing on the brick road. One of the fallen barrels burst with a half-dozen foaming geysers. The smell of hops was unmistakable.

Bingham's advance spooked the horses as would the first gust of a storm. In the distracted instant that the wraiths took notice of their distressed mounts, Bingham was upon them, swatting their guns from their hands. Not a man among them was aware that it was a human who had stripped them of their weapons. However, in the next instant they all saw a like-dressed form materialize from nowhere, moving immediately behind one of their intended targets. Disarmed and stunned into inaction, the men were reduced to spectators.

This intended target was a suited man fleeing the area from the passenger side of the wrecked truck. His partner was sprawled on the hood, grotesquely accordioned, much like the front of the damaged vehicle.

So as not to pulp the runaway into a gravestone, Bingham cut his pace by connecting the turf first with his heels. If only as a thrashing shadow, he was now visible to the Klansmen. Bingham plowed into the fleeing man's back, causing him to lose his grip on his gun and sending him roughly to the earth.

No one noticed the young boy on a bicycle quickly brake and dismount just behind. Elmer laid his bike in the uncut grass of an adjacent residence and took refuge behind a decorative shrub with a clear view to the scene ahead.

Bingham, gowned head to toe in black, rose from the earth like a vengeful spirit, bent, and pulled up his prey as if the burden were little more than a discarded sock. The terrified man whimpered as he gazed upon this grim reaper, and then gaped in astonishment at his own feet dangling off the ground.

Bingham sensed rather than saw the approach of the four horsemen behind him. Quickly recovering from the inexplicable loss of their guns, the cross-bearing member staked his flaming burden into the soft ground and joined his three brethren before they all approached this fifth member of their posse.

One of the four yelled, "Hot damn! You caught a live one! What's the name, son!"

"Cletus."

"Well, damn Cletus, it's me, Thomas, you told me you'd be visitin' family this week so's I didn't bother with the 'fiery summons' for this mission."

"Beg your pardon. I got back a bit earlier than planned. Heard ya'll shootin' and made a beeline outa the house to pitch in."

"Ain't no 'pardon' necessary Cletus. Don't know how you did it, but I ain't lookin' a gift horse in the mouth. 'Sides, we'll have to tend to the details later. We've got to take our prize and skedaddle. The police ain't swift, but they is sure." In the distance, the wail of a siren sounded. Presumably the entire community was not as cowed as Bingham had feared and someone had notified the authorities.

"Leave the stiff for the police, mount up and let's head down the ravine to the river." Thomas uttered from his shroud to the other three wraiths. As the three apparent subordinates quickly mounted, the speaker turned to Bingham.

"Here's some coil to tie up that scoundrel," he said as he handed Bingham pre-cut cords of twine, a handkerchief, and pointed with the other hand at a nearby horseman. "Toss 'em over the back a' my horse, and then saddle up with Harv...'less you got a thoroughbred buried somewhere?"

Bingham did as instructed, the hapless "scoundrel" too

stunned yet to resist. Without effort he slid the bound man, on his stomach, over the stirrup, between the neck of the horse and the robed rider.

Leaving the flaming cross speared to the ground, the riders, with their burdens, raced off through the damaged gates of the cemetery down the wooded ravine toward level, wooded ground below.

Elmer, letting curiosity get the best of him, fled the scene on his bicycle in pursuit of the trotting horses.

* * * * * * *

Infused with pride from their successful pursuit, the four horsemen bantered along the way to the as yet undisclosed destination. Bingham gathered merely that the site was in deep woods, along Alum creek, the sleepy waterway along which they were galloping. A narrow path along the bank served as passage for the horses. Piecing together the bits of information that flew among the riders, Bing eventually understood that this mission had been planned well in advance. The 'bootleggers,' as the truck driver and passenger had been tagged, were observed and tracked over a period of weeks. Their route was well known. Along that route, teams of black-clad Ku Klux Klan members had been posted to give chase and scare the bootleggers to the next team as the first team's horses tired and so on. The object was to corral the bootleggers and their "goods" as close to the Klan's temporary camp as possible. Apparently, the scheme went off rather well as the distance from capture to campsite was barely two miles—far enough from the scene of the wreck that authorities would not look that far, but close enough to make quick time with captive in tow.

En route, Bingham had gathered the names of his erstwhile riding companions. The leader and bearer of the captive was Thomas; Bing's partner was Harv and the other two were John and Eugene—indistinguishable in their all-black attire except for the color of their mounts. Last names were neither used nor requested.

The captive gave a muffled whimper once or twice early on but was violently lashed with Thomas' riding crop until he resigned himself to silence for the rest of the trek.

The camp was little more than flattened underbrush, roughly 100 feet in diameter surrounded by enormous beech trees. The calm flow of Alum Creek ran for a few feet along its side. Roughly a dozen black-clad Klansmen loitered about, their horses rustling and sniffing but not visible; presumably secured just outside the clearing. Likely, these were the men from the teams at the earlier stage of the "corralling," returned to the pre-determined meeting place.

Two or three of the Klan were tending to a glowing pit at the very center of the camp. Bright orange embers of smokeless coal had been heaped into a hole of unknown depth, flush with the earth. Whatever its purpose, this manmade oven had to be generating heat more akin to a kiln than a campfire.

A thick, grey pungent smoke wafted from a large black kettle suspended over the fire. The strong smell was familiar to Bing, but he couldn't place it. A black lid capped the kettle, audibly trembling.

This scene was visible now as the sunlight of early dawn shot faint rays of light through the dense foliage.

Having spent the last mile or so in defeated repose, slung over Thomas' horse, a glance at the kettle sent the captive boot-legger into apoplexy.

Bingham had no idea what he was witnessing. But seeing the captive's reaction he was beginning to have vague concerns about having bound the bootlegger so securely. Whatever was in store for him, he did not have a fighting chance of escape.

One of the black wraiths flowed into the surrounding foliage upon sight of the arriving posse and returned quickly with a full, seemingly weightless burlap bag. A few white feathers clung to the outside of the bag, one or two drifting in the currents of heat generated by the fire. He sat his burden upright on the ground next to the black kettle.

Even before their horses were brought to a stop, Thomas grabbed the thrashing captive by the seat of his pants and savagely flung him off the horse, head first to the ground.

Unconsciousness would have been a blessing to the bootlegger; however fate denied him even this small concession.

The four horsemen with Bingham quickly dismounted and secured their horses to nearby trees. Bing merely stood in place desperately trying to deduce the utility of these arrangements. Still clueless, he followed his "team" to the center of the clearing on foot.

His attention was drawn to the sound of tearing cloth. Bingham saw immediately behind him Thomas and another robed figure stripping the huddled captive to the waist. Thomas was shouting random epithets to his assistant's great amusement. It was then that Bing realized that he could distinguish the otherwise like-garbed Thomas from the others. Aside from being the one consistently giving orders, Thomas' voice was a distinctive octave or so higher.

The captive was dragged by his feet to a spot adjacent to the boiling kettle, surrounded, Bing noticed, by roughly six hardy ropes. The ends of each met at the center of a circle with their opposite ends extending like spokes on a wheel to stakes in the ground.

The bootlegger was bound with the free ends of the ropes by his waist and neck. The binding was cruelly ingenious, forcing the victim to remain in a seated posture with any effort at repose causing the binding around his neck to tighten.

Like most of the Klan members, Bingham placed himself just at the perimeter of the staked ropes, less than four feet from the captive.

Bing struggled in his own mind with how far he could let the anticipated events proceed. He could not stand by and watch a man die, but he had resolved that he could, and must, witness minor, even serious injury. After weeks of fruitless surveilling and investigation, he had now discovered and infiltrated his target. The survival of many depended on him seeing the larger scheme to completion.

Two shrouded men joined Thomas at the kettle with broad paintbrushes in their hands. One of them grasped the kettle's lid with a gloved hand, sliding it off to the ground. Together, they dipped their brushes into a black viscous material and approached the bound captive at three different points. The brushes made a trail of smoke from kettle to prisoner. On contact with the first brush the bootlegger spastically thrashed, oblivious to the ropes tightening round his neck. A guttural, baritone cry was caught and stifled both by his constricting neck and the binding handkerchief that Bingham had applied much earlier.

In what seemed like hours, but which amounted to less than two minutes, the bootlegger was slathered from the neck to waist in a black sludge. Mixed with a stench of burning flesh, Bingham could finally recall the stink. It was coal tar. His house staff used the concoction to fire the several boilers necessary to heat his Long Island estate, Myquest.

Smoke and steam rose from the bootlegger's coated torso and clouded his head in noxious fumes.

The two assistants eventually stepped away to join the encircling spectators but Thomas remained poised immediately next to the captive, a dripping, smoking brush in hand. His voice abruptly broke the silence.

"This...*cancer* comes to the 'dry capital of the world' after the states of our union and a God-fearing congress ratify the prohibition of alcoholic spirits from sea to shining sea and has the nerve, the *audacity* to distribute his hooch!"

Thomas' arms trembled and pumped at the elbows, splashing molten tar on the face of the captive. Nervous Klansmen took a few steps back, widening the encirclement, trying to avoid the spray from the backswing.

"We know now that this purveyor of poison isn't alone; that he is a member of a 'gang.' And that this 'gang' has come here— to the heart of Ohio, Columbus and Westerville—to tempt our young, our weak with volatile spirits. We cannot let this contagion escape, so recently contained by law; by our Constitution.

"This...dealer in death has a boss. And we, brothers, have cut a swath so deep in this bootlegging business that the 'gang' has sent their boss all the way from New York City, to stop us. They want the streets of Columbus and Westerville to flow again with booze and our blood. And they have sent their best enforcer to make it happen—Alphonsus Gabriel Capone."

Thomas' voice, though muffled by the hood, began to rise in volume and pitch as he continued. He sounded shrill, silencing man and beast alike. At the crescendo of his rant he purposefully kicked the kettle. The steaming kettle smacked into the unlucky bootlegger, splashing one last sizable glob of tar onto the captive's face.

Sweet unconsciousness had finally overcome the prisoner, and with it, the captive's ability to remain in a seated posture. He would surely asphyxiate from the weight of his now limp body on the noose-like ropes.

Thomas would not let this man off so easily. He lurched to the circle's perimeter and took hold of a hatchet. Klansmen backed away, clearly anxious as Thomas hacked away the restraints. On the second swing, the captive fell to his back.

Completing the circle, Thomas strode to the burlap bag next to where the kettle had sat. He up-ended the sack on the victim's torso unleashing a mass of downy, white feathers.

Pointing to the hapless, human sized goose, Thomas passionately gesticulated, "This is our message to organized crime!" Before Bingham could react, Thomas whipped a long stove match from a pocket on the outside of his robe, swiped it on the toppled kettle and dropped the flaming stick to the body of the captive.

...Swoosh!

Dry feathers and flammable tar ignited in a rush. The once limp down-covered man staggered to his feet, screaming now that the gag had burnt away. Flames and smoke whipped from the victim's waistline, to his head, catching spattered tar, feathers and hair aflame.

Bing snapped from his shock, resolved to his actions at

this critical point. He leapt to the gyrating, flaming form and straight-armed him at his back, near the shoulder blades. The ignited body launched off the ground by inches and landed in the knee deep waters of the creek.

Tossing smoldering gloves to the ground, Bing raced to the water. Slogging through the creek, he caught sight through the cattails of the opposite bank the smooth surface of a bicycle fender marked with a familiar engraving. In a flash of recognition, he spun around, his body blocking the view from anyone else who might approach.

Thomas had followed Bing but gave his attention to nothing but his intended victim. Each took the submerged victim under an arm and dragged him back to dry land. In a tone disturbingly calm after his recent tirade, Thomas intoned, "Thanks for the dowsing. We want to save this 'message' for other bootleggers and it would be nice if he were alive at least long enough to put the fear of God in others."

Bingham had feared his "cover" was blown, and had resolved to do so if saving this unfortunate's life was the price. Thomas was unfazed however, apparently finding Bing's actions in harmony with his plans. Bingham decided to exploit the opportunity and continue to play the part. In any case, the captive appeared to be breathing and Bing's quick grip on his wrist found a weak, but steady pulse.

"We'll tip off authorities about the location of our 'message' as soon as we reach town." Thomas announced. With that, he unceremoniously loosed his burden. Bingham, left with the near-dead weight, gently lowered the tortured man to the ground.

In less than a minute all, including Bing, were mounted and galloping out of the woods.

From the bank of the creek a terrified, slack-jawed face pushed from between cattails. As the hoof beats faded in the distance, Elmer sloshed through the creek, bicycle in tow, toward the steaming body. Curiosity overpowering his fear for the moment, Elmer knelt down at the head of the blackened, human shape.

With a sudden cough and gurgle, the head raised and maddened eyes, one entirely lidless, stared at Elmer. Lipless, exposed gums opened releasing a gout of creek water and vomit.

Young Elmer fell backwards, crab-walking away as best and as fast as he could from the suddenly animated carcass.

He backed into his bike, stood and slung his leg over the seat. To this point he had not taken his eyes from the undead. Far enough away now to avoid physical contact, Elmer peddled away toward the narrow path along the bank. The back fender of the bicycle, now facing the charred bootlegger, clearly displayed the name "Elmer" in the morning sunshine.

A crazed, desperate moan echoed through the woods as the only "civilian" witness to the torture hurtled himself away from the scene.

CHAPTER FOUR
A DEATH IN THE FAMILY

November 20, 1918; Greendale, Long Island, New York:

"I am very sorry for your loss Bingham, Katherine. Sterling was a good man, a dear friend. Had circumstances and the law permitted, attendees to his funeral would number a thousand or more. A life so long and distinguished deserved a greater 'sending off.'"

"I appreciate your condolences Mr. Redick. We cannot blame folks for failing to attend a funeral when doing so would likely cause their own. A criminal citation for public gatherings during this influenza would be the least of our hoped-for guests' worries. But for your quick work in securing the necessary permits from the city so that Mr. Chester could be laid to rest on the grounds here at Myquest, his body would have been consigned to a public charnel house like so many other unfortunates."

Glenn Redick, Esq., visibly shuddered from the image called to mind by Bingham Harvard's description. He was a spectacled, well-dressed, stout man, obviously younger than Sterling Chester's mid-seventies, but nonetheless well into mid-life. World-weariness had settled on him as Sterling Chester was not the first of his friends and clients for whom he was entrusted with "final arrangements." He would not be the last.

"Before we get to brass tacks, let me compliment you, Katherine, on your beautiful home and well tended landscaping.

Myquest is no doubt your pride and joy."

"Indeed, Mr. Redick, we have put much of ourselves into this estate. Thank you for the compliment. I would be happy to give you a guided tour once these matters are dispensed with."

"I would enjoy that very much, thank you. Now, Bingham, you have tasked me with various assignments just in these past few days and my staff and I have made great strides in accomplishing your goals. Indeed, to date, but for your signatures on a few documents, I believe we can formalize all of your plans this afternoon. That is a compliment more to the well-ordered and meticulous fashion in which you and Sterling documented your accounts than to the efficiency of my staff."

"Thank you, Glenn" Bingham responded. "You had a considerable task and your humility is noted, but I would entrust my affairs to no other."

"Thank you, Bingham. Well then, let us begin. Sterling's estate is...uh, considerable. He had remained thrifty his entire working life on a generous salary and family investments, but passed on before he could fully enjoy the fruits of his labors. He has willed absolutely every dime and all of his possessions to you, Bingham, his only living family and heir. Leaving all that you have attained personally out of the picture for the moment, I can say without hesitation that you are now a million-...a multi-millionaire. While some of these assets are available for immediate liquidation if need be, a good sum has been designated in a trust, from which the interest alone could support the two of you, your staff and this estate...indefinitely. Sterling likewise invested heavily in shares of Standard Oil, well before the company was divided, also the Ford Motor Company, and Mr. Edison's General Electric. You will see all of the details spelled out here." Glenn slid a three-inch-thick portfolio across the desk.

"On your instruction, Bingham, I have prepared the paperwork necessary to divest yourself from the day-to-day operations of the Centropolis Bank, designating you a 'board member at large,' with decision-making and voting responsibilities delegated to me. Also, I have secured the services of a property management company to tend to the day-to-day operations of your rental properties and real estate holdings throughout New York City—including maintenance of the structures and collection of rents, lease payments, etc., etc. Again, by your designation, I will be the gate-keeper between you and the property managers. In short, Mr. and Mrs. Harvard, you are in the enviable position of being entirely free from the burden of both employment and management of the assets set aside to sustain you. Congratulations."

Lady Kate broke down and wept. Not one typically to publicize her emotions, the past week of caring for the fast failing Sterling Chester had brought her passions to the tipping point. Even the announcement of dramatically *positive* news was too much.

If Katherine was the metaphorical ship lost at sea, Bingham was a port in the storm. He sat back in his own chair hands together, fingers steepled beneath his chin. Furrowed brow and a distant, far away look made one wonder if he had even heard the fantastic statement of this trusted attorney.

Bingham had had a reasonably good grasp of his and Mr. Chester's estates even before this solemn meeting, and had psychologically moved on to other matters. His conversation with his foster father on the day of his diagnosis with Spanish Flu—just a week ago—weighed oppressively on his conscience. Who would not feel the weight of the world on his shoulders upon having a father-figure on his deathbed so convincingly articulate the misdirection of his life to date; to challenge him to fulfill a destiny best suited for adolescent fantasy? Bingham Harvard had taken Mr. Chester's dying wish to heart; he had embraced it with his soul.

Bing interrupted his own weighty reflections, "I understand that you were to bring with you today, Mr. Redick some...family heirlooms?"

"Of course Mr. Harvard. Although I've never viewed them myself, Sterling told me that these were his most valued possessions. He was convinced you would feel the same way." The stout attorney rose from his seat and handed Bingham a single, slim folder, and a small lead box.

In the presence of his wife and lawyer, Bing rested the box on the desk between them and lifted the lid. He then placed the folder next to the box and opened it as one would a book.

Inside the metal box was a single three-inch toy soldier, typical of the lead toys manufactured in pre-war Germany and so popular with middle- to upper-class American children two and three decades ago. This particular specimen was distinguished from his brethren by four, unmistakable impressions spanning from the upper legs of the figurine to its face.

The open folder exposed a yellowed single sheet of paper, roughly eight and a half by eleven inches in size. It bore many, pronounced creases, as if it had spent much of its existence folded up in a small square. One of the long sides was frayed, like a page torn from a book. Indeed, as the banner on one side of the page announced, it was the cover of *Nick Carter Detective Library*, a 5¢ magazine popular with young boys at least three decades ago. The sensationalized cover illustrations depicted an armed man standing above a sprawled body, a hooded cobra rising from the vest of the prostrate figure, inches from the drawn weapon. Inset, to the upper right of that illustration was a smaller sketch showing a man, facing an awestruck crowd hurling another grown man by main strength at the spectators.

Bingham delicately turned the aged newsprint exposing handwritten text. On close inspection, it was a poem, with the author's name inscribed beneath "John Greenleaf Whittier." A single line of verse was underlined: "The hope of all who suffer, The dread of all who wrong."

It was Mr. Redick's voice that broke the silence, confusion clouding his face "This is all very interesting, Mr. Harvard, but what are these items?"

His expression still distant, Bingham answered "My foster father was understating things a bit when he said these would be my most valued possessions, Mr. Redick...." He lifted his head to look at the expectant lawyer and then to his flushed, but smiling wife. "...They are my destiny."

* * * * * * *

"You understand how important this is to me Rodney?"

"I don't know how it could be *more* important, Bingham." Cigar smoke expelled from the speaker's mouth congregating with the cloud already surrounding his head.

The two men sat in big chairs, upholstered in leather with high, solid backs in Bingham's den; just hours after the family solicitor had departed bearing the fantastic news that the Harvards would live a life of leisure. With only a small reading table between them, Bing pushed the two items just left by the attorney toward the ex-police lieutenant, Rodney Rushton. Puffing compulsively on a gnawed-on cigar, Rushton carefully slipped the lead box and thin folder into a leather portfolio and fastened it with metal clasps.

Rushton and Bingham's relationship spanned many years. The two had been mortal enemies when Rushton, irresistibly tempted by a corrupt 'system' in the New York City police department then framed Bing for theft from the Centropolis Bank. Bingham resisted apprehension by the law with a Samson-like strength that, until then, he had never had cause to exercise, leaving in his wake a trail of broken and maimed police officers. He was tagged a felon, wanted dead or alive, and marked with the alias, "The Night Wind" for his remarkable speed, stealth and force-of-nature strength. With the help of another under-cover police detective—the woman who would eventually be his wife—Katherine Maxwell, "Lady Kate," Bing turned the tables on Rushton. He exposed Rushton as the thief, redeemed his own name and saw Rodney off for a ten year 'vacation' behind bars, compliments of the New York City justice system.

Just two years later, when faced with over a quarter of a million dollar theft from Centropolis Bank and a threat to Katherine's safety, Bingham enlisted Rodney Rushton to work for him. He believed that it would take a thief to catch a thief. Exercising political connections afforded him by his foster father, and generous campaign contributor, Bing secured a full pardon for the fallen lieutenant. His trust was well placed. Rushton made good, his record was cleared and he began a new life helming his own private investigations agency, aptly named: the "Rodney Rushton Detective Bureau."

Now Bingham was calling upon his friend's uncanny investigative instinct and vast network of contacts—on either side of the law—to help him out again.

"I honestly don't know what could be more important to a fellow than discovering his heritage, Bingham. I'll find out who your mother was, I'll root out your father too. I won't rest until I do. You gave me back my life, Bing. I owe you this."

"Thank you, Rodney. If anyone can do it, I know you can. I fear, however that the trail is so old it has gone cold. I've written down for you every detail Mr. Chester conveyed to me, and you have absolutely all of the physical evidence." Bingham pointed to the leather portfolio in Rushton's hands.

Rodney stood from his seat, erupting from the cloud of his own cigar smoke, in preparation for his departure, "You leave it to me Mr. Harvard. I won't leave a stone unturned."

"Good luck. Remember that you need only phone in to Mr. Redick for any expenses. And you need not report to me or Redick with leads or progress—I'd rather not have scraps of disconnected facts unnecessarily raising my hopes—I want two names 'mother' and 'father' with addresses for them or any other immediate, surviving blood-relatives. Are we clear?"

"Like my conscience." The private investigator said with a touch of irony he knew only Bingham would catch.

"Now take yourself and that forsaken smoke-stack you call a cigar out of here before Katherine catches the scent of it and gives you, and I 'what for.'" Bingham did not smoke and his wife forbade it even of guests inside their home.

"I surely do not want to get on the wrong side of Lady Kate," said the former police lieutenant with a wry smile.

The two old friends shook hands and Rushton took his leave from Myquest on a mission to learn the identity and story of at least one female ghost—Bingham's biological mother—and one man, living or dead—Bingham's biological father.

CHAPTER FIVE
THE LADY OF THE NIGHT WIND

August 11, 1920; Westerville, Ohio:

Katherine Harvard wiped her sweaty brow with an exposed forearm. It was not yet 7:00 a.m., the coolest part of the day, outside anyway. Inside the printing plant it was at least eighty degrees Fahrenheit already. The brick construction absorbed and held the late summer temperature from the day before, and was compounded by the heat emanating from the vast array of machines, large and larger, dedicated to the dissemination of the noble cause of temperance. There were four Miehle printing presses, two the size of cars, two others roughly a third that size, typesetting machines, trimming machines, a gas-powered power plant, binding and folding machines, cutting and addressing machines all tended to by dozens of human operators that worked like ants on a loaded picnic blanket. The printing plant was just short of 20,000 square feet. Nearby, an unattached three-story house contained "the brains" of the institution: administration offices, copy-editors' room, etc.

This was the home of the American Issue Publishing Company, organized in 1909 and owned by the Anti-Saloon League of America. Its purpose was to build up a great publishing institution for educational work in the interest of the movement for an alcohol-free civilization. With the very recent ratification of prohibition—the 18th Amendment to the United States Constitution—its "purpose" was largely fulfilled. Even in victory, the presses of this publishing house continued uninterrupted 24 hours a day, employing 200 people, making it the life blood of Westerville, Ohio's economy.

The level of printing and readership for its principal periodical, *American Issue*, was vast. 1,746,184 copies were distributed in just the last month. During that timespan alone approximately 950 pounds of ink were used and fifty tons of paper. In addition to the *American Issue* magazine, thousands upon thousands of issues of the *Scientific Temperance Journal*, books, pamphlets, folders, leaflets, charts and posters were composed. They were printed, bound, addressed and distributed nationwide from this single location. By necessity, Westerville was the smallest town in America to have a first class post office. The trains stopped daily and picked up carloads of the printed material dealing with the beverage alcohol problem in its many phases.

A condition of employment with the American Issue Publishing Company was an oath of alcoholic abstinence:

> "Whereas, the use of intoxicating liquors as a beverage is productive of pauperism, degradation and crime; and believing it our duty to discourage that which produces more evil than good, we therefore pledge ourselves to abstain from the use of intoxicating liquors as a beverage."

While some would fête their newly attained employment with a generous swig from their vest flask, others embraced their pledge with religious fervor. The city itself was "dry;" not a saloon, distiller, retailer or even a restaurant or hotel would engage in the business within city boundaries. The last purveyors of intoxicating spirits, a Mr. and Mrs. Henry Corbin, had their saloon blown to kingdom come. Within a year it was rebuilt and then blown up again. Now, the rest of the nation was to follow Westerville's lead—or suffer the consequences of violating the new law of the land.

Eunice Parker strode through a door to the floor of the printing plant. She was easily within Katherine Harvard's view from her slightly elevated perch next to one of the two largest presses in the building. Unusually tall for a woman, Eunice was just an inch or two south of six feet. She was substantial; roughly 180 pounds, a corn-fed Midwestern lady. Her movements were much like an elephant, lumbering, but sure. While the first few days subjected to the round-the-clock cacophony of the printing plant had made Katherine irritable, Eunice was unfazed. Her long-term exposure rendering her virtually immune to the noise.

The single door to the office of the plant superintendent swung open with considerable force, its outer doorknob slamming into the unprotected plaster of the adjacent wall. Eunice, only a yard or two away with her back to the door en route to her station, slowly curbed her considerable momentum.

"Mrs. Parker! A moment of your *extremely* valuable time please?!" hollered the superintendent, sarcastically.

Accustomed to making himself heard over the roar of printing machinery, Plant Superintendent Jackson Knutson had no problem securing Eunice's attention, as well as the notice of everyone else in the plant at that moment.

After a brief pause to absorb the portent of the plant manager's tone, Eunice turned on her heels, gazed levelly at Mr. Knutson's ruddy face, and then proceeded, chin up, toward the office.

Though still a bit rattled by the violence of Knutson's entrance to the plant floor, Katherine was not entirely surprised by his behavior. In the few days she had been employed at the publishing house it was evident that the plant manager was suffering greatly under the stress of his job. The demands put on the presses had not let up even after the passage of prohibition, but the tired mechanical work horses were aging and in need of replacement. The generous funds originally donated by the likes of J. D. Rockefeller and others had dried up along with the public sale of alcohol. In the opinion of these philanthropists, the Anti-Saloon League had fulfilled its mission with the passage of a Constitutional amendment.

Knutson was told to do more, with less—or at least with inferior, dated machinery. Press breakdowns happened more and more frequently, causing the loss of hundreds of yards of press paper trapped in the stalled machine, and delays in printing and shipping of the *American Issue* to the thousands of subscribers coast to coast. While the oft confrontational plant manager accepted the frailties of machinery without histrionics, he made no such concession for employees. Unlike the costly Miehle presses, labor was expendable. Tardiness of five minutes or less got one warning. The second offense was summary dismissal. Those who were delinquent more than five minutes knew enough simply not to bother showing up, ever. The dismissal notice was mailed to their last known address. This managerial tact earned him the soubriquet "knut," "knutty," or simply "knutcase."

Even if he exhausted the labor pool of the 2500 or so citizens of Westerville, the growing metropolis of Columbus offered thousands more eager would-be employees easily brought to town via the street car service between the suburb and its larger, more populated neighbor.

Eunice was tardy by seconds. Katherine knew. Mrs. Parker had been scheduled to relieve Katherine from her shift. If anyone could or should be granted leniency from Knutson's draconian management style, it should have been Eunice Parker. She *was* a devout teetotaler. Plant gossip had it that Eunice shed a tear upon reciting her oath of alcoholic abstinence and had added her own passionate embellishment of "...so help me God!" She authored a well received weekly column in *American Issue* and was presently in contract with the publisher to complete her second of a projected series of fictional novels on the dramatic trials of a Clara Barton-styled nurse. The overriding theme in her tracts dealt with the medical and psychological impact of alcohol. Despite these intellectual contributions to "the cause," Eunice had insisted on adding her labor too. She had refused the relatively comfortable task of proofreading submitted text, or secretarial duties. She declined even to run one of the more manageable machines. She declared her intent to operate one of the two enormous Miehle presses, and met no resistance upon taking the challenge.

Where Jackson Knutson found Mrs. Parker to be as dispensable as any other machine operator in the plant, she was by contrast eminently *in*dispensable to the General Manager and Editor-in-Chief, Ernest Cherrington. Her vast and popular contributions to printed material dealing with the beverage alcohol problem so dominated any given publication, editors feared that the public's impression of the movement would be a one-woman crusade, and not a grass-roots, nationwide struggle. They veiled Eunice's true involvement behind at least thirty pseudonyms.

Observing the tirade of the overburdened plant manager through the enormous window that divided most of his office from the plant floor, Katherine was wondering if maybe Eunice would need to enlist the support of the Editor-in-Chief to avoid termination.

Although words were indecipherable through the plant's noise, Knutson's physical posture left little to the imagination. He was standing behind his desk, red-faced, pounding his fist on the furniture with abandon. He was a large man—both in height and girth. Aside from a very thin line of white hair terminating at his ears, he was bald. Eunice's seated, crossed legs, from the knees down were visible, and noticeably rigid. The rest of her body was out of view from the office door.

Knutson's Western Electric candlestick desk phone gave a ring, and he yanked it off the desk as if he were strangling a chicken. Indeed, as was his habit born of extreme tension, he jammed the black transmitter to his mouth and the receiver into the side of his head, mashing his ear.

With raised arm and a brushing motion with his hand and pointed finger, Knutson appeared to summarily dismiss his employee without even the courtesy of speaking. The telephone's transmitter and receiver remained stapled to his reddened head.

The rigid legs straightened and disappeared for a second. The plant manager's door opened and Mrs. Parker appeared.

As she exited, some machine operators looked on in sympathy, while others attempted to act as if nothing out of the ordinary had occurred.

To Eunice's credit, she admirably retained her composure. Indeed, a look of focused resolution appeared on her bull-doggish face. Whatever her intention, it was not to immediately relieve Katherine from her duties as assigned. Instead, she strode off to the storage room and shut the door behind her.

Presumably, Knutson's telephone conversation required his immediate departure. True to form, he was flushed and his face taut with anxiety. Upon mercifully pulling the phone from his head and returning it to his desk, he shut off his office light, exited his office, shut the door and hurriedly left the plant.

The drama over, the employees on the floor turned their attentions to their immediate tasks. Katherine remained on alert; not only bowing to her inquisitive nature, she also had a vested interest in Eunice's return to the plant floor to relieve her of her shift.

Her curiosity was quickly rewarded. Katherine noticed Eunice exit the supply room. In her hand, she clutched a kerchief-sized rag, typically reserved for cleaning the presses. While generally gray in color, this rag was saturated in reflective black.

She trundled to Knutson's office and entered. The door drifted shut behind her. The room remained dark. About a minute later, she emerged and casually tossed the rag into a nearby waste barrel.

Eunice slowly made her way over to Katherine and her press, the resolute, intent expression on her face now softened. She smiled up at Katherine and spoke.

"I do sincerely apologize Kate, for being late. I hope I haven't kept you from something."

"Uh...not at all, Eunice. You've got a good few minutes before this press needs restocked, and, so far, no breakdowns."

"You're a sport. But I won't let my neglect go unpunished...."

"It did not seem as if Mr. Knutson did...really, you've suffered his wrath. Your debt, if you had one, is paid."

Eunice's eyes flashed briefly at Katherine's reference to her recent humiliation, but the expression dissipated immediately. Katherine caught the reaction and was sorry for it. She rushed to account for the perceived slight.

"I have been here just over a week now and have not had the opportunity to know anyone socially. As we are the only two representatives of the fairer gender working the bigger machines, surely we must watch each other's backs? I would be gratified if you would dine with me. Your spouse, er...family would be most welcome too." Katherine offered this invitation not knowing if Eunice had a spouse.

"Oh, that would be lovely!" Eunice trumpeted with a feminine glee at odds with her hulking appearance. "Reginald and I would be happy to accept."

"Wonderful! Presently, my residence is undergoing a few... renovations...but I anticipate in forty-eight-hours time we should have things tidied up. Would August 13 be amenable to you and your husband? After your workday; 6:30 p.m.?"

"Perfect."

Thereafter the ladies exchanged addresses and telephone numbers in anticipation of their get-together. During their brief exchange, Jackson Knutson had returned to the plant. His complexion had reddened and his facial expression was pinched and angry, as if ruminating over some recent unpleasantness. His telephone was ringing even as he opened his office door. He ran the few feet to his desk, throttled the phone and pressed its component parts to his head. Sticky moisture on his ear and mouth immediately caught his attention. He threw the strangled phone to the desk and howled.

Like nervous sheep at the approach of the barking collie, all of the floor workers were startled to a halt when Knutson's door swung violently open for the second time that morning. A large black circle covered his ear and the whole side of his head. Another one shone greasily around his mouth and down to his chin. Neglecting his usual fastidiousness, Knutson violently spat on the plant floor en route to the sinks and wash room. Even contending with the rumbling presses, the sounds of vigorous scrubbing and phlegmy expectoration escaped the wash room.

As these events transpired, Katherine was successively fearful, then shocked, and, finally, when it was clear no physical harm had come to anyone, humored. The entire work floor shared her reactions, some attempting to suppress their laughter for fear of retribution, others exercising no restraint in raucous belly-laughter.

Katherine glanced over at Eunice, who slowly turned to face Katherine with a wide, closed-mouthed smile; much like the illustrations of the Cheshire cat in Lewis Carroll's *Alice's Adventures in Wonderland.*

It did not require Kate's considerable powers of deduction to piece together what had just transpired. In a somewhat juvenile effort at vindication, Mrs. Parker had coated the plant manager's telephone transmitter and receiver with ink from the supply room. It was just a matter of time before the phone rang and Knutson's habit of fusing it to his face would bring about his own sticky comeuppance. Katherine had plenty of articles of stained work clothing to testify to the fact that Knutson would bear the circular "tattoos" for weeks to come.

Conveniently for Eunice, Jackson Knutson's reputation among his subordinates was poor, at best. Had anyone on the work floor observed Mrs. Parker's actions, their common dislike of the plant manager would earn Eunice only respect, not tattling.

Katherine had to admit, at least to herself, that she too believed Knutson's gross overreaction to Eunice's tardiness was justly "rewarded." However, her good conscience could not permit her to openly endorse such a prank. Conveniently, Eunice neither acknowledged her role, nor sought approval— indeed, other than the smile; she seemed to quickly dismiss it.

"I look forward to our dinner two days hence, Katherine. I know we will get along like long-lost sisters."

With this seeming closure to their dialogue, Katherine returned Eunice's pleasantries, and retreated to the wash room herself before departing the plant for her residence.

CHAPTER SIX
THE FUNHOUSE

August 1, 1920; Greendale, Long Island, New York:

Thomas Clancy the Third drove his touring car along the gravel path to the columned façade of the Harvard estate, Myquest. He parked, alighted, walked a few steps to the main doors, uttered a frustrated "Tsk!," returned to his vehicle and grabbed wadded pages and a scroll from the front passenger seat. As he was none-too-delicately jamming the parchment into his suit jacket pocket, the oak door to the mansion opened. In the entryway stood Julius, butler, manservant, and sergeant-at-arms.

"Good day, Julius!" said a slightly winded Clancy, pattering up the stairs of the main porch. He carried himself with a comfortable familiarity at Myquest. Tom Clancy and Bingham Harvard had been close friends for in excess of a decade, beginning as roommates in college at Harvard.

Tom was a prosperous man, with a waistline to prove it. Despite his receding, reddish hair, Clancy had a boyish face, a turned-up nose, freckles, and the pale-pinkish skin tone of a man unfamiliar with the outdoors, let alone physical labor. He was third generation banker and commercial investor, yet his comportment belied the clichéd Wall Street blueblood. His wife of just a few years, Roberta, would say that Clancy "lived large." In his own mind, Thomas Clancy's piety to spouse and friends, his work and the Pope, afforded him a certain moral flexibility during his increasingly rare recreational time.

Tom gambled and drank, a lot.

"Seems you've made 'specially good time arrivin' this lovely early afternoon, Master Thomas. Mr. Harvard wasn't expecting you for 'nother hour, at least." Julius made a slow and deliberate show of brushing aside his suit jacket, pulling an antique pocket watch from his vest, dramatically raising the timepiece to eye-level, staring at its face, and mechanically turning his head to look at the banker. The chronometer was indeed a beautiful piece of Swiss craftsmanship, albeit incongruous with the spartan black and gray livery of a valet.

The manservant's skin was the blackness of a sealed cave. He would be a silhouette, except for the whites of his eyes and graying hair. Julius' facial features were distinctly Caucasian, as if somewhere in his lineage a Roman Centurion and the daughter of a Sudanese tribal chief made a family. His nose was razor-straight, lips tight and thin and he stood erect at well north of six feet.

"That's a lovely watch you've got there, Julius." Thomas spoke through gritted teeth.

"Why thank you for noticin' Master Thomas. Of course it came to my possession as a generous gift from you upon my birthday...if you recall."

"Oh, I recall." Tom said with a huff. He grudgingly kept to the script of the fiction the two of them had concocted to hide from Katherine Harvard the true nature of Clancy's "gift."

Tom had bet and lost the family heirloom on a wager with Julius that he could walk, without restraint or delay, from the main entrance of the mansion to Bingham's study at the far west wing. At any other residence no one in his right mind would bet against Clancy's success.

Myquest, however, was like no other residence.

On the day, now two years past, of Sterling Chester's deathbed epiphany that Bingham Harvard was destined to be the savior of civilization, the Master of Myquest had given his wife license to engineer their mansion in the image of her existing personal 'chalet' or retreat.

The 'chalet' had been a wedding gift from Mr. Chester, built to Kate's specifications. Employing craftsmen and mechanical engineers locally and abroad, the 'chalet' incorporated untold numbers of ancient or medieval methods of capture and restraint—mixed with modern-day mechanics and pneumatics—as a means to ensure Mrs. Harvard's privacy and safety. Now that the Harvards had embarked on this mission of fighting injustice, it stood to reason that this creative means of domestic security was necessary within the principal residence.

Katherine Harvard had granted only a select few the privilege of knowing where and how to engage the various snares: Bingham, Julius, and Clancy. This latter confidant was selected grudgingly, and only after Bingham had impressed upon his wife the near certainty that Clancy would otherwise seriously injure himself, or any number of the domestic staff whilst "mansion-sitting" in their extended absence.

And so Mrs. Harvard had given to Clancy the complete blueprints of the various tripwires, pressure points, and switches, their "surprises," and recommended maintenance. It was this paperwork that Clancy had crumpled into his jacket pockets.

Clancy had convinced Katherine that the best method of committing this information to memory was to see it in action. Katherine agreed on the condition that Julius supervise. And so the table was set for a manly wager.

Having grossly underestimated Katherine's degree of sophistication—and perhaps no small dose of paranoia—Clancy bet his grandfather's timepiece and took the maiden voyage through the 'funhouse.' Julius' mission was to engage whatever mechanisms he saw fit to restrain Clancy's progress. Certain traps had the means to incapacitate—not merely restrain. The men had agreed on "restraint only."

This proved to be one of Mr. Clancy's rare, wise decisions.

Had Clancy bothered to look at the blueprints beforehand he might have at least successfully scaled the master staircase. Instead, Julius nearly dropped him to the cellar through a collapsing third step. Clancy's portliness proved an asset as his protruding belly broke his vertical plummet. Stubbornly refusing to concede, he pulled himself up and soldiered ahead... four steps. Focused instead on collapsing stairs at his feet, Clancy wasn't looking forward and up to see the ceiling drop just above the landing of the master staircase. The opening belched forth a phalanx of medicine balls. As one unit, the mass of spheres succumbed to gravity and crowded down the staircase. With just a few feet to spare, Clancy threw himself horizontal upon a level stair, only to drop like an anchor into the mansion cellar when two steps fell away as one.

"I arrived a bit early, Julius, hoping I might interest you in a double or nothing wager in the funhouse. I've done a bit of homework and I think I've got your number...er...the house's number, anyway." To make the point, Clancy patted the blue-prints at his vest pocket.

"Well, suh, I do believe in givin' a man a fair shake. You was licked just about the moment ya got yerself started the last time. I suppose if ya mightn't make it at least to the second floor landing this time it'd ease my conscience a bit in takin' this here fine watch." Julius twirled the pocket watch around his finger. "Then again, I take no pleasure'n seeing my fellow man come inta harm's way. That cellar floor I done dropped you on hadta leave a mark. Did it Master Clancy?"

If Clancy's knickers weren't already in a twist, Julius' none-too-subtle efforts to further bruise his ego did it.

"Listen here, Julius...." Clancy took a deep breath. He'd thought of the funhouse as an amusing challenge before, but now Julius had gone and challenged his manhood.

"I get inside Bingham's study on my own power and you give back the timepiece. You incapacitate me beforehand and these wingtips of mine you've been eyeing are yours." Clancy jammed his finger down in the direction of his two-toned, white and tan footwear with perforations over the toes.

Julius cringed. He had been teasing a bit, but he'd underesti-mated Clancy's sensitivity. Perhaps he could talk this man back from the precipice. "You said 'incapacitate' Master Clancy. You meant just holdin' ya so's ya can't move no mo, right?"

Clancy could not be saved from himself.

"You heard correctly. If I've got an ounce of fight left in me, I'm getting into Bingham's sanctum...you drop me in the cellar I'll climb back up. You've got to take me down for the count." Clancy shuffled closer to the manservant and added in a conspiratorial whisper. "I swear Julius, if you don't play ball I'm ratting us both out to Katherine. Sure, I'll get an earful, but she expects this kind of conduct from me. But you? Her mighty man-nanny wagering personal possessions with the houseguests? Ooooh, she'll be devastated...devastated!" This last word burst from Clancy's mouth in a shout.

"Very well, Master Clancy." Julius stepped away from the open door and waved the guest to enter first. "You done dug your own grave, now's nothin' to do but lay in it."

Clancy disregarded the words as mere melodrama and charged through the door and across the marble floor to the grand staircase.

In no hurry, and seemingly without intent, the valet strode to the base of the steps, giving a slight hitch in a stride to stomp a heel into a symmetrical design on the terrazzo.

Clancy would not be fooled twice.

The disappearing third step, tidal wave of medicine balls, and collapsing seventh and eighth steps had actually been successive motor functions born from a single triggering mechanism. Or so the blueprints revealed. The sadistic engineer had designed the clockwork functions to anticipate a person's reflex reactions to simultaneous threats from below and above.

The means of foiling the trap, then, was to act like a simian.

Timed to the seven bars of "Shave and a Haircut,"—and singing the tune as he did it—Clancy bounded up steps one and two, leapt from the second to the fourth step as the third fell away, skipped up steps four, five, six, seven and threw himself bodily from the eighth step to the banister, as seven and eight, on a single hinge, swung down and away to the stygian cellar.

Like a desperate, portly monkey, Tom Clancy shimmied up

the banister as an avalanche of inflated leather spheres rumbled past.

Standing at the top of the staircase, Clancy performed a couple of victory jigs, his stomach flab out of synchronicity with the rest of his otherwise limber body. His successful ascension of the grand staircase surprised even him, so much so that he hadn't made sufficient study of the mantraps beyond. Being between-traps as it were, he might have made use of the schematics wedged in his suit jacket. Instead he forged ahead on the principle that perhaps he could out-race Julius to the next snare.

Tom Clancy's judgment was poor, even cold sober.

The Chinese silk mural looked innocent enough. It hung from corniced ceiling to floor at the wall of the hallway just off the staircase landing. In its original form, the Asian tapestry was a gift to the Harvards from Sterling Chester upon his holiday in Peking. Since then, Katherine Harvard had subjected it to a few alterations.

Clancy barely glanced at the image of the demure geisha in the foreground, a pond alive with koi at her feet, a craggy cliff in the background wrapped with a toothy winged dragon. Leafless stalks of bamboo peppered the crag between silken coils of dragon, each with a curious, three-dimensional appearance.

The appearance of depth wasn't a trick of the eye.

Poker faced and tired stride, Julius casually slapped one non-descript baluster with the back of a hand as he climbed the restored staircase.

A whirr and click of cogs precipitated a transformation of the Chinese silk. The culms of six bamboo dropped from vertical to horizontal, hinged at their bases. With a hiss of pressurized air, four of the culms protracted first one jointed segment, and then another in increasingly narrowing internodes like nested links of a retractable umbrella. Each of the four bamboo were threaded with wire, tipped with a pointed molly bolt, or grapple and shot with enough force to punch through and anchor themselves in the opposite wall.

In appearance, the extended bamboo looked to be a brutal

attempt at clothes-hangering a passer-by. However, the design was meant merely as brief restraint in anticipation of a second, malevolent function.

Clancy blundered into two of the bamboo culms at his chest and waist. He rebounded off the other two bamboo at his shoulder blades and buttocks.

The two remaining, unextended bamboo were not means of restraint at all, but blowguns.

With a wet pop from their "barrels" two anesthetic saturated darts jabbed Clancy at the thigh and shoulder.

Not wanting to stop the victim's heart with a general anesthetic, Katherine selected instead a means of effecting localized paralysis by use of an extract from an Amazonian jungle frog. This rare and exotic sedative came compliments of the Harvards' generous endowment to the New York City Museum of Natural History and thereby direct access to their field biologists.

The bamboo restraint was designed as such only to delay a pedestrian's locomotion long enough for the local anesthetic to take effect and thereafter freeze their motion entirely for the paralysis of half their limbs.

Tom Clancy's combined desperation and pigheadedness was rooted as much in his physiology as his personality. Even his body refused to oblige the funhouse's efforts at incapacitation.

Clancy gave a deep groan as he used his own weight to snap the bamboo in front of him and lumber between the now exposed wire as if breeching a cattle fence.

"Master Thomas, sir, I'm beggin' you as a humble servant of the Lord ta leash your's pridefulness and cry 'Uncle.'" Julius slowly shambled in Clancy's destructive wake, shaking his head.

"Now let's not drag the Holy Father into this, Julius." Clancy yelled over his shoulder. "It's just about a pocket watch, a pair of wingtips...and me making you sit down to a nice plate of crow."

His left leg—tranquilized at the thigh—was a dead weight, and his left arm just a numbed extension of meat at his shoulder. Clancy's movement now resembled that of Ms. Shelley's Modern

Prometheus.

The chandelier above the entryway to Bingham's study was a dead giveaway for a trap. Surely subduing quarry would be a simple matter of releasing the entire light fixture upon its head. Like a live laboratory specimen subjected to ample negative reinforcement, Clancy was catching on.

For what little good that would do him.

Clancy paused his pitiful slide-stepping just short of the chandelier's drop zone, and indeed, by means of a spool and pulley system in the attic, the entire decorative hanging dropped like a stone.

Hundreds of crystals exploded on impact, forcing Clancy back several steps and directly upon a brass grillwork at the floor. From this came a concentrated spray of wombat musk, soaking the seat of Clancy's trousers. Upon the hallway wall, at a ninety-degree angle from its twin on the floor, another brass grating spit forth a swarm of angry Australian ground wasps. Air blasted from their terrarium behind the wall grate, and intoxicated into berserker frenzy by the scent of their natural predator the insects commenced a two-pronged assault upon their perceived nemesis, simultaneously biting and stinging.

Abandoning even the pretense of composure, Clancy unleashed a banshee wail.

At this moment, Bingham chose to succumb to his curiosity about the racket outside his sanctum and opened his study door. Single brow and upper lip raised in tandem, the Master of Myquest stepped through the open portal and to the side.

Seeing the "light at the end of the tunnel," Clancy—screaming all the while—lunged toward the opening with his crippled stride.

Clancy was steps away from recovering a lost wager.

But he turned to look at Julius, now leaning against a wall of the hallway, and gave him a Bronx cheer.

In that instant, the manservant tapped a wall sconce. Before Clancy's head turned forward—the direction of his pathetic flight—the door frame to the study sprang apart, two oak pieces shot from one side of the opening and locked into place at the opposite side via industrial-grade magnets.

Tom Clancy rammed headlong into solid two-by-fours at his head—just above the browline—and at his belly. Total darkness descended.

CHAPTER SEVEN
THE MISSION

August 1, 1920; Greendale, Long Island, New York:

"So Bingham, can I borrow a pair of shoes?"

Bingham Harvard rolled his eyes and audibly exhaled. "It sounds like you've regained your senses...or at least conscious-ness, Clancy. I'm going to take the 'hear no evil, see no evil' approach—as I did with Julius—and won't even ask why our valet took the shoes off your laid-out body and handed me these old house slippers. When Kate asks...and she will...I'm just going to point to you."

Tom Clancy sprawled on his belly upon an oriental rug at the center of Bing's office. Facing, and looking down at his old college friend, the Master of Myquest sat with his elbows on his knees, chin propped upon a massive fist in a high-backed, leather upholstered chair.

"Oh, yes, and Julius gave me these...." Bingham placed a bottle labeled "apple cider vinegar" and a fresh onion imme-diately in front of Clancy's face on the floor next to a pair of threadbare slippers. "He said they were for your wasp stings. I'll leave it to you to make proper application."

"I'm surprised Julius didn't volunteer to pour vinegar on my behind so he could watch me thrash and scream." Clancy retorted from the floor.

"Actually, he did. I told him to leave the home remedies with me."

"Ugh! These house shoes smell like hound piss." Tom clumsily swatted the slippers away.

"Come to think of it, Kate uses those when she plays with the Foxhound pups.

Look, old man, can I beg you to take a chair...lean against the wall...anyplace but where you are. It's awkward and uncomfortable carrying on a conversation with the floor. Let alone take you seriously."

"Oh?" Clancy rolled tenderly to his side, propping his head with an arm, his hand cupping an ear. "And you've never struggled to take me seriously before?" He said sarcastically. "I'll stay right here for a spell, thank you. It just so happens that is why I came to your big meeting a bit early, Bing. I was hoping I could talk some sense into you before you go too far."

Bingham leaned back in his chair and gave a baritone chuckle. "I'm sorry Clancy, this whole conversation...or the part I'm anticipating from you...has so many layers of irony, it's got that onion beat." Bingham pointed to the vegetable on the floor. "You were just anesthetized, attacked by a swarm of bees and knocked senseless on account of, no doubt, some petty ante wager, and now you want me to seriously contemplate your plea to abandon my new life's mission at the eleventh hour of its launch?"

"'Life's mission?!' Bing, this is nuttier than squirrel breath!" Tom Clancy exclaimed.

"Really Tom?" Bingham Harvard responded. "I seem to recall that back when I was wanted dead or alive, you were itching to be in the thick of it. You wanted little more than to see me toss a few grown men around like so much dirty laundry."

"And I stand by my morbid interest in seeing you take out four or five men at once. Who gets to see something like that...ever? My word, Bingham, the strongmen at the circus are downright sleep-inducing compared to what you can do. Just for the record, let's not forget all the times I talked you into public displays of Herculean strength in college...all the pranks we pulled?! I'll never forget the look on the Dean's face when he found his half-ton oak desk hanging from the top of the flag pole! But what you are contemplating now, Bing, it doesn't compare."

"Oh really? How so?" Bingham retorted. Most other pairs of men would have been at fisticuffs after ten minutes of this back-and-forth, but these two were special among men. From their introduction almost twelve years ago it was apparent that their personalities complimented each other; they were either side of the same coin. Bingham was intensely focused, quiet, and self-conscious. By contrast, Tom was and remained considerably more outspoken and worldly, occasionally *over*indulgent, with irons in many fires at once.

Theirs was a relationship both a mile wide and a mile deep. Bing had saved Tom's life in the past from armed thugs—an event Tom would have loved to recall had he been entirely sober. For his part, Tom was the only person to stand by and help his college chum when Bingham had been framed for stealing considerable sums from Centropolis Bank. When even Sterling Chester, his foster father, turned his back on Bing, Tom took him in, and secured a private investigator who ultimately played a significant role in exonerating Bingham entirely.

It was this strong bond of mutual respect and brotherhood that kept the somewhat heated debate from erupting into battle.

"The college fun was just that. Had you not ratted yourself out, no harm would have come to anyone. Even then, the Dean refused to believe that anything but a large construction crane could be responsible; and there being none within a hundred mile radius, selected instead to simply give you a reprimand for 'making up' the story. And as for the experience being framed by the cops and so on, you did not really have a choice in any of that now did you? It's one thing to use your God-given gifts to get yourself out of a pickle, it's quite another to invite one. Going out into the world to right others' wrongs is just plain screwy."

"So a few years ago when I tossed away a couple thugs rushing you with lead pipes and black-jacks; that was 'screwy?'"

Clancy toned down the rhetoric. "Okay, I cotton to your

point. But Bing this is still different. You saved my worthless hide from a couple of desperate foot-pads armed with blunt objects. I'll make a reasonably educated guess that this 'mission' Roderick Maxwilton needs to meet with you about to-night is going to involve some ill-tempered, well organized folks. They will have big, multi-round guns with bullets to spare. Why else would Roderick's employer, the United States Secret Service, have to enlist *someone else* to do the job?!"

"I made this promise to my dying father." Bingham soberly announced. "Katherine is behind me all the way. She even commissioned a German craftsman to make a couple of suits of 'armor' for just the flying-bullets type of event that worries you so. Glenn Redick, Chester's trusted friend, is in my camp and is well suited to keep my affairs in good order. Old chum, I've known you longer than any of them. I suspect that getting into this game of 'good versus evil' my friends and family will become targets. It would help my conscience to have at least your tacit 'okay' to be placed in peril on my account."

"With all due respect to your beautiful wife, Lady Kate, she is...your wife. Also, if that Redick fellow is the salt of the earth you say he is, he's the exception in his trade. Ninety-nine percent of lawyers give the rest a bad name."

Bingham's response was a smile. He stood. "You are welcome to sit in when Roderick arrives. He expressed no objection when we spoke on the telephone to arranging this get-together. You are, whether you like it or not, a bit of an accomplice agreeing to reside at Myquest in my and Kate's absence."

Resigning himself to the temporary cessation of the debate, Clancy sarcastically responded, "Oh, cruel fate! That you would burden my dear wife Roberta and me with all the material temptations of Myquest, one of the largest of Long Island's notoriously huge estates, free of any responsibility other than managing a staff of domestic servants already capable of running this palace on their own. The stable stocked with Kentucky thoroughbreds, the golf course, tennis courts, the lake and beach. How will I ever bear this cross?"

Clancy's whole body jiggled as he laughed from the floor.

* * * * * * *

Roderick Maxwilton stood at the head of the long oak table in the well-stocked library at Myquest. He was Katherine's only sibling; the three Maxwiltons born between them had died in infancy or early adolescence. Roderick was tall, broad of shoulder, well built, and carried himself like a soldier. His hair was thick, but for his age of forty-six prematurely white. His face was handsome, and patrician.

Seated to Roderick's immediate right was his boss, Daniel Drake, head of the United States Secret Service. He was a smallish, thin man with a full head of blonde hair graying at the temples. On that same side, in order, sat Bingham, Glenn Redick, and Tom Clancy.

Clancy perched delicately upon a canvass bag of crushed ice, bandaged about the forehead like a war veteran, in his stocking feet.

To Roderick's immediate left sat his sister, Katherine Harvard, and next to her, Julius, loyal servitor from her birth to present day. Next to Julius was Ernest Cherrington, General Manager of the American Issue Publishing Company and next to him Harry Micajah Daugherty, a Washington Court House, Ohio, political manipulator and lobbyist and presently presidential campaign manager for the 1920 Republican Party nominee, Warren G. Harding.

"This may be an unnecessary admonition under the circumstances, but I must remind all of you that every detail of this get-together must be kept absolutely confidential." Roderick's glance stalled briefly upon Tom Clancy, the only party to this gathering known to be vulnerable to verbal indiscretions.

Somewhat sensitive to his earned reputation, Tom exclaimed, "I don't appreciate that look, Roderick! Assuming for the sake of argument that I do have loose lips, who in their right mind would believe me...about this." And he swept his arms wide to take in all present.

"Fair enough, Tom." Roderick conceded in a tone suggesting more an acceptance, than any heart-felt confidence. "Bingham, you remember just after Mr. Chester passed, almost two years ago now, you and Kate had me over for dinner and volunteered your services to maintain law and order in our country. I thought it was a bit over-the-top at the time, but it made sense, I guess. If you wanted to fulfill Sterling's wishes for your destiny you would ask a U.S. Secret Service agent for leads on troublesome cases of national interest.

"I've heard of your incredible physical feats...read about them in the newspaper, even before I met you several years back. Notwithstanding, taking on the role of a modern day Sir Galahad and righting wrongs that would otherwise overwhelm the usual institutions of public safety...well, I still think it's crazy."

"Here, here!" interrupted Clancy as he leaned forward in his seat catching Bingham's attention. "Well said, Roderick. Great minds think alike...right, Bing?"

Bingham didn't humor Clancy with an acknowledgment.

"Circumstances such that they are, and having casually mentioned your offer to my boss here, Mr. Drake, we thought there was nothing to lose in making a pitch." Roderick continued.

"Except the life of your sister and brother-in-law...there's nothing at stake at all," Clancy added sarcastically.

"Humph!" Mr. Drake audibly cleared his throat, signaling that Roderick should get to the point. Roderick quickly responded.

"Your government needs you, Bingham...Kate. You are aware that national prohibition was ratified just a few months ago. With all due respect to Mr. Cherrington and the fine, fine efforts of the Anti-Saloon League that spearheaded this, uh... social experiment...enforcement problems have arisen.

"Organized crime has significantly upped its bootlegging businesses as they are uniquely placed to take advantage of this once legal, albeit regulated, industry. One would think that members of this new black market would give gracious 'thanks' to the forces of prohibition for quadrupling the price of their product over night; with the added benefit of being entirely free of any regulation whatsoever. It has not worked out that way."

Roderick continued, "It seems that the more militant factions of the prohibition movement have taken it upon themselves to enforce this new law of the land. Specifically, the Ku Klux Klan get their robes in a twist when it comes to consumption of alcoholic spirits. As of this year, KKK membership is roughly four and half million folks, 15% of the nation's eligible population. They've got chapters all over the country, and when they've had the opportunity, they've torched saloons, organized armed patrols to intercept and apprehend bootleggers and, broken up 'speakeasies.'"

Leaning forward for emphasis, Roderick added, "And they are Red Cross volunteers, compared to their more mean-spirited brethren in bed sheets.

"Local police reports around the Indiana and Ohio area have described a wing of the KKK calling themselves the Black Guards, or the Black Legion. They are a security force for the officers of the KKK and are distinguished by their black robes and pointed hoods."

"And why precisely would a group of Klansmen freely exercising vigilante justice *need* a 'security force?'" Bingham interrupted.

"Good point, Bing." responded Roderick. "Seeing their businesses going up in flames, the mafia has been striking back. Men in white robes toting flaming crosses are pretty easy targets if you're patient enough to wait around. And the mafia's hit men have been very patient.

"Enter the Black Legion. They are usually led by a charismatic, literate local, who just happens to have more grudges and scores to settle than the others so they have the wit and the will to orchestrate lynchings, saloon arsons, and synagogue bombings.

"Now all these goings-on seem to be coalescing on one field of battle: Westerville, Ohio. When you put all the facts together, it makes sense in a disturbing sort of way. First, the State of Ohio rendered itself dry by popular vote two years *before* national prohibition. Near its geographic center is Westerville, the home of the Anti-Saloon League, the sole owner and shareholder in The American Issue Publishing Company. It's the mouthpiece for the national prohibition movement. The town is quite appropriately dubbed 'The Dry Capital of the World.' What better locale to draw the figurative 'line in the sand' for the mafia than the home territory of the KKK's pet social initiative? If that weren't enough to bait organized crime, the vast majority of the speakeasy fires, bootlegger tortures and saloon bombings have taken place just south of Westerville in Columbus, the capital city of Ohio. Six arsons and nine dead or dying bootleggers in just two months—all within a ten mile radius of Westerville.

"We have evidence to suggest that the mafia is done with random assassinations of Klan members. The latest activities in Westerville have shown that to be an ineffective tactic. Now they're sending in one of their go-getters, a twenty-one year-old by the name of Al Capone from here in Manhattan."

Roderick sat back, comfortable now in his recitation, "I know it is a sin to believe evil of others, but my experience has been that it is seldom a mistake. Capone is evil. Since his early teens he has worked as a gangster out of Brooklyn, keeping an 'honest' job as a bouncer and bartender at a dive called the Harvard Inn. Just recently he hospitalized a rival gang member, and his 'boss' sent him to Westerville until things cool off. We know he is personally behind at least two cold-blooded murders, but it's been tough to prosecute since witnesses either don't talk or have a strange habit of dying horribly violent deaths before trial."

Clancy interrupted again, "Seems to me you fellows have your work cut out for you. So far I haven't heard anything that Bing's hurricane strength can solve. What about the local police forces of Idaho? Besides, this is *national* prohibition. What are you going to do, ship Bingham off to every burg in the nation when someone dares make a toast at a wedding party?"

"It's 'Ohio,' Tom," retorted Roderick, "And if this sounds like a 'wedding party' to you so far, you haven't been listening. Westerville just hired its first paid police officers five years ago, all three of them. The city itself has a population just under 2,500. Columbus public safety forces are tending to their own and it wouldn't stand a chance of getting to Westerville in time for the 'fireworks,' when they start. In any case, it gets worse, much worse.

"Ohio has the largest KKK chapters in the country. The county just east from where Columbus and Westerville sit has membership of 50,000 or more. Also, Capone isn't settling down in Westerville alone. He'll get enough men from New York and Chicago to do the job right. Bluntly, major battles during the 'Great War' don't have a body count close to what we're expecting in Westerville."

"So call in the military," Tom interjected. "Bingham might have a shot at crippling an unarmed 'platoon' of Klansmen or mafia, but he isn't an army."

"We would prefer to avoid the battle altogether, Mr. Clancy." Roderick responded. "I haven't gotten to the heart of the problem yet. The reason the Secret Service and Mr. Daugherty are involved at all is that we currently have a presidential campaign going on in the midst of this gathering storm. Both of the major parties' nominees are Ohioans: the current governor, James Cox is the Democratic nominee, and United States Senator Warren Harding is the Republican nominee. Some of Governor Cox's campaign stops are scheduled in and around Columbus but, worse, Senator Harding has selected to conduct what he calls a 'front porch campaign.' That is, staying put in his own residence in Marion, Ohio, just 40 miles north of Westerville. From the comfort of his own front porch he plans to lecture to anticipated thousands upon thousands of supporters, the general public and national celebrities alike."

"Just out of curiosity Mr. Maxwilton, *which* national celebrities are we talking about?" Clancy asked.

"So far," the Secret Service agent replied, "Senator Harding has proven himself somewhat of a media darling. He's a news-paper man by trade. Owns and operates the *Marion Star* with his wife, he knows what the press likes, and he gives it to them. As far as Mr. Daugherty can tell us," Roderick pulled a slip of paper from his vest pocket and referred to it, "Al Jolson, Lillian Russell, Douglas Fairbanks, Mary Pickford, Thomas Edison, Henry Ford, and Harvey Firestone will make social calls and public appearances in Marion at the Hardings' home."

Clancy added, "Bing, you'll have to take along my wife's autograph book to Iowa; she just adores Douglas Fairbanks. Kate can ship it back home with your other personal effects and your coffin."

"Tom! Enough!" Katherine interrupted. "All of us are well aware of your opinion on this situation. Bingham, Julius, and I effectively committed ourselves to this 'mission' even before Roderick came here today to give us the details. As a close family friend, there is little left for you to do but accept our decision and lend at least feigned support."

Clancy's mouth clamped shut like a sprung trap. He had a fondness for Katherine Harvard that bordered on puppy love, despite his deep and loyal affection for his own wife. He disliked being on the opposite side of any opinion held by his dear friend's wife.

"Kitten...did you say 'Julius?'" Roderick interjected.

"Yes, of course Roderick. Julius has been the brawn and the brains on more than one trial we Harvards have faced. Julius?"

"Yes, Mis' Kittie...gentlemen," the man seated next to Katherine spoke nervously, but clearly.

"I've spent these last couple years since Mr. Harvard's epiphany trainin' and exercisin' with him. Seems you *can* teach an old dog likes me new tricks...Mis' Kittie here says I'm a natural with a whip and a six-shooter. Also, I built Mis' Harvard's roadster from the ground up and can fix or even build most any of her contraptions.

"All that aside, I's cradled Kate from her birth and wouldn't sleep right at all havin' her off gettin' in trouble. I's cradled you too, Roddy, least until your sister came along."

Earnest Cherrington and Harry Daugherty both sat bolt upright in their chairs while Julius spoke.

"Julius, I know," Roderick seemed pained to say more, "No one, least of all me, questions your proven loyalty to both the Maxwilton and the Harvard families...."

Harry Daugherty burst in, "...but your presence will no doubt jeopardize Mrs. Harvard's safety, not preserve it. Central Ohio is very...homogeneous. You would make yourself, and by association, Mrs. Harvard, a target of the Klan and Black Legion. Also, Mr. Drake, I've expressed to you previously the absolute necessity of dissociating the campaign of Senator Harding with the activities of the Harvards. As the Senator eloquently says, 'America's present need is *not heroics* but healing, not nostrums but normalcy'."

"Is 'normalcy' even a word?" Tom responded, not sufficiently cowed by Mrs. Harvard's pointed statements to cease interruption.

Ignoring Clancy entirely, the Secret Service director stood and spoke for the first time. "Harry, I've told you that to the extent this operation remains under the guidance and control of the Secret Service, our intention is to remain as discreet as possible. Hopefully, the details of the Harvards' assignments will put you at ease."

Drake continued, "Mr. and Mrs. Harvard, your task is twofold; we need someone to get at the root of the problem...that is, the vigilante attacks on the bootleggers and 'speakeasies.' Stop the attacks, and the mafia backs off. Mr. Cherrington has been invited here not merely because his publishing company seems to be sitting at the axis of this conflict and stands to suffer greatly if things worsen. He also has suspicions that the Black Legion itself has been meeting at, or very near his printing plant in uptown Westerville during the very wee hours of the mornings. We suspect that some of the members of the Legion, possibly even their leader, are employed by Mr. Cherrington, unbeknownst to him, of course. For that reason, Mrs. Harvard, we have arranged for your employment by the American Issue Publishing Company. Your brief tenure as a New York City police department undercover detective should see you in good stead. Discover the Black Legion members, pinpoint the identity of their leader and report to Roderick or myself for the arrest. We will be in Marion, with the Senator. Communication via telephone cannot be counted on for privacy, so Roderick will have you and Bingham both outfitted with the very best wireless transmitters and receivers with our direct frequency pre-programmed."

Drake turned to Bingham. "Mr. Harvard, yours is the fall-back plan. Failing some immediate progress from your wife, we have to force at least one of the combatants from the battle line. There is no time to infiltrate the mafia. Suspicions are high even when tensions are low in that camp and we don't think you would stand a chance of blending in. On the other hand, toss a black hood on anyone's head and you become indistinguishable. So here you are," Drake bent to the floor next to his chair, picked up a paperbound package the size of a phonograph and placed it on the table in front of Bingham.

As Bingham opened the package and pulled the item from its wrappings, Drake explained, "That is the 'fighting togs' of a member of the Black Legion; ankle length black robe with black hood—pointed, like a dunce cap, ironically. Of course, this is a very special model robe and hood; it is made entirely of tightly spun and layered silk, 'soft body armor,' if you will, effective against low-velocity bullets.

"For reasons that are not exactly clear to us now, the Black Legion members remain in 'uniform' even amongst themselves. It's relatively easy to get initiated—seems little more than the proper attire will do—just damn near impossible to ferret out the proper names of members. We have a man currently among them, shares your general physique well enough. We've got a script for you and our plant to identify one another so you can swap places. As an accepted member, your approach is pretty blunt really:

"Beat the living hell out of as many members of organized crime as you can.

"In addition to whatever intelligence the Legion might gather on the whereabouts of Capone's troops, the Secret Service will provide all intelligence it can secure. Cripple enough mafia boys, as high as you can get in the chain of command, and we think the mafia will cut their losses and run. The big bootlegging money is in Chicago or New York City. Other than their grudge against the KKK, there isn't a lot of profit to be made in Central Ohio. We think if pressured to choose, the mafia will favor their bottom line to personal vendettas."

Clancy, again: "Wasn't Archduke Francis Ferdinand of Austria wearing 'armor' like that when he was killed by a shot to the head, precipitating 'the Great War?'"

"You are a stickler for detail, Mr. Clancy," Drake responded. "You happen to be correct. Two differences from that tragic event however. Unlike the unfortunate Archduke, Bingham will be covered, from head to ankles. Also, this robe is just the outer layer of protection. Mrs. Harvard?"

"Thank you, Mr. Drake. I'll be happy to explain what I've come up with by way of 'armor,' later. First, however, it is plain that my intentions of bringing Julius with me to Westerville are being summarily dismissed or ignored. Do I understand, Roderick, that despite being set up in a separate residence from my husband and told not to interact with him lest we double our chances of being 'uncovered' you are also depriving me from having my most valued assistant and protector at my side?"

"That is precisely what I'm saying dear sis...," Roderick bluntly replied before being interrupted by a metallic *clank*. A flexible steel bar rapidly snaked around from behind, crossed in front of him and locked on the other side of the seat. Roderick was effectively pinned in place. "What in God's na...." He couldn't finish his startled question before his entire chair dropped below the floor like a rock in water. The trap door swung closed barely muffling Roderick's unrestrained cursing below.

Bingham, Julius and Glenn barely restrained their laughter

at the other participants' shocked expressions. Clancy enjoyed a brief moment of relief seeing someone else suffer at the hands of the 'funhouse.'

Wired for emergency and action by trade and experience, Secret Service Director Daniel Drake shot upward from his seat. His chair behind him, he landed, cat-like, with his legs and feet spread wide and positioned such that if the floor should drop he would safely straddle the edges of the hole.

Poised thus, Drake spat through gritted teeth, "Someone better explain what's happening. Now!"

As if in response, there came an audible click, this time emanating from the oak table. Drake's eyes were lured to the edge of the table directly in front of him. As only he could observe precisely what was transpiring, Katherine narrated for the group.

"That is the muzzle of a seventeenth-century 'blunderbuss,' extending from the edge of this table and pointed directly at your vital organs, Mr. Drake. As you likely know, the blunderbuss compensates in sheer destructive force what it loses in accuracy. At its present range, with the small collection of children's lead jacks in the barrel, you will be deceased before your organs hit the floor."

Drake's face turned red with fury. "And what exactly do you think you are doing, threatening me with this miniature cannon?!"

Katherine continued, her brother's spirited profane protests from below the floor only barely audible, "Really, I have no intention whatsoever of causing you or anyone else in this room any harm. It is merely an admittedly rude demonstration of my ability to know precisely what is or is not in my best interests and to protect those interests, even unto death. Is my demonstration getting through to you Mr. Drake?"

"I believe I take your point, Mrs. Harvard," Drake said in a barely controlled grumble.

"Messrs. Cherrington and Daugherty?" Katherine added.

"Yes, indeed," Cherrington quickly spoke up. "I think I

speak for both of us."

Daugherty nodded in acknowledgment.

Katherine leaned back in her chair. Simultaneously, a trap-door opened where her brother's chair used to sit, and he and his seat gently rose to its former position at the head of the table. The steel arm that held him fast was released; it flew back to its former position as if it were one of the braces at the back of the chair.

Drake restored his chair to the table, and furtively glanced at the others around the room. He quickly straightened his tie and collar, and with obvious irritation took his seat.

Roderick Maxwilton, although clearly angered and embarrassed, had managed to compose himself during his extended captivity in the darkened recesses of the Harvard's cellar. "Kitten...you are such a...brat!"

"That's all you can come up with, Roderick? By the way, in your absence, your boss has exercised his sage wisdom and permitted me to have Julius along at my residence in Westerville."

Mr. Drake only smiled thinly at Roderick and nodded his head. By then the blunderbuss had magically folded itself out of view.

"And Mr. Cherrington, in light of your sightings of the Black Legion operating in the vicinity of your plant, I would like a position running one of your biggest presses, third shift."

"That is not typically a function assigned to the fairer sex, but I...uh...think we can arrange that for you, Mrs. Harvard." the General Manager responded.

"Very good. Thank you. Now to the subject of my husband's protective gear." Julius hefted on to the table a box even bigger than the one containing the Black Legion regalia. Katherine stood and pulled articles of clothing from the box giving description along the way.

"This is a considerably advanced model of the 'Brewster Body Shield,' developed by our government during 'the Great War.'" Kate lifted what appeared to be a padded, long sleeve shirt from the box and held it at the neck and shoulders for display. It was a deep gray color, with five, thick scarlet stripes, front and back. Three stripes at the front and back ran from neck to the trim at the bottom of the shirt. Two stripes on each arm, front and back, ran from the neck to the wrists.

"What you see is the same silk 'soft body armor,' as the Black Legion outfit, but dyed scarlet and gray. However, woven inside is a chrome nickel steel breastplate and back plate connected with overlapping steel scales, fixed to a leather lining." Katherine sat the 'shirt' on the table for all to see and lifted a gray headpiece from the box. "This 'helmet' has plates of chrome nickel steel sewn inside, the distance between each not large enough for any sized bullet to pass. These deep scarlet 'pants' are designed much the same way, with chain mail at the hip joints and knees for movement.

"Unlike the 'soft body armor,' this outfit is virtually indestructible. It can withstand Lewis Gun bullets at 2,700 feet per second. Of course the whole uniform weighs just under fifty pounds, and was therefore impractical for our dough boys in battle. But Bingham's enhanced strength makes it comparable to the rest of us wearing bathrobes.

"You will notice that the complete ensemble, and I've secured two of them, just in case one is damaged, resembles today's fully padded football player uniform. The similarity is not accidental, nor are the colors. I understand that a local Columbus college, the Ohio State University, has a very popular football team whose season begins in late summer and runs through the fall—precisely the duration of the presidential campaign. The team is called 'The Ohio State Buckeyes' and they sport similar scarlet and gray uniforms. I am hopeful that should Bing have to abandon his black robe and hood and be seen in this 'secondary' armor, he might be mistaken for a peculiarly avid sports fan."

Brokering no interruption, as her two passions—her husband and her hobby—were at issue, Katherine ignored Clancy's posture suggesting that he had something to add.

"These are the only 'weapons' Bingham would permit me

to commission." Katherine held up what appeared to be a pair of scarlet gloves each with unmistakable protrusions where the knuckles at the hands would be. "Roman gladiators wore these in boxing matches...to the death...they are cestuses, the classic world's equivalent to brass knuckles. The name notwithstanding, they are made of steel, molded from a caste of Bingham's own hands, and secured by scarlet silk and leather."

Katherine went on: "Bingham may have incredible physical strength, but he bleeds like you and I. Because he is mortal, he has at least a subconscious anxiety about harming his own hands when striking. The cestuses eliminate that fear and allow him to punch or hit harder than even he would consider 'normal.'"

Refusing to be ignored any longer, Clancy interjected. "Do any of you seriously envision a happy end to this 'mission'? If there is a light at the end of this tunnel, it's the headlamp of an approaching train!"

CHAPTER EIGHT
A DOUBTING DRAKE

"Sir, is this really necessary?" Roderick Maxwilton whispered quietly to his boss, Daniel Drake, as the participants of the secret meeting on the Harvards' 'mission' rose from their seats in anticipation of dispersing to their respective homes.

"We've had this discussion, Roderick. I never once doubted your faith in your sister's ability to pull off her part of the deal. Her credentials are in order, her background is documented. Great Scott!, I just 'okayed' her plan to reside with a black man in the heart of KKK territory! But I absolutely must see this 'Night Wind' fellow in action. This mission is too important for me to take on faith the existence of a modern day Hercules."

"Very well, sir. I'll leave it to you to explain it to my sister, then." Roderick lamely responded.

"Plan on it." Drake said. "Just as soon as we're out of this 'funhouse.'"

Engaged in more casual banter, the other members of the group ambled toward the main doors. Harry Daugherty and Tom Clancy gave a quick handshake, and Daugherty strode ahead placing a controlling hand on the shoulder of the man just in front—Bingham Harvard.

Gripping what felt to be solid brick, and failing even to slow Bingham's tread, the portly politico snapped his hand away as if bitten and spoke, instead.

"Mr. Harvard?"

By response, the Master of Myquest looked over his shoulder, raising one brow in acknowledgment.

Daugherty continued. "Mr. Clancy has just this moment staked a goodly sum of cash, in exchange for my Italian business shoes. To win the wager, I need only get you to speak three words. I am a well regarded broker of political power and...."

Cutting off the politician, Bingham neither broke stride nor looked at his insistent house guest. He said merely, "You lose."

A flummoxed Daugherty cut his pace and looked aghast at a now beaming Tom Clancy.

Julius held the main door as the party exited single file, the first in line lingering briefly until all stood on the wide veranda together. As Clancy made a step to the staircase and his waiting car, Drake announced, "A moment more Mr. Clancy...please.

"Mr. Harvard," Drake spoke in a voice intended to capture the attention of all present. "I hope you might understand my apprehension in sending a respectable citizen like yourself into the 'lion's den,' so to speak. I have some eminently capable men in my agency, Roderick included, who I would not dare ask to do what I have just asked of you. So please pardon me, sir, when I say that I must have some demonstration of your fantastic abilities."

"What!" Katherine exclaimed, "You mean to put my husband in harm's way for your own lack of faith?!"

Cherrington and Daugherty, convinced that Mrs. Harvard's exasperation signaled another demonstration of creative restraint or threat of death, scurried down the front steps to the gravel driveway. Daugherty gave a piggish squeal as jagged rock pierced his sock feet.

Drake stood his ground, "Do you mean 'in harm's way' like threatening to disembowel him with a set of kids' jacks, Mrs. Harvard? Is that what you mean?

"I have no intention of causing your husband harm. But if, by happenstance, he does suffer some injury, here in the controlled environment of your own estate, we can stop this charade right now and spare him, and others, the slaughter that's waiting for him in Westerville. I have hired several men recommended to me as 'peerless' or 'superlative,' Mrs. Harvard—or at least that was how they were described by the pastor at their graveside.

"I mean no offence to either of you, Katherine, Bingham. Consider it a selfish act on my part in wishing to be able to look myself in the mirror certain that I did not just send a good man to sure death."

"What do you propose, Mr. Drake?" Bingham asked.

"Thank you, Mr. Harvard. It is a simple 'game' really. My hat is resting on the stoop of the unused lodge at the entrance to your estate. Get it and return it to me."

"It isn't really that simple, is it?" Bingham mused out loud.

Drake gave a sly smile, "Of course I have eleven trained Secret Service agents stationed along your quarter mile route who have been promised a week's vacation and a $100 bonus if they can stop you from returning my hat to me."

Remaining within earshot, and intrigued by the challenge—not to mention being comforted by the fact that no one had disappeared through the floor—Cherrington and Daugherty carefully ascended the porch steps and rejoined the group.

"Very well. I accept your 'test.'" Bingham was off the porch and into the driveway before his wife could open her mouth to protest.

"It is a very cruel thing you have done just now." Katherine sighed.

"Your husband will be fine Mrs. Harvard." Drake snapped irritably.

"It's not my husband you've been cruel to, Mr. Drake. It's those eleven men of yours to whom you will be making apologies."

* * * * * * *

The sun had set hours ago but the cloudless night sky provided enough star and moonlight to make out at least the silhouettes of anyone on or near the gray gravel road to the Harvards' estate. Bingham was fifty yards along the path, making no effort whatsoever to conceal himself along the thick-boughed balsam lining the road, before the first agent got within striking distance. He came on just in front of Bing, in a waist-high football tackle. A sharp, but restrained drop of his right elbow to the agent's head smacked his would-be attacker abruptly to the road, face-down, and horizontal. Bingham barely broke his stride.

A circle of four agents—two from behind, two from the front—came at Bingham together. Bing skidded to an abrupt stop, forcing the two agents at his front to try to slow their momentum or fly right past their target. They couldn't stop fast enough. Bingham dodged the closest agent, sticking his foot out for good measure and sending him flying to the jagged gravel road. He grabbed the extended arm of the second agent in front of him and using his own forward momentum launched him directly into one of the agents racing up from behind. Like a 'keystone cop' the fourth and last agent tripped over his fallen comrade, taking him out of the picture.

Bingham paused only briefly to ensure that the five agents left in his wake were getting back on their feet. As the last man arose, the Master of Myquest turned back to his target— the lodge gates—and throttled forward like a sprinter from the starting blocks. Bits of gravel and dust erupted with each footfall. At his present pace in the cover of darkness, the dust trail was the only thing visible. Pursuing Secret Service agents would later describe the sight as if a very narrow fault line in the earth's crust was opening directly down the center of the road, spewing smoke and dirt in a rapidly lengthening line.

Not entirely comfortable with physically engaging the Servicemen for fear of causing them considerable injury, Bingham was satisfied to simply outrun his pursuers. However, he failed to consider that the agents would not rely entirely on physical contact to apprehend their target. In fact, they had had considerable time—from Roderick and Drake's arrival until the end of the secret meeting—to prepare for Bing's "test."

Within sight of the gates, but still hundreds of yards away, he felt a sudden, brief tug at his forward ankle and then a feeling of weightless flight. With his speed and dimmed vision, not to mention the dust kicked up by his own momentum, Bing did not see the trip line strung across the road and secured to balsam trees on either side.

Instinctively, Bingham tucked and rolled. He hit the gravel upside down, just on the shoulder blades, completed a half circle role and then snapped-to, on his feet.

Convinced that brute strength alone could not win the day, Katherine had insisted that her husband train with masters of various fighting techniques. Until he was forced to fight for his freedom years ago, Bingham had relegated the display of his physical acumen to parlor tricks, usually for Clancy's amusement. As he would discover, even his fisticuffs with the police force of New York City didn't truly exhibit the full extent of his physical capacity. His so-called trainers read like the competitors at an Olympic game.

Their injuries read like autopsy reports of gladiatorial combatants.

Master sensai Konishi, karate, suffered a ruptured spleen and shattered right wrist. Master Devillèrs boasted expertise in savate, French kickboxing. At least for a time, he was unable to say anything due to his compound jaw fractures and collapsed right lung. Grandmaster Prajadhipok made a sincerely beautiful demonstration of Thai boxing, Muay Thai. Sparring with Bingham left him paralyzed from the waist down.

Glenn Redick's 'release from liability' forms, a predicate to entering into a contract to train Bingham, saved the Harvard fortune many, many millions in lawsuits.

It seemed Bingham's bare-knuckle pounding and uncanny reflexes needed no refinement after all, but restraint.

At the moment, the back of his suit jacket was in shreds, as was his dress shirt. Stubborn bits of rock that might have punctured normal skin created irritating indentions in Bingham's more resilient hide.

Along with the bothersome throbbing, anger began to flare. Where his conscious mind accepted, even invited Drake's challenge, Bing's subconscious had unleashed his "fighting" instinct. For others, this would have been a *"fight or flight"* instinct. But Bingham Harvard did not possess the latter in any measurable degree.

Rousing this violent passion was something his wife avoided at all costs. Indeed, in the past, she had permitted herself to be blackmailed and threatened, rather than subject the villain to sudden and violent death at the hands of her husband. Lady Kate feared Bingham's explosive strength more than anything that a plotting rogue could let loose.

The Secret Service agents were not so informed. Indeed they, like their director, brushed aside the history of the 'Night Wind' as folklore if not complete fantasy.

Having brought their prey to a stop, two agents raced from either tree line facing Bingham, blocking him from view of the gates. Each was armed with nun-chucks—wooden handles connected by foot-long, steel-link chain. The weapons moved like angry bees around their nest as the agents made a show of their exceptional skills in brandishing these tools of the Orient.

They faced Bingham, two black silhouettes outlined by the light coming from the lodge gates at their backs. Designed originally as an agricultural implement to thrash grains of rice from stalks, necessity had turned the nun-chucks into a means of pummeling a target into submission.

Thoughts of history, culture or the skill with which these weapons were wielded did not enter Bing's rage-clouded consciousness. He dashed toward the agent to his left, clasped an upraised arm at mid-swing with one hand and unleashed a lightening blow with the other into the agent's stomach. Red rage notwithstanding, Bingham was careful to slightly hold his punch for fear of putting his fist out the agent's back. He wrenched the nun-chuck from his victim's grasp and flung it at the neck of the second agent. The tool made a graceful, rapid arc around the agent's raised arm and neck. Bingham was upon him at once, gripping both handles in one hand and constricting his target's head and arm whilst forcing his victim to his knees.

Once kneeling, Bing used his free right hand to slide down the agent's back, grasp his pant's belt and lift him completely off the ground.

Slinging his burden over his shoulder, Bingham marched several feet to one of the lit lodge gates, hooked the agent's belt loop to the overhanging lamp, six feet from the ground, and let the nun-chuck drop to the gravel. The agent swung helplessly, unable to make purchase with his hands at either Bingham or the nearby gate post.

From first contact to the submission of the second and final agent, only seconds had elapsed. The two men had as much chance of laying hold of Bingham's flashing limbs as a person would have trying to grasp the wing of a humming bird in flight.

As promised, a nicely creased dress-style fedora rested on the ground just at the stoop of the vacant lodge. Parked nearby and only partially shadowed in the gloom, three black convertible Ford Model Ts sat near the lodge gates.

Ignoring the swearing of the suspended agent and the groans from the second clutching his stomach on the gravel, Bing bent and picked up the hat. He turned and walked back the direction he had come.

Careless of where his next assault would come from, Bingham slowly dragged his feet in the vicinity where he had been tripped. He quickly uncovered the trip line, bent and ripped loose the hemp rope as if it were a dry weed.

With his next step, Bingham first heard and then felt the whistling lassos: two of them, one from either side of the road. Both were expertly thrown, snaring their intended target over his head and tightening just below the shoulders, pinning his arms. Bing casually dropped the fedora at his feet, and then, as if shucking an unbuttoned dress shirt, he expanded his chest and swiftly raised both arms, tearing the looped cords into pieces. He grabbed one of the loose ropes and pulled with considerable force, yanking the man at the other end off his feet and onto the gravel, raking him along the path as he stubbornly held the remains of his lasso.

Bingham raced to the prone agent first, hog-tying him like a seasoned rancher subduing a calf. With the final loop of his knot around the first agent's limbs, the second agent raced up from Bing's back. Distracted for an instant from the weight of a full-grown man on his back, the agent had the opportunity to get a rope over Bing's head and around his neck.

Unfazed, the Night Wind reached back, grabbed a tuft of the agent's hair and effortlessly flipped him over his shoulder and on top of his hogtied partner. Before the dazed second agent could come to his senses, he, too was prone on the gravel road and hogtied.

Bingham stood, recovered the hat, none the worse for the wear, and resumed his direct course up the center of the road to his home. So focused was he on his return flight that he didn't even hear the two bolas. The pain from the constricting ropes was bearable, but rugged skin would not preserve his balance. He went down like a felled tree.

As he hit the rocky path, yells of triumph erupted behind him from the bola throwers, and in front from the five agents he had leveled at the start.

Fury blinded Bingham to the biting from the bola cords. He found it inconceivable to submit this close to the "finish line."

He could see the five agents immediately in front of him, cautiously approaching, illuminated by the mansion lights. Behind them, Harvard made out the group of people poised upon his veranda, his dear, no doubt distraught, wife among them. He likewise heard the crunch of heavy footfalls on gravel behind him as the triumphant bola throwers moved toward their downed prey.

Bingham quickly brought himself to a seated position and felt down his legs for the weighted ends of the bolas. Using both hands, he quickly snapped the solid lead balls from the ends of the cords as if beheading dandelions. Without pause, and seemingly without taking aim, Bing pitched a sphere from each hand.

He was careful to check both throws.

The two bola throwers were not expecting return-fire.

Two meaty thwacks confirmed impacts. The first agent was hit at the right thigh, separating hip from socket. He was fortunate, by comparison to his partner. The second bola master was hit at the knee and would live out his life with a limp.

Cries of agony stopped the five approaching agents in their tracks, giving Harvard the critical time he needed to snap the two weighted ends from the final bola and to delicately shrug the cords from his legs.

The Night Wind slowly stood, lead projectile in each hand, a simmering volcano of rage. What had begun as an admittedly violent game of tackle football had evolved into a no-holds-barred safari with Bingham as the game animal. Nun-chucks, even from practiced hands, could have brained him. The bolas, but for the unusual density of his superhuman muscle fiber, would have cut him to the bone, crippling him for life.

The five standing agents, the only obstacles between Bingham and the success of his 'test,' separated and quickly moved to let him pass. All five had suffered by Bing's impressive strength at the beginning of his ordeal. They could still hear the agonized wailing of two of their own, crumpled on the gravel road, leveled by lead ball-bearings, two of which Bingham still held.

Seeing his challengers cede the field, Bing dropped one bearing and bent to pick up the fedora. Despite the disheveled appearance of its bearer, the fedora remained in remarkably fine shape.

From behind Harvard, the sound of a car engine kicking into life broke the temporary silence of the night. Not all of the once-felled agents had resigned themselves to defeat. Unbeknownst to Bingham, the belt loop of the agent strung to the gate post only briefly held his weight. Unceremoniously dropped to the earth, the Secret Service man got to his feet and cranked up one of the three Model Ts at the gate, hopped in and began to speed toward the main house.

It was not the agent's intention to harm Bingham, but simply to get quickly to the scene of battle so that he might help his comrades. Nonetheless, with the power of the Model T's engine, and the give of the drive's gravel, the agent found himself stomping for dear life upon the brake as he raced, full bore, directly at the only figure in his path, Bingham Harvard.

The Night Wind had hesitated at the incongruous sound of grinding gears and automotive backfire. He turned to the sight of the onrushing convertible, the headlights blinding him in their glare.

"Master Bingham, sir!" Julius, shouting from the porch, caused Bing to look over his shoulder.

On Katherine's instruction, as Bingham was running the 'gauntlet,' Julius had returned inside for first aid equipment—iodine, bandages, etc. On a whim, he also brought out the unusual cestuses that Katherine had displayed to the assembled group earlier that evening. He clutched the cestus for the left hand as he shouted Bingham's name over the roar of the fast-approaching automobile.

Bingham understood Julius' intentions immediately and raised his arms as if to receive a pass. Julius hurled the heavy cestus in a beautiful, arcing toss. For a moment, the pitch seemed destined to fly over Bing's head, but he quickly launched himself from the ground, intercepting the cestus in flight with both arms straight over his head. In one seamless motion, Bingham slipped the gloved weapon over his left hand and slapped his right hand over the now gloved left, just below the steel "knuckles."

The skidding Model T's hood was nearly upon Bingham. But for his leap, impact was certain. Gravity pulled Bingham back to earth, but not before he brought both arms down, bare hand gripping the wrist of the "brass-knuckled" appendage in a double-armed swing.

The steel-plated gauntlet, with all of Harvard's weight behind it, rammed into the front-mounted radiator of the Model T's hood. Radiator and engine block caved in on impact, driving the face of the vehicle piston-like into the soft road beneath.

The scream of the hapless driver was masked by the double *boom* of the bursting front tires. Without a roof to protect him, the Secret Service agent catapulted into the air uninhibited. His body broken, he crashed at the base of the front porch staircase immediately in front of the spectators. He would live, and even mend, but his pride would never be restored.

(page 106) **The steel-plated gauntlet with all of Harvard's weight behind it, rammed into the front-mounted radiator of the Model-T's hood.**

Bingham recovered the fedora from the ground and turned to face the observers from the porch. The Model T behind him was mashed, hood first into the earth like a mechanical ostrich burying its head in the sand. A geyser of radiator water shot into the air. Nearly a dozen torn, bleeding men limped or crawled to the house. The piteous moans of those who could do neither played as a gruesome background chorus.

His anger spent, Bingham climbed the steps of the veranda and held out the still unmarred fedora to Dan Drake. "Satisfied?" he asked, rhetorically, and brushed past the Secret Service Director to Julius' waiting first-aid supplies.

CHAPTER NINE
A SILLY LITTLE BOY'S FANTASY

August 11, 1920; Westerville, Ohio:

Elmer Pfleager stood outside on his back porch, a cake of soap poking from his mouth.

His mother bellowed scolding words through the back, screened door. "Y' can take that bar of soap out of yer mouth just as soon as y' can tell me the truth about getting home so late from yer paper-route this mornin'!"

For emphasis, Wilma Pfleager pressed her worry-worn face to the inside of the screen and continued to chastise her young son. "An' I'm not buying yer 'I met a superman who chased down gangsters an' Klansmen' story. Ain't nothin' more than a silly little boy's fantasy, an' you know it."

The lecture continued, but by then young Elmer had plopped himself down on the first step of the wooden-plank stoop, his back to his ranting mother. Only fragments of her oratory interrupted his already wandering thoughts: "...if yer father would stop bringing home those wretched magazines...those pulps are gonna rot yer brain, mark my word...."

Shortly, Mrs. Pfleager withdrew from the screened door, her words clattering along with the pots and pans in the kitchen.

Looking left, a somber Elmer spied his father's legs protruding from underneath the family car just a few feet away.

Elmer, Sr. fancied himself a master repairman. Truth be told, his own wife wouldn't trust him to fix a bent spoon. As the saying goes, "he had two left feet, and was all thumbs."

Notwithstanding, Mr. Pfleager's confidence and enthusiasm were irrepressible. It was understood even among Elmer's three younger siblings, that items in disrepair were hidden from view, or repaired on the sly, lest father inevitably injure himself or permanently damage the object in "fix it" zeal.

The family auto's size, and the fact that only Elmer, Sr. drove, necessarily exempted it from this unwritten agreement between mother and children. The sound of metal on metal and random swearing emitted from underneath the vehicle.

Just at his back, Elmer, Jr. heard the gentle impact of the back screen door on the frame followed instantly by the shuffling of tiny bare feet on the wooden porch. Feeling a light tug on his shirt sleeve, the boy turned his head toward his youngest sibling, two-year-old Clary. Seemingly born with the capacity for empathy, she was the self-appointed family peacemaker, a junior Clara Barton.

Her dishwater blonde, shoulder length hair was generously suffused with curls, messy and tangled as always. Her chubby cherubic face expressed heart-breaking, genuine sorrow for her brother's persecution. "Eat soap again? I sorry."

Without further comment, the little girl seated herself snuggly against her brother, crossed her arms at her chest and slouched forward, duplicating her older sibling's posture. As an additional expression of solidarity, the youngster carefully wedged a plump, dirty hand into her mouth just past her knuckles.

This was the tableau that greeted Bingham Harvard as he strolled down the alley abutting the Pfleager's backyard. Unlike his wife, whose "cover" was daily employment at the American Issue Publishing Company, Bing had nothing to occupy his day-light hours. Consequently, he had taken to enjoying brisk walks through the community for exercise and fresh air, abandoning black robe and padded uniform at his lodgings in favor of normal, "civilian" garb.

Unlike the more whimsical walks he had taken of late, this day's stroll had a definite purpose. Elmer's presence during the violent events of that same early morning compelled him to seek out his new acquaintance. A quick telephone call to Elmer's known employer—*The Ohio State Journal*—provided Bingham the name and address of his newsboy.

Bingham halted mid-stride upon catching sight of the only friendly face he'd come to know in Westerville, Ohio. With a wave of his hand in greeting, he casually walked up the dirt driveway from the paved alley toward the seated children.

Elmer saw Bing approaching and reached to his mouth to extract the bar of soap. Before his lips could form a single word, his mother's voice exploded through the open window above the kitchen sink. "Less'n yer planning a' honest explanation for yer tardiness this mornin' y'd best insert that soap back in yer pie hole, young man!"

"But...!" Elmer turned his head to see his mother's face peering through the open window.

"No, 'buts,' Elmer." Mrs. Pfleager interrupted. "Yer first words gotta be 'here's the truth, ma'am,' or I'm gonna switch that there store-bought soap with granny Pfleager's home-made cow-fat bar."

Elmer gave an unconscious shudder at the thought of consuming grandma's rendered animal fat soap. With a "humph" of frustration, the boy popped the commercial bar-soap back in his mouth.

Elmer turned to face Bingham as the man stopped and stood with only the front-end of the family's automobile separating him from the two children on the porch.

Although just a few feet from both of Elmer's parents, Bingham's location was such that neither could see nor hear him. Elmer, Sr. was prostrate under the jacked-up car. His unrestrained cursing and clattering masked any awareness of their guest. Likewise, while Mrs. Pfleager's view of her children on the porch was clear, a projecting corner of the house blocked her line of sight along the dirt driveway where Bingham stood.

This was not accidental, for Bingham Harvard had made the conscious decision to spare any additional persons from becoming material witnesses to his purpose here in Westerville. As it was, he had slept very little those few remaining hours of the morning, worrying of the consequences of young Elmer's involvement.

With a view to making a quick departure, Bing got to the point. "You did not abide by my instruction to flee when I ran off in pursuit of the Klansmen and their prey this morning, did you?"

Impressed by Bingham's demonstrated great strength and confused that he appeared to be a member of the KKK, Elmer's response was hesitant, but honest nonetheless. Soap still firmly in mouth, the young boy slowly turned his head from left to right.

"I fear that you have made yourself known to either member-ship of the Black Legion or organized crime...or both." Bing continued, "Even if they don't know of you, it's clear they're most active when and where you're delivering newspapers and you will get in their way, sooner or later.

"I do not suppose I can convince you to abandon your duties as a paperboy?"

By response, Elmer gave a firm jerk of the head from left to right again.

Bingham went on, "In that case, you have earned yourself a personal escort during your morning paper deliveries. By that I mean from your departure from your home until you return, every morning." Bing had resolved already to make regular, early morning "patrols" of Westerville and this plan had the double purpose of protecting his youthful companion.

This declaration might have frozen a less active mind in fear. But Elmer was a thinker. All last school year he'd only had to wear the dunce cap once.

The newsboy recalled that the poor man who had been tarred and feathered was saved by a Klansman who had sent him airborn for several feet into the water with just a push. He'd only seen a demonstration of strength like that from one person. And that fellow was talking to him now. Perhaps it was the soap chemicals disturbing his brain, but he would go along with Bingham's dictate. Surely no one would mistake him for a bootlegger. He was just a kid.

The more he ruminated upon it, young Elmer was relieved to have the company of this 'superman' during his morning route. He would not soon forget the violence and horror of that same early morning and welcomed any chance to avoid a similar experience. His internal reflections notwithstanding, the boy merely shrugged his shoulders and slowly nodded his head up and down.

"Very well then...." Bingham turned to take his leave. Fate had other plans. Suddenly a high-pitched whine of rending metal cut the air. Elmer and Clary's eyes bugged. As if choreographed they wordlessly pointed to their father's feet protruding from under the car. Clary yanked her hand from her mouth and chirped "Daddy!"

In an instant, Bingham grasped the situation. The owner of the protruding feet was about to be reduced to pulp under his own car.

Without a word, and with his usual sanguine expression, Bing stepped forward and against the sagging vehicle and raised a foot just under the running board. The muffled *clang* of the broken jack signaled that tool's demise. Bingham Harvard thus carried the full weight of the automobile.

Elmer, Sr. remained blissfully ignorant of all of this, being by his nature oblivious to the hazards to which he subjected himself and too preoccupied with the task at hand.

Bing quickly looked around his immediate vicinity for some means of relief, and found it in the form of a broken elm-tree branch just above his head and extending perpendicular to the dirt driveway.

The two children looked on, mouths agape such that Elmer's bar of soap soundlessly slipped from his mouth.

Bingham raised himself upon the toes of his grounded foot, extended his arm above his head and grasped the overhead tree branch. With a twist and a barely audible *snap* he wrenched the massive limb free at the trunk.

Thereupon, with his free hand, he stripped the log of branches as if husking an ear of corn, dispensed with the thinner and weaker portion of the limb with a snap over his raised leg and a toss over his shoulder. With the hardy elm branch thus reduced to a sufficient size, Bingham wedged it between solid ground and the under-carriage of the car. Satisfied with the balance and support of the single log, Bing released his foot from the running board.

Content that his visit had served its purpose and that Elmer was reconciled to constant escort, Bingham waved good-bye. He turned and departed the scene casually, not the least fatigued by his exertions. He was gone before Mrs. Pfleager, entirely ignorant of the events of the last few minutes, stepped from her screened back door to the stoop where her two children sat.

Before she could utter a word, Clary sprung from her seat next to her brother and let loose a torrent of excited, barely comprehensible words, pointing in the direction Bingham had walked: "Ooh, Mommy, Samson right here...Goliath...."

Clary's mother could see a chunk of tree precariously balancing the family automobile over her oblivious husband. But this was just the sort of hair-brained retro-fitting for which her spouse was infamous. Mrs. Pfleager shook her head in frustration and directed her comments to her eldest son.

"Now look what your fanciful story tellin' has done, Elmer! You've filled yer sister's head with nonsense! You've just bought yerself another ten minutes of mouth cleansing, young man!"

To this, a defeated Elmer sank his head into the open palms of his hands, expelled a sigh, and with it several soap bubbles.

CHAPTER TEN
DESCENDING THE FAMILY TREE

May, 1919; Dutchess County, New York:

Rodney Rushton guided his roadster along the narrow path en route to the City of Beacon, New York and the Matteawan State Hospital for the Criminally Insane. Cigar smoke wafted from open windows as if the car's interior had caught flame.

It had been roughly six months since Bingham Harvard had given him the assignment to find his father and the identity of his deceased mother, and he had only just a week ago gotten his lucky break. That is, if you call being "lucky" discovering that almost all of the members of your benefactor's maternal side of the family tree have suffered violent deaths and the one survivor is a criminal lunatic.

It had been a long road from the start of this investigation to now. The tiny lead toy soldier and the inscribed cover of the nickel adventure magazine that Sterling Chester had bequeathed to Bingham turned out to be the critical pieces of evidence that led to Rushton's present mission.

At the beginning, Rushton had hoped to discover a memorial marker with a matching date of death and records of Bing's mother's internment and from there trace backward to his parents' identities. He found no evidence of this kind. From Chester's description of Harvard's mother's physical symptoms, she was likely the victim of tuberculosis. In which case, county health officials would have lost no time in disposing of the potential community health risk. If present day protocol at the county coroner's office was any example, the unclaimed, unidentified body spent less than 48 hours in a morgue before it was dispensed with in a mass "paupers'" grave. Shoddy record keeping and Chester's distraction due to the abrupt shift from busy professional banker and bachelor to father of an infant child coalesced to create an utter void in the last, tragic chapter of the life and death of Bingham's mother.

After this disappointment, Rushton's only recourse was to attempt to trace the origins of the lead soldier and the old magazine cover. A former NYPD colleague and a hobbyist in the growing field of forensics subjected the "Nick Carter Detective Library" cover to intense analysis. The bright light exposure and fine, impression-disclosing powders wreaked terrible destruction on the already fragile piece of pulp wood paper, but the sacrifice was not without rewards. He found a name—first and last: Teddy Garrett. Where the vast majority of nickel novels were sold via newsstands, more rural markets were served through subscriptions. Teddy or Theodore Garrett was a subscriber. However, the trail stopped there.

"Teddy's" address was indistinguishable. Not surprisingly, the publisher's and distributor's records did not reach back over thirty years to include that information.

Fortunately, the toy soldier supplied its own scant facts. It was a product of Dresden, Germany, hand-painted and sold in sets to parents of middle- to upper-class American children. The cost of the toys and limited chains of distribution here in the States narrowed down the list of possible retailers considerably.

Rushton was left to discover through rural land records a family in the right economic class with the surname of Garrett, living near one of the few rural toy retailers. For better or for worse, Rushton's weeks of property searches proved fruitful.

He discovered Abraham and Wilma Garrett of the Town of Fishkill, New York. The information on the deed suggested that these could not be Bingham's parents—ownership went back over twenty-five years before Bing was born. In all probability, these were Bingham Harvard's maternal grandparents. From there, Rushton's search shifted from property records to criminal records.

The home no longer stood on the listed acreage. It had been burned down many years ago by Wilma Garrett, with Abraham Garrett's mutilated body inside. The arrest reports indicated that upon responding to a report of a fire, the volunteer fire brigade discovered a Mrs. Wilhelmina Pearl Garrett, axe in hand, dancing in circles, "covered in blood and whooping like an Indian" in front of her blazing domicile. Court records showed that Mrs. Garrett was found incompetent to stand trial and committed to the nearby Matteawan State Hospital for the Criminally Insane.

Birth certificates for the Garrett's child, Bingham's mother, or children were non-existent as most childbirths took place at home. However, old local newspapers from 1918 noted the passing of "Private Theodore Eugene Garrett," presumed killed in action on a battlefield in France.

Discouraged but not entirely resigned, Rushton had posted a letter to Mrs. Garrett at Matteawan. If she had been entirely incoherent, he wished to spare both of them his personal visit. On the other hand, if she possessed even a passing hint of lucidity, and had interest in discovering the identity of her grandson, a responsive letter would help Rushton decide if a face-to-face would be worthwhile.

The letter, or rather the epic treatise, back from Mrs. Garrett inspired some hope in Rushton's mission. It was dozens of pages of ranting, stream of consciousness blather evidencing feelings of grandeur and paranoia interchangeably. She was President McKinley's secret assassin - ordered to do so by the voice in her head. In retribution, she was ceaselessly hunted by agents of the United States government, posing as janitors, wardens, and squirrels to keep tabs on her. Oddly, just in the middle of this tome, in slightly darker ink from the surrounding text was inscribed: "Please visit. Bring chocolate."

And so here he was, driving his tin lizzie through the scenic countryside, the Hudson River on one side and the Fishkill Mountains on the other. Six pounds of assorted chocolates sat in a bag on the passenger seat and fifty miles between him and an insane, homicidal grandma.

* * * * * * *

"Mr. Rushton, my name is Hilda. I am Mrs. Garrett's...care-taker, and chaperone for your visit. Dinner for our patients will be served in just forty-five minutes, no guests allowed, so we must move along. Please follow me and stay close. I will take you to Mrs. Garrett's quarters. Oh, and please dispense with your cigar; this is a facility for the ill of body as well as for the ill of mind."

"Hilda" was gorgeous...that is, in the vein of an Amazon woman of Greek myth. She stood nearly six feet—just a couple inches shorter than the stout private detective. Her hair was long and blonde, pinned up tightly above her ears with a common nurse's cap perched atop her head. Despite her size, the asylum worker was quite proportional to her surroundings. Matteawan State Hospital was an enormous castle-like structure, complete with four-story central clock tower and turrets at either end. The wings of the facility, which branched out for hundreds of yards, were multi-storied with numerous, massive chimneys jutting from the roof every dozen feet or so. The "hospital" had 550 beds—all reserved for not yet convicted females too "unsound" even to stand trial.

Walking just in front of Rushton, Hilda made conversation. "So, Mr. Rushton, your letter said that you are not a police officer or government investigator?"

"Uh, yeah. That's right. Just a private dick trying to earn a buck." Rodney was distracted by the sight of a middle-aged woman in institutional gown pressed against a corridor wall as if she were a child at a swimming pool, fearful of the open water and hugging the pool's walls for dear life. She was making forward progress—albeit at a snail's pace—in the direction

Rushton and his chaperone were walking.

"I hope you do not take this in the wrong way, Mr. Rushton, but as Mrs. Garrett's...guardian, I make a point of...looking into her guests' backgrounds. She is such a fragile, elderly woman with a very...delicate constitution. It would take very little shock to disturb her emotionally. I have discovered that you have at least two years of, um, experience in an...institution?"

Rushton was surprised and annoyed at the intrusion on his personal life, but chose to stifle his feelings. Hilda was beautiful, and this was his only lead to the ultimate discovery of Bingham's heritage. "Yeah; I spent a couple years in the lock-up. Nothin' I'm proud of. What's y'point?"

"I suspect that being a former police detective in prison along with some of the persons you may have had a hand in imprisoning might have made that experience especially difficult? You may have been forced by your unfortunate circumstances to do things to protect and preserve yourself to which those... outside...would not necessarily subscribe?"

Rushton's feelings alternated from anger, to embarrassment, to professional suspicion in Hilda's motivation for bringing up the topic of his tarnished past. "Look, I don't know what you're chinnin' about, but I'll humor you. Sometimes the 'system' ain't too fair—it's a 'one size fits all' arrangement, and, well sometimes folks don't get the right 'fit.' I did what I thought I had to do to get through—to pay my dues, without paying with my life. Satisfied!?"

"More than you understand at the moment, Mr. Rushton." Hilda stopped quickly, turned and looked Rushton dead in the eyes—a feat no woman had ever accomplished to date. "So... based on your own personal experience, you would understand, maybe even sympathize with someone who was trying to make the best of a very bad situation...someone who was compelled, by circumstances, to do something objectively 'bad.' Someone who was willing to pay her debt to society, but not with her life?"

Still confused, but speaking from instinct, Rodney replied

slowly "Well...sure. That's copacetic with me. I wouldn't wanta cause someone in that jam any more grief."

"Mrs. Garrett will be very pleased to know that, Mr. Rushton. Please, will you follow me? We've arrived."

Hilda grabbed a doorknob to an impressively solid looking, windowless door, opened it a crack, looked in for an instant, and then waved Rushton ahead.

Hilda spoke over Rushton's shoulder to the petite, white-haired woman and only occupant in the room. "Mrs. Garrett, this is Mr. Rodney Rushton, private detective. He would like to speak with you about Eve."

The room was sparsely furnished, a single bed, bed stand, small bookshelf, wardrobe, and a comfortable-looking chair next to the room's only window, tall with a wooded view, criss-crossed with bars. A couple mismatched folded chairs and a rickety card table completed the fixtures. By Rushton's esti-mate, Mrs. Garrett had to be into her seventies. She was very small in stature, withered, with huge, sad eyes. She moved with glacial speed and had a distant, vacant look in her eyes.

"Teddy? Teddy is that you?" she croaked in an almost whis-pered but gravelly tone. "I chopped up papa, Ted, so now you can stay home with me. I chopped him up, fed him to Barney, your spaniel. Thought you'd like that touch, sinse papa took to kicking him wherever he saw him. 'Cept Barney died just after the meal—that mean bastard causes hurt even in the after-life...."

Hilda interrupted, "Wilma, Mr. Rushton is 'okay.' I've had the talk with him that you suggested, and I think we understand each other." She stared hard at Rushton, willing him to respond in agreement.

Suddenly Rodney put together the crux of the obtuse conver-sation he had had with Hilda in the walk to this room. "Yeah, I'm with you."

Instantly, the slack jawed expression on Wilma's face disappeared. Likewise, the vacant eyes focused into a sharp-ened intensity. Spectacles that she had buried in her lap upon

Rushton's entrance popped back into view and were perched on her nose. She snapped from the chair and marched toward Rodney on slippered feet. Still physically small, and aged, Mrs. Wilma Garrett displayed the exuberance and intelligence of expression of a much younger person.

"So glad to finally meet you Mr. Rushton. I hope that bag you are carrying is for me?" Wilma grabbed Rodney's right hand even before he could raise it and pumped it like a seasoned politician.

In the confusion of his veiled interrogation and the shock of Mrs. Garrett's lucidity, Rushton had entirely forgotten about his burdens. He held the leather portfolio containing Bingham's 'artifacts' tucked under one arm. In the other arm he had the six-pound box of chocolates. He held the latter out for Mrs. Garrett. Hilda attempted to intercept the exchange with her own outstretched hand, but Wilma snatched the package with lightening speed and hugged it close.

"Hilda likes to filch my treats on the pretext that they disagree with my constitution. I've no doubt she would eat them herself." Wilma smiled while sliding the treasure under her bed.

Hilda merely shook her head "Tsk, Tsk, Mrs. Garrett. You know what Dr. Cleary said about too many sweets...."

"Well, *you* know where Dr. Cleary can put his advice!" Wilma retorted.

"We will discuss this later, ma'am." Hilda finished.

Mrs. Garrett gave Hilda a withering stare upon seating herself on her bed, legs and slippered feet blocking access to the bag of chocolates on the floor. "Please, Mr. Rushton, have a seat." Wilma indicated the cushioned reading chair immediately next to her. Hilda turned and grabbed one of two wooden chairs at either side of a card table at the other side of the room and sat next to Rodney.

"So sorry about the crazy talk, Mr. Rushton. One can never be too cautious...and if Hilda here had spoken a bit sooner...." Wilma glared at Hilda again in a playful expression.

Hilda smiled, "You are such a wonderful actress. I cannot

miss an opportunity to see you perform."

Wilma's response was a girlish giggle, cut short by a rap on her door from the main corridor. "Come in, Gladys...," Wilma called from her bed.

The latch clicked and the door eased slowly open revealing a female face, cheek against the door frame. A grasping hand clutched for purchase upon the interior wall and the rest of the body followed. Rushton recognized the woman as the one he and Hilda had passed in the hallway en route to Mrs. Garrett's room.

Wilma directed an inquisitive look at Hilda who responded with a nod and a shrug. "Gladys dear, it is okay." Wilma interposed. "This is Mr. Rodney Rushton, a private investigator hired by my grandson to discover his 'crazy' grandma. Hilda says he is on our team."

"Oh, goody!" Much like Wilma's prior transformation, Gladys swiftly abandoned her guise as an anguished wall hugger, and padded with healthy stride toward the seated nurse and Mrs. Garrett. "This routine is getting tedious. Had I known the size of this place before I was committed I would have taken on a few nervous ticks, or some other eccentricity. My word! It takes me twenty minutes just to get to the 'john' hugging the walls like I do."

Not easily embarrassed, Rushton nonetheless flushed red at Gladys' indiscretion. "Gladys, please!" Wilma scolded, "I said Mr. Rushton is privy to our circumstances, I did not say he had even the slightest interest in your 'washroom' habits! I do apologize for my friend here, Mr. Rushton, it is not often that we have guests of the opposite gender and I believe Gladys is a bit out of practice."

"Oh pooh pooh to you, Wilma," Gladys retorted as she took hold of the last available chair in the room, plopping her well-fed frame on to the seat.

Interceding in what was evolving into a verbal sparring match between the two 'patients,' Hilda turned to Rushton and explained. "Mr. Rushton, as you are no doubt aware, things are not quite as they appear here at Matteawan. Murder is frowned upon regardless of circumstance, regardless of the gender or the age of the 'perpetrator.' Convicted murderers are 'hanged from the neck until they are dead,' period. It is, as you so artfully titled it, a 'one size fits all' institution."

Hilda continued, "I do not condone murder. I do not believe that one should get a 'pass' on the death penalty on the basis of gender or age alone, but I do passionately embrace certain, unusual mitigating circumstances that the State does not recognize as yet. Even then, there is some price to pay for the transgression—institutionalization for example, but death seems too extreme a price."

No stranger to the system of criminal justice, Rushton remained naïve to the unique circumstances faced by the 'fairer sex' caught up in this bureaucracy. "You can take my honest word that I won't gum up your game, Hilda, but precisely what 'mitigating circumstances' are we talking about?"

"I'll be happy to tell you Mr. Rushton," Wilma interrupted. "My husband, Abe, may he burn in eternal hell, was hardly fit to wear human skin. I know that sounds a bit cruel, but you don't have to take my word for it. You have gathered enough facts to see the big picture—or at least understand it when I tell you.

"Without the excuse of drunkenness or mental frailty, Abe was just a mean, hateful, cuss. I wasn't perfect, but I had the basics nailed down: I was honest, faithful, hard working...gave him two honest, and hard working children...a girl, Eve, and then a boy, Teddy. But Abe needed more from life I guess. He needed a punching bag. I blamed myself for many years. I thought I could 'change' him. Of course, I was wrong, but I was willing to suffer the consequences of my choice of a husband... that is until our children came along. He didn't beat them. But seeing their mamma take the brunt of their papa's frustrations was just as bad. Not knowing what to do, and for lack of any action by their mamma, Eve and Teddy just got themselves out of the situation as best they could.

"Eve went off to school in Ohio. She wanted to be a school

teacher and attended Ohio Central College in Iberia, just north of Columbus, Ohio. Teddy ran away to the east coast and joined the U.S. Army, lying about his age of fifteen to get in.

"Soon, too soon it was just Abe and me again. One more fearsome beating finally put me over the edge. Abe may have felt the first whack of the axe, but I promise you he couldn't feel the second since his head had already come unhitched from his shoulders."

Rushton had read the coroner's report amongst Wilma's commitment files. He knew she hadn't stopped at two "whacks." Had there been anyone to give a damn about the man to identify the body they would have mistaken him for butchered livestock except for the bits of clothing mixed in. Yet Bing's grandmother delivered her recitation with cold composure. A testimony to her sincere belief in the justification of her acts.

"You would hear variations of this same story from roughly half the female inmates of Matteawan, Mr. Rushton, including Gladys here," Hilda exclaimed.

Gladys nodded her head in affirmation.

"Half!" Rushton exclaimed. "You mean to tell me that more than a hundred of the ladies here are as lucid as you and me? That they have accepted life in a lunatic asylum?!"

Gladys interjected for the first time. "Absolutely, Mr. Rushton. Life here is not worse than the death sentence we would certainly get from a jury and judge. For most of us, considering the violent environment we came from, this is a considerable improvement. My unfortunate selection of feigned mental incapacity aside, it is somewhat liberating to be thought of as 'crazy.' It is like living the girlhood of which so many of us were deprived. Our every action; throwing food, public nudity, belching etc., etc. is simply dismissed as acts of the insane; excusing us entirely from responsibility."

"Speak for yourself, Gladys. I may be guilty of launching a few spoonfuls of mashed potatoes at that nasty commissary woman, but I leave the public nudity to the much younger generation." Wilma said.

"Suit yourself," Gladys responded. "Since you're occupied Wilma, I'll just start off for the commissary now. Dinner is in twenty minutes and it will take me roughly that long hugging the walls to get there." Gladys arose and walked to the door. She turned briefly to Rushton. "It was a pleasure to meet you Mr. Rushton. Good day." She cracked the door, slithered out, and pulled the door shut behind her.

Not missing a beat, Mrs. Garrett continued, "Mr. Rushton, I understand that each of us has some very important information to share. Could you humor an old woman and enlighten me first? Tell me about my grandson."

Still a bit rattled, but quickly regaining composure now that his obsession of the last six months was the topic of concern, Rushton explained. "To be fair, Mrs. Garrett, there remains a possibility that the magazine cover and toy soldier that came into the possession of my benefactor's mother did so by happenstance. I hope I have not raised your expectations too sharply. There may be no link."

"Tut, tut, and piffle, and fudge. I'll hear nothing more on that point." Wilma arose from her seat, shuffled to her massive wardrobe and swung the doors wide. She knelt briefly and hefted up a wide box, plopping it on her bed and sitting herself next to it.

"You no doubt know more than most grown men about the toy soldier sets whence my little Bingham's figurine came from?" Wilma smiled, continuing.

"Each set came with a regiment of 'blue-coats' and 'red-coats,' each regiment had one 'commanding officer' distinguished by the headgear." She upended a small box she had taken from the large one, spilling out little lead soldiers, and grasping the 'red-coat' version of the 'commanding officer' she had just described.

"Here is the 'limey' officer, but as you can see, no American officer. I trust you brought Bing's soldier with you?"

As she had been talking, Rushton was retrieving the portfolio he had layed on the floor, and pulled out the toy. The damage caused by Bingham's infant grasp was not bad enough to blur the stark similarity of the two 'commanding officer' figurines. Other than the impressions, the only difference between the two was the color of their coats. Rushton's was obviously blue.

"But...." Rushton's attempted interruption was quickly silenced by Wilma's raised index finger.

"Here is the remaining portion of the adventure magazine that you wrote about." Mrs. Garrett reached into her box and delicately extracted a thin eight and a half by eleven inch pile of newsprint quality paper glued at a spine and wrapped with a paper cover, or at least a back cover. The front cover was missing.

With equal tenderness, Rushton slid out the folder containing the inscribed "Nick Carter Detective Library" magazine cover and opened it for inspection. Where the bright-light analysis and powder bath it had received had faded the imprinted image on its front, the paper's shape was entirely intact.

When laid upon the coverless magazine, even a cursory inspection would reveal the precise line-up of cover to the tiny tear marks left upon its extraction. It was as if two puzzle pieces had been connected.

"This was my son, Teddy's magazine. He just loved Nick Carter. This is his soldier set, too." Wilma pointed to the strewn lead toys on her bed.

"Eve came home from college one summer, and, knowing her father's hypocritical religious zeal and short temper, confided in me alone that she was pregnant. She wasn't heavy with child yet, for a time anyway; so I cared for her from her room at the house. Eve refused to disclose the name of the father, but she had no doubts herself as to his identity. She told me that he was a college boy, fancied himself a fairy tale hero...Sir Galahad, she said.

"She could hide her condition just so long before even my thick-headed husband found her out. Abe gave her two choices: disclose the name and location of the father so he could track him down and force a 'shotgun wedding' or leave the house permanently so as to cease disgracing him."

Wilma continued, "Eve was a charitable, big hearted young lady, but she had too much of her father's stubbornness. She left one night without a word to anyone but her younger brother. A few weeks later she sent a letter addressed to him using a pen name only he recognized. He told me later that she had delivered a baby boy in a homeless shelter in New York City and that the infant had immediately demonstrated unusual 'gifts' of strength. Teddy responded with his own letter, the toy soldier, and one of his sister's favorite poems on the back of his treasured Nick Carter magazine."

Wilma began to cry. First noiselessly, then with heaving sobs. Hilda left her seat and sat next to her charge upon the bed, putting her arm around the old woman.

Gradually, Wilma composed herself and lifted her head to look at Rushton. "I use my daughter's name in the past tense, because if she were alive I know you would have found her and she would have come here with you."

"Yes, ma'am," the burly detective was not unshaken by the old woman's story. His words barely escaped his choked, tightened chest. "I know she passed on when Bingham was just a month or so old. Her last deed was to secure for her son a very honorable and successful banker to raise him as his own. She did that, with her dying breath." Rodney resolved to give no further details about Eve's wretched physical condition or likely cause of death by tuberculosis. The elderly woman was clearly overwrought as it was. To his great relief, Mrs. Garrett made no further inquiry to her daughter's last moments.

"Please tell me about my grandson, Mr. Rushton, and then tell me how we might communicate with one another?" Wilma asked.

"I will do just that, Mrs. Garrett. But first, is there anything more you can tell me that could help me to locate, or at least identify your grandson's father?" Rushton inquired.

"Well, young man, Ohio Central College matriculated only three to five students at a time back then. If my grandson's father was one of Eve's schoolmates it could be only one of thirty five souls at most. Surely the college keeps tabs on alumni for future donations."

"That sounds logical enough, ma'am. Thank you. Now my part of the deal...." Thereafter Rushton gave a detailed accounting of Harvard's life to date to a very grateful grand-mother. He made his "good-byes" promising himself to return if for no other reason than to re-acquaint himself with Hilda once his mission was completed. He then set off for the Ohio Central College in Iberia, Ohio.

CHAPTER ELEVEN
ELMER'S ORDEAL

August 13, 1920; Westerville, Ohio:

"Tony I'm begging ya, can we put the top down!? Just for a few minutes. It smells like a damned cannibal cook-out in here!"

"Ya think I ain't gotta nose, Mikey?! Ya know I hate your damned stogies but they smell like daisies to me now! Hell, anything's better'n gettin' a lung full a' Vincent's charred carcass, but if that news kid sees us he'll be halfway to China before we can snag him. You wanna explain to Capone that it was too stinky, so's we let the kid get away? Be my guest, pal. I'll probably get tagged to dump your ventilated body some-wheres."

"Yeah, okay, fine." Mikey fell back to his seat in the rear of the Model 38 Pierce-Arrow. It was a mercifully big seven-seater, but not half as big as Mikey would have preferred. Tony pulled the long straw and was in the driver's seat while he was stuck in the back with Vincent, the human-sized burnt camp-fire weenie. Mikey took three quick puffs from his cigar and blew a cloud of smoke directly at the shrouded figure. Although bearing the shape of a human covered in a dark sheet, it neither moved nor reacted in any way to the gout of smoke. Only a phlegmy, pained moan escaped the figure; the same noise it had made every five minutes for the last hour the men had been tracking Elmer Pfleager, newspaper delivery boy.

"Ahhh, I just hope we ain't gotta do this twice." Mikey continued to whine. "Wouldn't surprise me none if once that kid saw deep-fried-Vinny here he quit his paper route and waved off eatin' meat forever. Who could blame 'im."

"And that's just the reason Capone had us drag Vincent along." Tony intoned. "If he can I.D. the brat what saw him at his tarring and feathering, we've got our guy. We just grab him, bring him back to Capone for a little interview and get the goods on where to find the super fella."

In what had been Vincent's only moment of coherent thought upon having been tarred, feathered and lit aflame just 48 hours before, he had articulated to his 'gang' a muddled description of an unusual man, dressed in Black Legion garb who moved like lightning and tossed him around in a fashion unthinkable for his 240 pound frame. Vincent had likewise coughed out the memory of a young boy with a bicycle at the scene of his torture, the name "Elmer" inscribed on the back fender, with a newspaper delivery bag flung over the seat.

Al Capone, newly arrived from New York City to give "personal attention" to the situation, ordered Tony and Mike to hunt the newsboy down and bring him in. Although a veritable zombie, verbalizing little more than anguished moans of obvious agony, Vincent was ordered to join the hunting party. Cooked black from the waist up, Vincent lacked upper body strength to toss away the dark sheet Mikey had thrown over him. Mikey and Tony had agreed that Vincent's mug was just too horrible to have to look at and that they would expose his face only long enough for him to I.D. the newsboy and then cover it again.

The Pierce-Arrow was parked at the curb, on Park Street. If the gloom of pre-dawn weren't enough to blacken the view of the occupants of the expensive roadster, the cigar smoke completed the effect. Following his mapped route, Elmer peddled directly up the center of Park Street, stopping periodically to hurl a newspaper to a subscriber's porch.

Tony lurched to attention in the driver's seat upon seeing the approaching newsboy. "Give Vinny a peep Mikey, here comes a newsboy."

With slight trepidation, Mikey grasped the shroud at Vincent's head and pulled it down, shuddering when the cloth resisted his pull from burnt, seeping skin. Unable to look at the unfortunate bootlegger's face, he turned his head away before asking, "So is that the kid, Vinny?"

As previously agreed, like a trained horse, Vinny thumped his foot on the floorboard twice. Recognizing the signal as a "Yes," Mikey announced to the driver, "It's him." He blindly flung the sheet back over Vinny's face.

Mikey reached down to the floor of the car and tipped a bottle of chloroform onto a gauze cloth lying there. He sat up and paused as the unsuspecting newspaper carrier pedaled toward him. He swung the car door outward, into the street and directly into Elmer's path. Elmer spun his pedals in reverse, but too late to avoid impact with the long, heavy car door. Mikey was out of the car almost before the newsboy's bike fell over. He ran around the door and pounced on the bike with the young boy struggling beneath it. Elmer managed a quick scream before the gauze covered his nose and mouth, instantly rendering him unconscious.

Just one block away, on West Plum Street, Bingham Harvard was exiting his house when he heard Elmer's scream cut short. The unfortunate timing of a call of nature had separated him from the boy for just a brief moment.

His acute hearing pinpointing Elmer's location, the Night Wind blew forward like shot from a cannon. Emergency robbing him of the luxury of neighborly courtesy, Harvard raced through private lawns taking the most direct route to the source of the scream. Fear for Elmer's well-being haunted him. Of course, it was Elmer's own curiosity that made him witness to the brutal torture of the bootlegger and a potential target of both the mafia and the Black Legion. But Bing knew well that but for his engagement with the warring parties two mornings ago, Elmer would not have had the opportunity to be in the wrong place at the wrong time. A feeling of responsibility notwithstanding, Bingham found his pre-dawn trot with Elmer to be refreshing and a good opportunity to 'break in' at least one of the two scarlet and gray suits of armor Lady Kate had commissioned for him.

This was his first occasion to run full tilt in his uniform and Bing could only hope there weren't complications. He was quickly disappointed. The armored football uniform gave added weight and virtual invulnerability that made the Night Wind a veritable human tank. On the other hand, these same features made maneuverability difficult at Bingham's super human speed.

A four-foot wide section of a chest-high hedge row exploded on impact as Bingham attempted unsuccessfully to check his pace. Two crude openings appeared in a residential wooden fence as Bing plowed through one, and then another. Wildly out of control, Bingham hit a buried support post for two frames of fence causing both to cave in like unhinged shutters on a house.

The coast was then clear to West Park Street except for a chicken coop. The wooden coop stood on six legs, about chest high and eight feet long. But for a timber frame, the sides, ceiling and floor were all of fine gauge chicken wire. Resigning himself to an unerring, headlong rush, and inspired that the hedge nor the two frames of fence had caused him physical harm, the Night Wind blasted through the near center point of the coop—a spot blessedly unoccupied by sleeping chickens.

The human torpedo of nickel-plated steel cut the coop in two, forcing Bingham to pry severed chicken wire from his armored chest. The impact was so sudden and the separation of the coop so clean, the sleepy chickens did not immediately react. However, the shocked silence was instantly followed by feather-flying chaos as either side of the coop fell into the gaping center.

Slowing his pace through the final lawn and coming to a stop in the center of West Park Street, Bingham saw the rear brake lights and distinctive back of the Pierce-Arrow. It was on the move, and as Bing approached, it carefully turned on Grove

Street.

No stranger to automobiles—he had several high-powered roadsters in a garage back at Myquest—Bingham knew of the expensive and rare Model 38 Pierce-Arrow. Until now he had not seen an automobile of this type in the neighborhood. The hourly wage laborers could not afford it and the salaried executives at the American Issue Publishing Company, the local toy manufacturer or the administrators at Otterbein College were not so ostentatious. This was an out-of-towner's conveyance, and likely from New York, where the Pierce-Arrow was manufactured. Elmer's bicycle lay on its side just at the curb line, front tire turned at a sharp angle and still spinning.

Elmer was in that car!

Fearing harm to Elmer should he aggressively run down the automobile, Bingham selected instead to race behind the car just out of its wake—and the sight of the occupants. Once the car had stopped, Bing would attempt a stealthier, less risky rescue.

Bingham's endurance was not without its limits. Back home on Long Island he reveled in the slack-jaw surprise of motorists as he kept pace with their 40 mile per hour touring cars. Every now and then, feeling his manhood, or at least his motor car's performance being challenged, a determined driver would hit the open road and begin to out-strip Bing within fifteen to twenty miles.

However, good luck materialized when the car kept a slow, legal speed and pulled off to a nearby farm just a mile or two away. By the time Bingham arrived on the scene, the occupants had left the vehicle and had entered the imposing red barn on the property. Another Pierce-Arrow was parked near the barn doors as well, suggesting that others awaited the group inside.

Tasked by the Secret Service to "beat the living hell out of as many members of organized crime" as he could, present circumstances forced that mission to the back burner. The longer he stuck around pummeling mobsters, the better chance one of them would cause harm to Elmer. The Night Wind needed a few minutes and some reconnaissance to come up with a plan.

* * * * * *

Fearing the wrath of Capone should their captive die of excess chloroform, Mikey had been unusually careful not to overdo it with Elmer. Consequently, Elmer's condition would be best described as a lethargy rather than unconsciousness. In any case Mikey had to carry the young boy into the barn, happily leaving Tony to assist Vincent and his chronic stench. Don, who had arrived earlier, opened one of the barn doors and ushered his burdened fellow gang members inside. He shut and latched the door just as Tony hauled Vincent past the entranceway.

The barn's interior was more shadow than light. Elmer heard plenty of shuffling feet and muffled conversation, but saw only an occasional figure outlined by the early morning sunlight shining between the wood slats of the barn. He was deposited on his rear on a bale of hay with his back against the wooden barn wall. One of the figures approached him. As it neared, Elmer was able to tell that it was a man. The man knelt eye to eye with the young boy. A deeply receding hairline emphasized a cherubic almost childish face. His voice had a harsh Brooklyn accent, though it only sounded "funny" to Elmer, never having crossed the county line.

"I've got better things to do than shake down a kid. But it seems my boss wasn't satisfied with the progress of this band of knuckleheads, so here I am." As he spoke he waved one arm behind him, directing Elmer's attention to the other men who were vaguely visible in the gloom of the barn interior. He counted six standing men including the speaker. A seventh was huddled, moaning on the ground, just at the closed doors.

"You saw one a my guys get torched a couple days back by the Black Legion." The man barked. "There was some gazebo among 'im what can be best characterized as really, really strong...."

"Helppp Meeee...!" Cried the figure on the floor.

After a momentary pause, the talker continued, "...My guys ain't too quick on the uptake, but they can count and they's saying that the strong guy is a newcomer, probably an out-of-towner. You and the muscle-man showed up at the same time, so I'm guessing you either know him or know of him. Ya following me here pal?"

"Y....yeah." Elmer stuttered.

"So's you can just tell what ya know right now about the strong fella and my guys here will drive you back home to your mommy and daddy. No harm, no foul, okey-dokey?"

"No." Elmer whimpered.

"Oh lord, augh, it hurts!" The burn victim interrupted again, loud enough this time for all inside, and possibly outside to hear.

"Mother 'a...! Frank, give Vinny a drink a water or some-thin'...shut 'im up!" The speaker yelled impatiently and then continued, to Elmer, "'No' what, kid? 'No,' you don't know nothin' or 'no,' you do know somethin' but ya ain't gonna talk?"

"I've got nothing to say to you, mister."

"Whoa! We got a fighter here boys." The speaker announced to the group in a raised voice.

Although noble, Elmer's knowledge of loyalty and honor came from adventure fiction magazines starring Tarzan and Zorro, among others. Even his recent exposure to the Black Legion and their cruel methods of torture could not overcome his youthful optimism, nor enlighten him to the concept of human mortality. Elmer was destined to age quickly this morning.

The speaker turned his back to Elmer and snapped his fingers to the men behind him. "Phil, Frank, take hold of the burnt bacon and bring 'im right up close here."

The still-shrouded, moaning man was unceremoniously grabbed and dragged across the hay-strewn, dirt floor. He was dumped on the floor, arms akimbo, his covered head just inches from Elmer's. Moans and whining came in muffled bursts through the cloth.

"Kid, I ain't a monster." The speaker resumed, "In fact it's more'n fair to say that the Klan drew first blood. They got wits, I'll giv'im that. They trailed our suppliers, like we'll trail their fire bug. We got the guns and the money to match their cleverness and numbers, but I wasn't counting on dealing with a Hercules too. I ain't a monster. I wouldn't cover a guy in tar and feathers and light'im up like a roman candle like your pal did here." With the last word the baby-faced man tore the sheet from Vincent's head.

If the bootlegger looked frightful the first time Elmer saw him, he was infinitely worse now. Vincent's hair was entirely burnt off except for a few gnarled tufts. His nose, ears and lower lip were shriveled or gone, as was the lid of his left eye. The exposed left eyeball was a seeping, blackened sore. The skin on his face was grayish-black, cracked like ancient parchment and oozing translucent fluid. The abrupt removal of the sheet tore off more remnants of flesh from his head and Vincent let loose again with moans, insistent and pitiful.

In a much louder voice the mobster continued. "We didn't start this fight, kid, but I'm gonna finish it here, in this godforsaken 'Dry Capital of the World.' I ain't a monster, but I gotta think of the bigger picture. I'll light a kid up...make 'im look like Vinny here, if it means I can take out the Klan's muscleman and shut down the damn bedsheet bandits!"

Suddenly, two scarlet fists exploded through the barn wall just to each side of the paralyzed Elmer. Wood slats collapsed behind his back and he disappeared instantly, feet kicking through the hole.

"What the...! Phil! Frank!" Cutting himself off, Capone lunged away from the hole in the barn wall and directed two of his armed men to action. Phil and Frank rushed to the hole, crouched and fired their revolvers in unison.

Bingham didn't bother to veer and zigzag out of firing range. He held Elmer snug against him, face to face, keeping himself between the boy and the hole in the barn wall. Bing had relied on the surprise of his intrusion and his armor to overcome the mafia men. Fortunately, that faith was well placed.

Phil and Frank rushed to the hole, crouched and fired their revolvers in unison.

He felt two focused impacts, one at the right shoulder, the other at the lower back. Bingham would later find fist-sized bruises at those locations, but that was all. At the moment, the bullets' impact pushed Bingham forward, like a tail wind on a sail boat.

"Son of a...! Hercules and bullet-proof?!" Capone had crawled to a position to see out of the hole, careful to stay out of firing range. He stared in undisguised awe at the rapidly departing scarlet and gray streak.

"Aaarrrhhhh!!!...I'm hurtin' real bad." Only temporarily masked by the firing guns, Vincent's wailing continued. His body thrashed on the straw-strewn dirt floor as spasms racked his tortured nervous system.

"Arrgh! Enough!!" Capone lurched to his feet and took the revolver from Frank's grasp, blasting two shots into Vinny. The moaning stopped.

"Leave the cinder behind. Let's go boys! 'Farmer Brown' here may be a late riser, but he's gotta be phoning the cops by now. Mikey! You emptied the kids pockets on the way here... right?" Capone shouted orders as the group hurried for the exit to the barn.

"Yeah, boss." Mikey handed the gang leader a weathered piece of folded paper. "Looks like he ain't been doin' the newspaper delivery thing long. He still needs this list of customers for his route."

"Perfect." Capone interrupted. "I want a stake-out of every damned house on that list. You find me the guy what matches that scarlet and gray torpedo and let me know! Got it!?" Capone slapped the list back in Mikey's hand for emphasis.

"Yeah, boss."

The gangsters fled to their respective vehicles, gunned engines and shot up loose gravel in their haste to exit the scene. In the passenger seat with Phil and Frank, Capone continued giving orders. "I'm gonna need a few dozen more guys. I'll make the call to Brooklyn and Chicago. Phil, I want each and every bartender at the seven torched speakeasies given the third degree on customers. Physical descriptions...whatever. The fire-bug was a customer or someone tailing a customer or they wouldn' a known where all our places were. The same guy goin' to all or most of the seven places is likely our man...or someone watchin' 'im. Let's watch 'im for a few days and if he ain't got a shadow, take 'im out, if so take 'im both.

* * * * * * *

Kneeling, Bingham looked closely into Elmer's eyes for any sign of shock. The two escapees from the barn paused for breath at the back of Towers Hall, just a block or two from Elmer's overturned bicycle and easily a mile away from the now fleeing mobsters.

With his hands on the boy's shoulders, Bingham attempted to calm him, "Take a deep breath, Elmer. That's it. Look at me now." Bingham raised a red, gloved finger in front of his face, "How many fingers do you see, son?"

"Wh...one. So what happens if I get scared half to death twice?" Elmer recovered.

"If you can come up with that line, I wonder just how 'scared' you were." The Night Wind stood in place, extended his arms to the sides and twisted his upper body at the waist. His eyes squinted and he visibly cringed. "Uggghh! I know how a Matador in training feels."

The first glimmers of early morning light hinted at a sunny day, but ominous storm clouds were fast filling the sky from the west. The rumble of thunder could be heard in the distance.

"You took a couple bullets, didn't ya?" the boy inquired.

"That or an elephant kicked me. Are you going to be okay?"

"I suppose, so long as you can stand guard. I don't mean to be disrespectful...sir. But, normal people can't do what you do. I just nearly got wind-burned from you holdin' me and running so fast. Ya hitched yer stride a time or two once ya got started scedaddling so I'm pretty sure you got popped by one a'the cannons those guys had. Yer still standing. That ain't normal.

Pa shot a deer last fall. Made me climb a tree as a lookout. That deer just dropped where it stood...just like its legs turned ta mush. You ain't even cussin'. Does it hurt much? Why did those guys grab me in the first place? Why was they askin' about you? Are you a wanted man? Does that make me a wanted kid?"

Bingham's head was beginning to hurt as much as his bruised back. Elmer had spat out his barrage of questions in less time than it took him to catch his breath and regain his posture. Despite the fact that it seemed the paperboy was already a target, there remained some tiny shred of safety for him in knowing as few of the details of Bingham's assignment as possible. He cringed even pondering the appropriate expression, but it fit; you can't squeeze blood from a stone.

For response, Bingham settled instead on a bit of mis-direction. "I was a wanted man...once. I had an alias, given me by the New York City Police Department."

It worked. The child's eyes bugged, and his jaw dropped. Elmer gave Bingham a look of awestruck hero-worship. For a moment, Bingham was certain the boy would raise his hand and touch him as if to confirm his proximity to a deity. "So what's yer alias? Hercules? Samson? Mercury? Elmer gasped.

It's "the Night Wind." Bingham said, simply.

"The Night Wind?" Elmer's posture deflated. The look of admiration wilted. "My pa gets the night winds. Happens every time ma makes chicken and dumplins'. It's gettin' so's I can't eat the stuff just knowin' what I'm in for later."

Despite his injury, Bingham laughed out loud.

"You wouldn't be laughing if you shared our family bed, mister.

I guess this means my newspaper route is done for?"

"Yes...," Bingham replied, reaching backward to touch his own bruised back, "if there was any question in their minds before about our acquaintance, it's confirmed now. They will be looking for you for no other reason but to get to me."

"Great," the boy sarcastically replied. "So how am I gonna earn my dime magazine money? I can't miss my Tarzan and

Zorro stories! Hey...?" Elmer's face suddenly lit up as an idea occurred to him. "...since the bad guys are gonna be razzing me anyway just cause I know you, how about you take me on as a partner or somethin'?"

"Ah...no. That is not even open to debate young man. I think we can come to some arrangement for remuneration...I can use some help making repairs in my house...where you are out of sight."

"Oh...come on, please!" Elmer whined. "I gotta red winter coat and some grey galoshes...you can call me 'Gusty'! Hey, what's so funny?!"

Bing could not restrain his laughter. "You can wear whatever you please and call yourself whatever you choose, Elmer... while you're fixing my broken banister and polishing the floor. Okay?"

"Fine." Elmer huffed.

CHAPTER TWELVE
SAID THE SPIDER TO THE FLY

Lightning ripped the sky to pieces, followed almost instantly by a torrent of marble-sized raindrops. The sudden sound of seeming cannon-shot impacting the glass and metal roof of the American Issue Publishing Company made Katherine Harvard jump in place at her post at the largest of the Miehle presses. The early morning shower coincided perfectly with the change of shifts at the printing plant so that employees both coming and going were certain to be caught in the downpour.

All except Eunice Parker. Religiously punctual even before being reprimanded by the plant manager, Jackson Knutson, just two days ago, Eunice had now taken to arriving fifteen to twenty minutes before her day shift began.

"A little jumpy, aren't we?" Eunice said as she lumbered from the direction of the plant manager's office toward Katherine at her post. She patted her co-worker on the shoulder with one hand while laying one of the tin funnels used for adding ink to the presses' reservoir on the metal tool tray next to Kate.

Katherine noticed the glistening moisture of fresh ink at the inside of the funnel.

"You should have been here early spring last year. Hail the size of peas made such a ruckus on the glass and tin roof of the plant you could barely hear the machinery. I do hope you've brought an umbrella, Kate?"

"Why, certainly, Eunice. Thank you. I leave one here at my locker." Katherine left her chair, trading places with Eunice at the roaring press.

"I am so excited that you and your husband will be dining with me at my residence this evening. I have so little opportunity to interact as we are all so intent on our work here and my husband is not with me presently. I must hurry on and oversee preparations."

"Reginald and I are also looking forward to our get-together. He is a man of few words, leaving that much more for we ladies to discuss. I will see you soon. Good day." With those words, Eunice turned her back to Kate, attending to a discordant sound coming from the old press.

Lingering only long enough to confirm that Eunice would not need her assistance, Katherine turned to the employee cloak room to retrieve her wrap and umbrella. Mr. Knutson, umbrella in hand, propelled his girth toward the plant's main exit, brushing by Katherine in his haste. His vain attempt to use ladies' make-up to cover the ink stains from Eunice's sabotage were evident. Katherine suppressed a smile.

"Good day, miss," he said, with a quick tip of his bowler hat in Kate's direction. Katherine made a quick nod of her head in acknowledgement and continued on her course past Mr. Knutson.

A primal howl stopped her in her tracks.

She turned quickly to find Jackson Knutson standing at the exit door, coat on, hat in one hand, raised umbrella in the other. His bald head, shoulders and the front of his coat was flowing with viscous black ink. Its apparent source, the inside of his umbrella, was still dripping thick dollops onto the plant floor.

"What in the name of all that is sacred!" Knutson shouted over the roar of presses and the now fading downpour. The plant manager dashed to the washroom as fast as his chubby legs could move. His feet left dark prints on the concrete, each one a permanent reminder of his humiliation.

As Knutson disappeared around the corner, Katherine turned her attention to Eunice, almost hidden by the Miehle press. Against a background of the poorly suppressed snickers of the other plant employees, Eunice laughed outright, full of vengeful pride.

Katherine had dismissed Eunice's prior behavior toward the plant manager. The ink on the phone trick may have been juvenile, but somewhat justified. This time, however, Eunice's actions were unprovoked.

Once challenged, Katherine Harvard's sense of justice could not go unrequited. In acknowledgement of Mrs. Parker's reputation, she would not confront Eunice at the workplace, but candid discourse in the comfort and privacy of Kate's residence, to-night, would suffice.

With this resolution, Mrs. Harvard retrieved her umbrella, cautiously inspecting the inside of it first, and proceeded out of the plant for the short walk to her house.

* * * * * * *

For the second time in less than twenty minutes, Kate was subjected to a relentless torrent of shouted expletives, this time coming from the inside of her own residence. The tirade was of such volume and passion that she felt a vibration as her bare hand clasped the outside doorknob to her front door. Her hesitation vanished upon hearing the distinct baritone laughter of her friend and protector, Julius. She cautiously opened the door and stood at the entryway, looking down into a darkened pit opened up at what was once the floor of her foyer.

Julius stood roughly six feet away at the opposite side of the chasm, a mortified expression on his face.

"Miss Kittie I do most sincerely apologize. I just plain lost track of time. I wasn't expectin' you at this instant. You just take a tiny step back there and I'll set things right."

Katherine's servitor popped away from the entrance and Kate heard a faint *click*, followed by the subtle rattle of chain, and then Julius returned to her view again.

From the rising foyer another figure emerged. He was a small man. Kate could see Julius from the chest up, over the newcomer's head. He was lean and solidly built with a posture most likened to an excited wolf, poised for attack. He was covered, head to toe, in powdered white plaster. Random, small splotches of red dotted his exposed skin, his own blood marking injuries common in his craft.

"Mrs. Harvard, ma'am." The man said, facing Kate. "You haven't been at the door long...I hope?" A wisp of white plaster dust floated off of each word.

"Long enough, Mr. Hanshaw...."

"Mr. Hanshaw's" weathered face blushed red even through the white coating.

"...but please do not worry yourself. I am not a stranger to salty language, and I can sympathize with your frustrations with this...project. Rest assured, the craftsman I lured from Europe to install these very same devices at my home on Long Island entertained me unashamedly with the coarsest of tirades, albeit in German, Russian, and Greek."

"Thank you, ma'am. Julius here thought he'd have a little chuckle at my expense and sent me on a quick ride to your cellar. The floor was still covered in plaster dust from installin' window snares and it seems I'm wearin' it now."

"Window snares?" Kate inquired, as she kicked up plaster dust walking across the foyer floor past the workman and toward Julius.

"Yes, ma'am," Julius added, for the first time stepping fully into the doorway, where he had been mostly hidden from view.

"Now what is that, Julius?" Kate stared at the black man's right arm. Despite his considerable size of six feet, and athletic physique, Julius stood like a scolded child. A heavy tangle of metal bars and springs firmly gripped his arm, just below the elbow. Julius scowled at the now smiling Mr. Hanshaw, and then turned sheepishly to his employer.

"Fred thought it was kinda' silly puttin' all this work inta fallin' floors and graspin' furniture, when we might keep the baddies from gettin' in in the first place. He come up with a pretty smart design for a spring-loaded window frame that grabs and holds anyone tryin' to get in. And, well, he tested it out on me."

Fred's ornery expression vanished in a heartbeat as Lady Kate turned an angry face on him. "I do not recall 'spring-loaded window frames' in the blueprints I gave you when I retained your services, Mr. Hanshaw. Nor do I recollect authorizing the additional expenditure for their construction."

Behind Mrs. Harvard, Julius pantomimed a cutting motion with his finger across his neck. All business now, Mr. Hanshaw repressed an angry retort and composed his thoughts for further explanation to the mistress of the house.

"There were no such blueprints, ma'am. Had it all in my head. Used the same type a snare over ground hog holes so's farmers don't snap an axel or two rollin' over their pitted dens while they're tillin' their land.

"And as for cost I just used the scrap from the pulley tracks and spring shock absorbers from the droppin' floor material. Before ya blow a gasket and have me tear'm all out, could I talk ya into having a look at'm? If ya don't like'm, it won't take nothin' to pull'em."

"Very well. But first, would you be so kind as to unshackle Julius?"

"I was kinda hoping I could leave it on him for a few days so's I could hear the big sneak comin' before he drops another floor outa under me...but, okay.

"Julius, put that arm on the floor here so's I can get a foot on one side of the frame and then the two of us can pull up the other side."

Julius stepped around Katherine, careful to avoid hitting her with the awkward metal frame. "Yes, sir, Mr. Hanshaw."

With considerable effort the two men pried the contrivance open just enough for Julius to slip his arm free, letting the now harmless device clang to the floor.

Fred stood straight from the task and directed the other two with a sweep of his arms. "If you will follow me to the cellar, I've got a little demonstration set up for you Mrs. Harvard."

The handyman led the way through the cellar door and down the steps. He nursed a slight limp from his drop through the trap door, but had worked off the hitch by the time his booted feet touched the cellar floor. Kate followed, with Julius taking up the rear, rubbing his sore arm.

The windowless basement was cluttered with sheet-covered bits of furniture and bales of old newspapers, most of which were not discernible under the single incandescent light. Immediately under the exposed bulb sat a dusty, straight back chair, with what appeared to be a glassless two-paned, metal window frame perched upon its cushioned seat. On the floor lay bits of metal shavings and the tools and implements of an experienced metal worker.

Fred paused briefly, then approached his device with arms extended, hands open like a salesman presenting the latest household convenience.

"It's simple, really. Two straight horizontal tracks—one at top, the other at the bottom." Fred pointed at two narrow metal troughs about two and a half feet long. "Two vertical bars of metal connect the two horizontal pieces, their ends inside the extreme ends of each track, making the rectangle shape. Three industrial strength springs...."

"Excuse me, Mr. Hanshaw, sorry to interrupt. It is all very good that you can recite the schematics, but they will need to be documented for future repair, or at the very least for the new occupant to refer to upon removal. I am anxious to freshen up just now. A simple demonstration of functionality will do."

Having taken the wind from his sails, Fred continued with less enthusiasm. "A couple pounds of pressure against any one of those metal projections and the three sets of rods slip out of alignment and loose the springs, and...." Thereupon Fred slid an empty propane tank through the frame, over the very bottom track.

Whommppp! Before the tank penetrated a foot through the frame all three springs simultaneously contracted, instantly drawing the two vertical steel bars together, caving in the metal tank in a pincer grip.

Kate jumped back in shock. Catching her breath, she uttered "Well, Mr. Hanshaw, that's brilliant. A few questions?"

Beaming, Fred responded, "Why certainly ma'am, fire away."

"Should Julius and I need to extricate ourselves through the windows...say, in case of a house fire or some similar emergency would not this device catch us too? And how about house guests innocently opening a window?"

"Good questions, ma'am, but not a problem. Assuming I don't put the things in backwards, the snare won't work from the inside. The metal tabs sticking up through the bottom spring can't bend backwards, just forwards."

Katherine nodded, then in a relieved exhale stated, "I must confess, I had my reservations when Mr. Cherrington recommended you and conveyed to me your preferred method of recompense, but you have truly lived up to your billing."

"I thank you kindly for the compliment, Mrs. Harvard. And as for the payment, I suppose bartering my labor for firearms seems odd to you coming from New York City and all. Then again, folks anywheres might find it a bit odd you fortifying this here house the way you've done. I'll take a guess that all this expense and labor ain't fer protectin' yerself from groundhogs?"

"You would be correct in your guess, sir. And as you are aware, Mr. Cherrington's referral was based as much on your mastery of mechanics, woodwork, and electrical wiring as your capacity to remain discreet."

"Yes, ma'am, well said. Rest assured, with or without the several Browning Auto-5s you promised me, there just ain't no profit in flappin' my yap."

"Very well then, you have earned them and more. I expect this petit arsenal here by train any day now. Meanwhile, how far have you progressed in installing your remarkable 'window snares?'"

"Just a couple in the foyer to put in and that should wrap-up the entire first floor. Julius and I could have'em ready in a couple hours. Cleaned up in another hour?"

"That will do nicely for the day. We should have plenty of time then to prepare for our dinner guests this evening. I have some errands to attend to outside of the house, so if I do not see you again sir, please give my regards to your lovely family and we will see you again bright and early tomorrow?"

"Yes, ma'am, good day to you."

CHAPTER THIRTEEN
SWORDS INTO PLOWSHARES

"It is sure kind of you to invite the missus and me to your home to break bread, Mrs. Harvard," said Reginald Parker from his seat in Katherine's parlor. His enunciation was slurred, and the words escaped in a droning monotone, as if it were a line poorly spoken from a script.

If his speech was unsettling, Mr. Parker's appearance was patently eerie. He was dressed well enough: a pressed three-piece suit of a cut only five to six years dated, and loose-fitting. His abdomen appeared swollen.

Mr. Parker's complexion commanded the most attention. None of it good. It was abnormally yellow, more so for the lamp light reflecting off his perspiring face. His hair was thin at the sides and entirely gone from the crown of his head, except for the amateur comb-over. His teeth were in need of serious, basic hygiene—and much of his mouth would require far more intrusive dental treatment. Dark, tired eyes shrank back in his head like cornered mice in a shallow hole. They lacked even a spark of life, and were noticeable only for the deep, dark half-circle bags under each.

"You are most welcome, Mr. Parker," said the hostess. "From the moment Eunice proposed such a get-together, I have thought of little else. It is so nice to have an opportunity to see and socialize with one's co-worker outside of work. I get the warm feeling of knowing another as a person, not so much as merely the laborer who must relieve me from my shift at the presses."

As Katherine spoke it was apparent that Mr. Parker had disengaged almost from the moment he uttered his rehearsed courtesy. His sunken eyes never met hers, but remained distant and vacant.

Katherine attempted to engage him. "Eunice tells me that you make play guns and caps at the Kilgore Manufacturing Company here in town? It immediately struck me as ironic, the name of your employer, and its products: 'Kil-gore.'" Katherine and Eunice gave polite laughter to the comment. Reginald remained quiet, the irony, if not the humor entirely lost on him.

Then he spoke. "Dear Katherine, could I bother you to direct me to the water closet?"

Kate left her seat and directed Mr. Parker to the rear of her house. Eunice quickly struck up a conversation the moment Katherine reappeared.

Mrs. Parker was dressed impeccably. Her hair was done up in the latest fashion - uncommon for mid-westerners, let alone the residents of this suburb of Columbus, Ohio. Unlike her husband, Eunice was the picture of health. Although large of frame, she retained a full, womanly figure. She had attempted beautification by way of make-up, but unfortunately no amount of cosmetic could improve her pinched, bull-dog countenance.

Avoiding eye contact, Eunice said, "Reggie will be indisposed for a considerable stretch, I'm afraid. He has a very sensitive disposition which has preyed upon him particularly harshly of late."

"That is unfortunate." Lady Kate responded.

"But it gives us ladies more time for feminine banter, without fear of putting poor Reginald to sleep for boredom."

"Why, yes it does, Eunice. How nice. In fact I do have a matter I would like to discuss...just between we ladies. I fear, however, it is not the casual banter you would hope for."

"Oh?"

"I have noticed your...relationship, with Mr. Knutson."

"Oh, yes, that."

"I trust my knowledge of your treatment of the plant manager of late does not come as a surprise? You have not been subtle in your expression of displeasure with him. The very open layout of the plant floor seems to have made your actions quite the subject of break-time chit-chat among the persons in my shift, at least."

"Oh, to be sure, staining Knutty's worthless hide has been my open objective...except to maybe him." With these words, Eunice metamorphosed from superficial conversationalist to a cleric of fire and brimstone. Never entertaining a fully relaxed posture, she was even more taught and rigid than normal.

"Surely one must question his loyalty to the mission of the Anti-Saloon League in ridding this land of intoxicating beverages when he continues to make a living hell of the lives of we disciples of Prohibition. He pays mere lip-service to the word of the Lord and I am merely a bulldog running along at the feet of Jesus, barking at all that is unrighteous. I can make no apology for my passion, for it is a sacred union of my faith and the law of the land."

Katherine was somewhat taken aback by Eunice's vitriol, and wisely selected to abstain from a direct attack on her expressed, twisted motivations. Surely no one conveyed the passion and commitment to Prohibition as deeply as Eunice Parker. Jackson Knutson was destined to fall short of Mrs. Parker's notion of "loyalty to the mission." Nonetheless, Kate's concerns were with the consequences of Eunice's actions, not her intentions.

"I do not disagree with you that Mr. Knutson's managerial methods are harsh. I cannot tell if he is simply a man suffering from too much pressure from his superiors and consequently lashing out at his subordinates, or if indeed he is ruthless by nature. It seems to me that either alternative speaks poorly of his character generally. It is this very pitiless trait that forces me to address the matter to you."

Katherine continued, somewhat reassured by the fact that her consoling words of agreement on Knutson's character settled Eunice down to her usual posture.

"You have just said that Knutson may be unaware of your

objective. Indeed, I believe that you are the *last* person he would suspect. Your efforts to the cause are singularly unique for being the only person exerting both mind and muscle. Even Knutson must believe that the events he has suffered would be beneath you. My fear is that especially after today's...incident, Knutson will engage in an inquisition-like investigation, causing more than one innocent laborer to lose their job, or to wish they had."

Katherine pressed on, "I do not ask you to apologize, Eunice. You are entitled to your passions. I ask simply that your feelings be expressed more directly, and that you spare otherwise innocent employees the wrath of Jackson Knutson for your past actions."

Katherine folded her hands in her lap, lowered her eyes, and steeled herself for continued rancorous diatribe.

It did not come.

"You are absolutely right, dear Katherine." Eunice replied softly. She had already witnessed the fallout of her behavior. While Kate was home making preparations for their evening dinner, Knutson had paraded at least a dozen plant employees through his office. A few returned to their posts, clearly flustered from their meeting. Others were escorted from the manager's office to the cloak room to gather their belongings, and then out through the plant entrance. Eunice remained at her post, a placid spectator to these events.

"You flatter me with your suggestion that I am above reproach," she continued. "Upon reflection, it is probable that Mr. Knutson shares your belief. If it suits you, to-morrow, at our change of shifts, I will disabuse our plant manager of his belief that I give even tacit approval of his management technique."

On whole, Kate satisfied herself that Eunice had acceded to an unconditional "clearing of the air" with Jackson Knutson. Tragically, she did not have the luxury of probing the details of Eunice's promise as Mr. Parker, followed closely by Julius, entered the room. There would be no further reference that evening to their shared workplace or the plant manager.

"Ladies and gentleman, dinner is served." Julius intoned.

Eunice made much ado of Katherine's table service: Gorham's Chantilly pattern china, and flatware, French cut crystal, and a Tiffany silver repoussé tea set. She was likewise effusive over the Georgian sterling silver coffee pot, making Biblical allusion to its ivory handle in the shape of a snake. It would never occur to Katherine to boast of her possessions, but Eunice assessed the finery with the skill of an antiques appraiser. She quickly determined that the Parker income would require at least four years of frugal investment to acquire such accoutrements.

Over the main course of pheasant, Eunice inquired, "So Katherine, what does your husband do for a living?"

Mindful of her instruction to abstain from reference to her husband's current activities, Katherine was nonetheless careful not to utter a blatant falsehood.

"Bingham is in banking. He has pursued that vocation for the whole of his adult life."

"And clearly found much success in it." Eunice declared, inclining her head toward the spread of the dinner table.

Mrs. Harvard did not take the clear opportunity to brag, but responded simply, "My father-in-law preceded my husband in the business and left him with a very solid enterprise."

"And where is the dashing Mr. Harvard while you toil away for the Anti-Saloon League?"

Katherine responded somewhat elusively, hoping that her pre-scripted explanation left the impression that Bingham Harvard remained on Long Island, tending to the business of banking. "I am surely blessed with a husband who will entertain my philo-sophical interests to such a degree that he would consent to our physical separation for months on end."

Eunice's change of subject spared Lady Kate the risk of even suggesting that her husband, alias the Night Wind, was pres-ently charging about the local neighborhood in scarlet and gray body armor waging war on organized crime.

Fortunately, for the duration of the evening, this was as close as conversation touched upon Katherine's family or personal life. To her relief, Eunice was content to make herself and her accomplishments the focus of all further discussion. Mr. Parker contributed absolutely nothing to the conversation, though anyone would be hard put to interject upon Eunice's life-narrative.

Seeing her guests to the door, Katherine, with Julius just at her back, made polite "good-byes."

"We had such a wonderful time, dearest Katherine. Didn't we, Reggie?"

After hours of enduring his wife's relentless airs and graces Mr. Parker's fleeting responsiveness had degraded to catatonia. "I had a lovely evening Mrs. Harvard, the meal was superb and you are a gracious hostess." If the lifeless monotone of his delivery did not betray his ambivalence, the fact that he barely consumed a bite of the "superb" meal lent certitude. Being physically closer to Mr. Parker than she had at any time that evening, Lady Kate caught the distinct and near overwhelming scent of male cologne.

"Julius, Mr. Parker and I would be happy to take you home. You are familiar with *that* part of town, right dear?" Mr. Parker gave a ponderous nod to his wife's suggestion.

"Oh, that will not be necessary Eunice, Julius will be staying here."

"Well, surely Julius deserves an early evening home with his *people*. Your maid seems to have the clean-up well in hand."

"Oh no, Eunice, you misunderstand. Julius resides in this house with me."

"Is that so?" Mrs. Parker's ramrod posture returned.

"Well...eh, yes. My husband sent Julius along as a condition of my...adventure, if you will. You cannot doubt a negro of his virility can be depended upon in time of need." Her words barely escaped Kate's lips before she blushed at her obvious poor choice of expression.

A chill ran down her spine as Reginald Parker displayed a rare instant of animation. Looking at Kate and Julius as if seeing them for the first time, "Reggie" offered up a rotted toothful grin over his wife's shoulder. It was clear that even his muddled mind had both heard and made the most salacious of possible interpretations of Katherine's assertions about her valet.

Eunice's clipped inhalation, and raised brow intimated her disapproval, but the expression dissipated nearly as fast as it appeared. A look of composure, if not resolve, softened the lines around her mouth and relaxed her brow.

"Very well then, dear. If there is nothing Reggie and I can do for you at the moment then?" Eunice smiled thinly, avoiding her hostesses' eyes.

"You are very kind to offer, however, as you said, 'clean-up is well in hand,' and we all must get our rest for an eventful work day to-morrow."

"Oh, yes, and you with the third shift and all." Eunice turned to the front door, catching sight of her husband's dodgy smile. In the span of a single heartbeat, her eyes blazed directly into her spouse's, melting the leer from his face.

As the Parkers' automobile sputtered away from Katherine's residence, she turned to her loyal servant and spoke, a hint of worry in her voice. "Surely there can be nothing to the Parkers' reaction to our accommodations? Why even the suggestion of impropriety is not worth contemplation. You could be my father, Julius; indeed you have cared for my older brother and me from birth, much like a father."

"That's sure enough the truth Miss Kittie. Mrs. Eunice struck me as a God fearin' woman. Sure enough she ain't got no quarrel with you."

Having known her valet for a lifetime, Katherine could rely as much on Julius' non-verbal communication, as his verbal. It was clear to her that her protector did not believe his own assessment of the departed guests.

Her nervous chill returned in force as Julius turned toward the kitchen with the words, "Jus' the same it won't hurt none to keep our guard up. Those who beat their swords into plowshares will end up plowing for those who didn't."

CHAPTER FOURTEEN
HATS OFF

"Jackson Knutson, you are a horse's ass." Eunice's tone was hostile and vicious and she was only getting started. Oddly, the invective came with a smile, and was delivered in an eerily composed matter-of-fact posture. Mr. Knutson and Katherine Harvard could not have been more caught off guard.

This confrontation was not what Lady Kate had imagined when Mrs. Parker pronounced her intentions the evening before. Indeed, every word up to this point suggested a simple, direct and honest dialogue, until taking this nasty turn.

Eunice had arrived early, as had been her routine of late. She first wandered into the binding area, then marched to Kate's workstation at the big Miehle press. She exchanged pleasantries with Katherine, thanking her again for the lovely dinner, and then caught sight of the plant manager exiting his office.

"Oh, Mr. Knutson, sir!" Eunice cried while waving her arm in the air. "A moment of your *extremely* valuable time please?!"

The plant manager wore his derby hat when he left his office. Since having the top of his bald head stained with black ink, he had taken to donning his bowler nearly round the clock, inside and outside.

"Please, Mrs. Parker. I am in a hurry. Can't this wait for a more opportune time?" Knutson approached within a couple of feet of the two ladies at their press.

"I beg your indulgence sir, I do have some important information to convey." Eunice extended her right arm toward Knutson as for a handshake.

Knutson hesitated. It was not customary for a woman to greet a man by handshake, but he'd been acquainted with Mrs. Parker long enough to not question her eccentricities. He firmly clasped his subordinate's extended hand. Katherine smiled, content that the discussion was off to a gracious start.

But for the roar of the nearby press, the sticky tearing sound of separating, glue-soaked palms would have been obvious. Knutson gave a disgusted snarl. Eunice instantly and expertly diffused his anger with fervent apology and explanation that she had just been to the binding machine and must have inadvertently set her palm in spilled adhesive.

The plant manager shuffled within inches of the spinning rollers of the press to locate a rag from the work station to wipe his hand. He was still vainly searching when Eunice's tirade began.

The contrast between Mrs. Parker's delivery and its content was intentional. A less calculating soul might have spat the same vitriol with clenched fists, a red face and a menacing posture. However, Eunice endeavored to communicate two entirely different messages to two different audiences. For Knutson, a spiteful tirade, and for witnesses outside the range of hearing, a composed, routine discourse.

"It sickens me to be in proximity to your abhorrent carcass. While your brutish, sadistic mode of communing with your fellow man is common knowledge to we few at the plant who must suffer it, the outside world stands unsuspecting and vulnerable. That is why I have endeavored, successfully I might add, to brand you, like many cultures tattoo their convicts. It humors me that you are self-conscious of the black ink stains about your face and head, when nature had already made your appearance so repellant that mothers hide their children from its sight. Do you see how useless it is to hide your true character with this silly hat?"

Before Knutson could react, Eunice snatched the bowler from his head and sent it tumbling end over end toward the exposed, whirling spools of the nearby printing machine.

Instinctively, the plant manager reached for his hat, growling with anger. His hand connected as did the hungry maw of the press. In a trice Knutson knew who would win this tug-of-war and endeavored to release his grip, but the binding glue forbade it.

The earth's rotation seemed to slow as Knutson's visible frustration and anger at the loss of his hat transformed into a rictus of terror upon realizing that he could not release his hand from the chapeau.

Knutson was pulled off his feet. Fingers, hand, and forearm were instantly pulped; their unrecognizable remains extruded onto the floor and back of the press. The massive Miehle gnawed at the elbow briefly before grinding it, too. Thereafter, the press rapidly drew in Jackson Knutson's limb up to his shoulder, snagged an ear and then spooled in the flesh from his head just above the jaw line. The rest of the body shivered and shook as the machine tried, and failed to suck in his slick, round skull. A terrible falsetto scream exploded and then as quickly died in the plant manager's mouth.

Knutson's violent expiration took just seconds. Throughout, Eunice Parker casually re-arranged maintenance supplies at her workstation. She glared at Kate Harvard with a burning, hateful stare, a self-satisfied smirk on her mouth. She was indifferent to the blood and flesh flying in spatters on to her work frock.

It was Kate who first snapped from the morbid trance and hammered with frenzied fists at the emergency, full-stop button. Chaos ensued.

Other machines were shut down and the plant erupted with shouts.

Her withering glare unflinching, Eunice whipped a rag from her waist pocket and methodically wiped the binding glue from her hand. She jammed it back into her pocket, securing on her person the only bit of evidence that would distinguish this tragic accident from calculated murder. Like a striking cobra, she grabbed the collar of one of the few composed plant employees, drew him to her and spoke into his ear. He nodded his head in understanding and skittered out the plant door.

Eunice calmly strode to the cloak room and exited the plant with as much poise and composure as if it were lunch break.

Kate leaned heavily against the press, fighting for balance against her trembling legs. Her hand still gripped the full stop button, willing it to reverse the cycle of carnage she had just witnessed.

CHAPTER FIFTEEN
FIERY SUMMONS!

"Hello?"

"Who is this?"

"Cletus."

"What's your number, Cletus?"

"46."

"White Man's—" The first half of the Black Legion's current secret password.

"—Burden." Bing replied, returning the countersign.

"Birth of—" The voice on the telephone continued.

"—a Nation." Bingham finished.

Satisfied that he was speaking with a brother black knight, the voice on Bingham Harvard's telephone continued. "This is the Grand Wraith, and this is a Fiery Summons! Remember your oath to be ready when called! Bring your robe and seek the 'burning bush.' That is all."

The line went dead in Bing's hand. He placed the receiver back on its hook. It was two in the morning. Despite the early hour, the Night Wind's heart was racing. This was his first "call to arms" by the Black Legion—excepting his earlier run-in in the midst of their successful pursuit of bootleggers.

The unhesitating, staccato dialogue set him at ease that all the code information given him by the Secret Service infiltrator disguised as a Black Legionnaire was accurate. All that was left for him to do was suit up with both layers of body armor—the scarlet and gray "football uniform" covered by the black robe and hood—and race off for a block or two to the "burning bush."

He had discovered in the course of his involvement with this especially vicious sect of the Ku Klux Klan that they did not in fact conduct meetings at the printing plant for the American Issue Publishing Company. This was merely the location of the "burning bush." The "bush" was in fact a well manicured, waist high shrub at the back yard of an unsuspecting single-family residence that happened to abut the Anti-Saloon League's printing plant property.

Immediately upon a "Fiery Summons," members were to go to the bush and look for one of three colored kerchiefs tied to an exterior branch of the shrub, red, white or blue. Each color represented a location known only to the black knights within a mile or two of the bush itself.

This bit of cloak and dagger was not without its purpose. Telephone lines in this area were party lines where multiple residences shared the same connection. It was common, particularly during peak line use, for anyone to pick up his receiver and listen in on an ongoing "private" conversation, unintentionally or not.

On the chance that there may be an unintended listener at two in the morning, and that he or she could accurately translate the cryptic secret society dialogue as a call for a gathering of the Black Legion, they would have absolutely no idea where that gathering would take place.

Bingham laced his scarlet breeches and pulled on his steel-toed boots. He shrugged into his gray armored shirt with prominent crimson striping, and reached for his black robe, slung over a bedroom chair. The tightly layered silk robe now sported a hand sized white skull and crossbones insignia at the upper left chest-area, where a vest pocket might be. Along with the white piping around both cuffs, similar to officer's stripes, the "pirate" symbol was a very recent mandate from the Grand Wraith, or principal Black Legion organizer and boss.

Some members had taken to donning a black felt, pirate hat, complete with white trim and another skull and cross bones symbol front and center. Bingham spared himself that further indignity and stuck with the already ridiculous pointed black hood.

The Night Wind thudded down the stairs from his bedroom to the first floor, pulling on the red cestuses, and the oversized black leather riding gloves as cover. As he drew his door shut behind him with one hand, he yanked the black hood down over his face. Before he turned to walk through his yard, Bing caught sight of a parked car on the street in front of his residence. He had seen it only with his peripheral vision, but the image was unmistakable. It was a particularly weather-beaten Ford Model-T and it was occupied. Bing had seen it once before in the same location since Elmer had had his run-in with the mafia.

Then, as now, Bingham thought little of it. No question that the mafia would be interested in anyone participating in the tarring and feathering of one of their members, but Bing had been cloaked and well away from this residence. Even so, he'd seen firsthand the mafia's chosen means of conveyance— a Model 38 Pierce-Arrow. A road weary Model-T wasn't their style.

He had only been in Westerville less than a month and was still reasonably unfamiliar with the day-to-day comings and goings of his neighbors. In any case, on this occasion he was far too preoccupied with his current mission. It would prove to be an unfortunate oversight.

The handkerchief was blue, meaning that black knights were to proceed northeast to a densely wooded area just outside the grounds of the Kilgore Manufacturing Company.

Black clad members of the secret society seemed to converge from all points of the compass, first to the "burning bush," and then together in twos and threes to the "blue" meeting place.

The Grand Wraith, known by all members generally as "Thomas" of the earlier tarring and feathering atrocity, awaited his Klan along with a few subordinate officers in a clearing in the woods. Five or six oil lanterns were held by Klansmen to give a view of the entire conclave. There were roughly twenty in all. All of them armed with at least some form of weapon. If challenged, Bingham kept a blackjack in his robe pocket. However, most members' arms were much less discreet. They bore Springfield rifles, Browning shotguns and many had long knives. Several clutched a leather-bladed bludgeon used to beat their victims. This flogging whip was made by sewing a piece of sawmill belt to a sawed-off baseball bat handle.

One of the officers did a quick head count and turned and nodded to the Grand Wraith. From somewhere out of Bing's immediate view a gong was struck twice. Like sheep to a barking collie, all in attendance fell silent and looked as one to their leader.

The Grand Wraith, "Thomas," stood on a wooden soap box and addressed the Legion. "Brothers, we have a rare opportunity this night to kill two birds with one stone: A Negro who fancies himself our social equal, and a member of the patrician class who not only agrees with, but encourages the offense. She...yes I said *she*...is the wife of a successful banker, no doubt a Jew, from New York City. She has come to this city on the pretense of serving the cause of Prohibition, but has only tainted the effort with her liberal, socialist ideology. Indeed, my fellow black knights, this white upper-class woman who lords her east coast wealth over us all, chooses, nay *desires* to cohabit with a nigger.

"You all remember your 'oath of allegiance' to the Black Legion," the speaker continued, "'The native-born white people of America are menaced on every hand from above and below. If America is a melting pot, the white people of America are neither the aristocratic scum on top nor the dregs of society on the bottom, which is composed of anarchists and Communists and all cults and creeds believing in social equality. We regard as enemies to ourselves and our country all aliens, Negroes, Jews and cults and creeds believing in racial equality or owing allegiance to any foreign potentates. These we will fight without fear or favor as long as one foe of American liberty is left alive.'"

Bingham's stomach burned and his fists instinctively clenched. His erstwhile brotherhood had identified Lady Kate and her servitor, Julius, and had planned an assualt. Kate had been cautioned about the risks of bringing her black valet into KKK territory, but that fact seemed to be only one mark against her. The Jewish inference was just that, but how had the Grand Wraith come to know of Bing and his profession?

Bingham struggled with his responsibility for the burnt bootlegger. He let that ritual go too far, and someone was seriously injured for it. Perhaps the victim wasn't entirely innocent, his eventual rescuer not the most experienced, and doubtless Dan Drake would give him a medal for taking at least one mafioso off the streets of Westerville, but Bing would not forgive himself. He would not make that mistake a second time.

With the immediacy of the planned "event," Bingham knew well that there was no conceivable way to warn his wife and protector ahead of time. The assault would begin. Bing would have to see that its intent was never realized.

CHAPTER SIXTEEN
TEMPEST IN A TEAPOT

Katherine Harvard lay on her back in her bed, eyes wide open. It was three in the morning. She had been unable to sleep or even relax. It had been less than twenty hours since the grisly death of the American Issue Publishing Company's plant manager, Jackson Knutson.

The brief inquiry into the events had concluded that Knutson had made a thoughtless error reaching into a running press, and paid with his life. Kate was deemed "too devastated at the moment" to warrant questioning. Her contrary testimony notwithstanding, the tide of other witness statements and forensic evidence would dictate no change in the investigation's outcome.

Eunice's plot had proved genius. Physical evidence of the binding glue was entirely destroyed in the gore left at the press. The precipitating conversation between Mrs. Parker and Mr. Knutson was interpreted by eye witnesses just as Eunice had planned. Although varying slightly at inconsequential facts, all of the half dozen statements shared the same critical elements:

"Well, inspector, Mrs. Parker was her usual fulsome self.... No, I did not hear any words for the loud machines, but she was smiling and nodding her head as if in agreement with something Mr. Knutson was saying.... Yes, he seemed a little bug-eyed, but that would be nothing unusual for the plant manager. He was always a bit impatient and excitable, you know."

And so it was that Eunice Parker was well on her way to

getting away with murder.

The sudden, unexpected loss of management in the plant and the damage to one of the two big Miehle presses forced a shutdown until further notice. It was bad enough that Lady Kate experienced the horror of murder at all, but now she had plenty of free time in which to ruminate.

As she lay staring toward the ceiling of her room, she heard the faint tinkle of glass as a darting flame pierced her field of vision.

Alight from point to feathered fletching, the arrow pierced the upper pane of the window immediately above Katherine's head and speared into the opposite wall.

Her body surged with adrenaline. She, like her husband, lacked the capacity to respond to a threat by running, or seeking safety. Indeed, Lady Kate was instantly imbued with a sense of mission, relieved to be freed from her funk of helplessness and inactivity. Besides, she had meticulously planned for just such an assault.

She threw herself from her bed, simultaneously slapping the pressure-sensitive "call button" at the nearby wall with the palm of her opened hand. Of the many devices Fred and Julius had installed of late, this convenience pre-dated Kate's residence. The simple buzzer system linked the master room with the servants' quarters as well as the parlor, dining room, and kitchen. With the push of the master bedroom button a metallic buzzing alarm coursed throughout the house for so long as the plunger remain depressed.

A brief second or two of the grating noise sent Julius into action. He too had slept as restlessly as his charge.

Kate swiftly grabbed a brass, bulbous two gallon container resting on the floor just inside of her door. By means of an attached hand pump she sprayed a chemical concoction upon the arrow, extinguishing it on contact. This was a carbon tetrachloride or CTC fire extinguisher and it was just one of a dozen such contraptions spread strategically throughout the house.

While Kate dispensed with her small fire, she heard Julius

racing up the staircase.

"Miss Kitten, you okay!?" He shouted as he ran.

Kate met him at the open doorway to her room, donning a house coat and holding the extinguisher. Julius was a large black silhouette on the white plaster walls.

"Yes, Julius, I am fine. Someone is trying to smoke us out. I'll check the other rooms for fire, and you get the shutters."

Upon seeing Katherine unharmed and alert, Julius didn't pause to absorb instruction. He knew his duty and raced past Kate in the pitch darkness to the farthest of the five other second-story rooms, his employer right on his heels.

The "shutters" were devices conceived by Katherine and installed just days before by Fred and Julius. They were spring-activated steel window shutters affixed to the inside walls of each of the second-story windows. The foundation walls and the slate roofing were naturally fire proof, but the wood window frames had been vulnerable. Now sealed in steel, the entire structure was primed for any attempt at arson.

Two other rooms glowed with flickering firelight. Only one had advanced to more than a square foot. Kate quickly smothered both, set down her extinguisher and hurried on slippered feet to help Julius.

Just as the last steel shutter connected, Kate and Julius clearly heard a *crack* followed almost simultaneously by what sounded like a hammer blow to the metal window cover.

"They's moved from primitive weapons to high-powered rifles Miss Kittie." Julius observed correctly.

His words were evidenced by a volley of rifle *cracks*, some bullets bouncing harmlessly off the metal shutters, others ripping through the unprotected first floor windows and lodging in plaster walls or furniture.

The two besieged occupants of the house ran single file down the steps. Julius, in the lead, stomped out another burning arrow speared into the first step of the staircase.

Katherine had to shout to be heard above the clamor of rifle fire. "Whoever they are, they have to move quickly to kill us or take us prisoner. Surely they must know that even though Westerville may be a sleepy burg, police will respond eventually—particularly here so close to the center of town. I don't think they have the luxury of time for a siege. If the fire and the bullets don't work, they'll have to think of something else, fast."

As if Lady Kate had plotted the raid herself, "something else" arrived in the next breath.

Glass erupted into the first floor as stones and brick parts shattered both the upper and lower panes of all six front windows. The thundering sound of body blows to the single first floor door was followed swiftly by the snap of cracking wood as the exterior door gave in.

Without another word, Katherine raced to the interior door. She placed her eye to a tiny peephole in the solid oak portal. Her hand skittered along the adjacent wall, brushing aside a small framed oil painting and resting on a tiny chrome toggle.

The view through the peephole and into the foyer would have rendered a less hardy soul instantly incontinent. An adult sized black robe shuddered and flowed. Stomping in bitterness on the flattened exterior door, the wraith shouted, "Come on, I got the front door!"

Three more hooded apparitions stormed in through the shattered entrance. As the first wraith turned to face the door separating him from Kate, she discerned a white skull and crossbones adornment at its chest. Its three brethren specters wore black pirate hats displaying the same skull and crossbones emblem and white trim.

Despite the security of the reinforced oak door, Kate flinched when the futile twist of the exterior knob was followed by a full body slam.

Undaunted, Lady Kate pressed her eye to the spy-hole again. She had waited but a few seconds for the foyer to fill to its capacity of four persons, and then she flipped the chrome switch.

Just as the lead wraith had stepped back to make a second run at the interior door, its body dropped from sight—as did its three compatriots.

A thunderous *boom* echoed from the basement of the house as the foyer floor with its four burdens plummeted twenty feet down to the windowless cellar.

Kate was confused by the sound. She expected no sound at all. The dropping floor mechanism included a pair of pneumatic shock absorbers, designed to slow the initial precipitous drop. The depth of the cellar and a collapsing staircase from the basement to the first floor ensured captivity for otherwise unharmed detainees.

Presumably, the weight of four bodies had overwhelmed the shocks. This black clad quartet would be exiting the cellar only with the aid of stretchers.

Julius had not been idle during Katherine's trap-setting. As Lady Kate turned toward the parlor, Julius sprang into view from his quarters near the kitchen. A vicious looking whip was looped through his belt, an enormous pistol in one hand. Large even in proportion to big Julius, the gun appeared almost comically gargantuan as he placed it in Kate's waiting palm.

The gun was a Webley Mark VI, the most powerful top-loading revolver ever manufactured. Complete with a speed-loader device that simultaneously charged all six chambers for quick firing, this was a wedding anniversary gift from Kate's husband, Bingham. Persons uninformed of Lady Kate's predilection for weaponry might have questioned Mr. Harvard's sanity in thinking this massive British service revolver an appropriate expression of love and adoration. Yet, Katherine was so taken by the firearm, she gave it a name: "The Warhorse."

Kate held the Warhorse lovingly to her cheek. The feel of cold steel on her skin fanned the flames of her resolve and hinted at a maternal attachment to her weapon. Her reverie was interrupted by a baritone, agonized wailing from *inside* the house.

The six front windows were shared evenly by the two rooms at the front of the house on the first floor, the parlor, and an adjacent dining room. A solid wall separated the rooms, and double French doors connected them. The pained bawling was coming from the dining room.

As Julius and Kate scrambled from the parlor to the source of the howling, Julius unwound his whip and Kate cracked open the Webley to ensure a full load.

A black-robed person hung halfway in one of the shattered dining room windows. He was lying on his stomach at the sill. The two vertical sides of the frame pinched the figure securely in place, pinning his arms to his sides. Unable to bend or reach backwards, the black knight could only writhe like a beached fish.

"The windows are booby-trapped! Watch out!" he screamed.

The warning came too late.

The near simultaneous double *snap* of collapsing springs, followed closely by groans announced the capture of two more Black Legionnaires, this time in the parlor. An instant later another trap sprang back in the dining room.

Careful to not make too much of a target of themselves through the caved-in windows, Lady Kate and Julius crouched just inside the wide open doorframe of the French doors. Over the cacophony of inarticulate swearing and gasping from the predators turned prey, the two defenders, huddled close, were able to converse.

"Kitten, its lookin' like we'll be runnin' outta window traps any second. I've got an idea if you can jus' hold the fort here for a minute while I gather what I need."

Implicitly trusting her guardian's instinct, Kate nodded. Julius made a crouching run to the darkened passageway connected to his room and then the kitchen. He was back at his employer's side before two minutes elapsed, arms laden with an unusual collection of gear: an empty coffee tin with a lid, a handful of pre-made cotton fuses, a pair of pliers, and a leather powderhorn.

As Julius set to work on his mysterious apparatus, Kate remained riveted to the gaping windows. The ferociousness of the besiegers convinced her that their remaining membership would not hesitate to climb atop and over their own helpless brethren to gain their prize.

Again, Mrs. Harvard's assessment of the low character of the Black Legion proved dead on.

Sometime during the raid an enormous cross was planted in the front lawn and set aflame. The growing blaze served as excellent backlight to any figure attempting to enter from the windows.

Kate watched and listened as the volume of cursing and wailing from one of the window-snared black knights increased precipitously. A black silhouette outside was attempting to yank his trapped compatriot free. Finding the job impossible, he instead used his fellow Klansman as leverage to pull himself through the window frame.

Before he could put his feet to the floor inside, Lady Kate blasted three successive shots to either side of the invader, into the plaster walls.

"Aaaaaaa!" The interloper roared. Not expecting armed resistance at all, let alone the cannonade from the Webley .455 caliber cartridges, the terrified trespasser threw himself backwards out the window.

"Almost done," Julius yelled in his excitement.

Kate looked down to see her valet crimping the lid securely to the coffee tin with pliers. The leather powderhorn lay deflated on the floor. A few inches of a fuse stuck out of the can at the top, pinch marks at the lid to each side fixing the wick in place.

The thud of booted feet on a wooden floor jerked the defenders' attention from their respective tasks. A raider had made it through one of the kitchen windows at the back of the first floor and was making haste to the front.

Julius moved as if hit by lightening. Done with his tinkering, he brushed away the heavy can along the floor behind him and shot up from his crouch to face the attacker.

Emerging from the passageway, a six-foot tall phantom donned in Black Legion regalia burst into the parlor. It swept its head from left to right in an effort to survey the battleground. The reflecting orange flames from the burning cross danced on his shiny robe as the hooded wraith froze in place on seeing Julius.

The loyal servant lashed out with his whip the instant their eyes met. With precision born from two years of training by experts hired by his employers, Julius caught his target about the neck, the force of his lash looping around and then constricting like a snake.

Julius' mouth erupted with a warrior's primal roar as he yanked his strangling victim toward him. Although proficient with a whip, Julius' forte was close quarters, hand-to-hand combat. He had even sparred the super-endowed "Night Wind" to a draw more than once in the last year or two.

Black gloved hands grasped the squeezing whip and a gurgling sound was barely audible through the pointed black hood, as Julius drew back a massive fist and unleashed a power house undercut to the wraith's abdomen. The destructive force of the blow doubled the black knight in half, throwing him off his feet.

Curiously, Julius clutched his fist as if stung. "Oh, lordy, that phantom has a brick for a belly." He cursed to no one in particular.

"Julius, it's me! For the love of Pete, let up!" The gasping plea was barely a whisper through the shroud of the floored Legionnaire.

The voice, though tortured and rasping, was unmistakable to Lady Kate. "Bingham!" she whispered.

Clutched for a follow-up punch, Julius' hand went instead to his own mouth in shocked expression. "Heaven preserve us!" he muttered.

Julius and Kate rushed to the downed man. The valet unwrenched the leather from his neck an instant before Katherine threw herself upon the prostrate black form, pulled back the hood and revealed her husband's face.

Before saying another word, however, Kate interrupted her unexpected reunion. "Julius, the can, now!" Astride her husband but facing the standing valet, she pointed toward the neglected container.

The loyal servant needed no more direction. He turned on his heels and gripped the coffee can in one hand while swiping a stove match on the plaster wall next to him. Fuse lit, Julius stood with his back to the wall immediately next to a gaping window, a thrashing black knight affixed to the sill.

After a quick peek out the window to confirm a clear shot, Julius lobbed the sparking container purposefully in the direction of the fiery cross.

The resourceful servitor had hastily constructed a crude black powder bomb. The three pounds of exploding powder alone would do little more than cause a ringing of the ears and temporary blindness. The seemingly innocuous coffee can was the real threat. On detonation the brittle tin would disintegrate into hundreds of jagged bits of shrapnel; propelled with a force and speed capable of piercing cloth, flesh and muscle.

Julius selected his target on the assumption that the largest density of remaining besiegers would be congregating near the cross. He was correct, and his aim was true.

The Black Legionnaires pinned in the front windows violently lurched and gyrated in unison as the zipping metal shards riddled the backs of their legs and organs of generation.

Abandoning caution for the moment to assuage his morbid curiosity, Julius stepped from his place of protection next to the window and stood exposed, gaping at the destruction.

Two black-clad raiders, a dozen feet apart thrashed about on the darkened front lawn, clutching perforated limbs. A third lay still between them. The burning cross had toppled—likely the result of a flailing black knight. A human torch danced a macabre jig in an erratic course around the lawn, bounced off a tree and fell immobile to the ground. The flames from the corpse lit up a large enough area to convince Julius that those Black Legionnaires physically capable of doing so had abandoned the field of battle.

The first thing Julius heard as his ears recovered was the piercing wail of a police siren. The deeper-pitched chorus of wailing moans of the injured black knights made for a ghoulish accompaniment.

CHAPTER SEVENTEEN
FORCES UNITE

"I'm supposin' this ain't a hog roast gone terribly wrong?" The police officer poked at the smoldering corpse with his baton. His patrol car was parked diagonally in Katherine's driveway, headlights illuminating the front lawn, a single red flashing light mounted on the hood in front of the driver's seat.

"Uh, no sir, officer, sorry to say," Bingham replied. Before the police arrived at the scene, he had barely managed to change from black gown and battle togs to civilian attire. The clothes were Julius' and were at least one size too big. Completing the disheveled look, Bing's hair was sweaty and plastered to his head; the product of the constricting armored football helmet and concealing black hood.

Two other policemen were in the front lawn also, tending as best they could to the wounded Klansmen.

These three men represented the whole of the Westerville police force. The single patrol car had only recently replaced a stable of horses as the sole means of conveyance for Westerville's public safety force.

"Yeah, I was just makin' a funny, pal. Had about six telephone calls to the police station in five minutes' time 'fore I was able to gather the guys and get here. Was kinda hopin' it was just something in the well-water making the neighborhood jingle-brained, but I ain't so lucky. Damn, why do they's always gotta be burnt up! What happened to folks just dyin' in their sleep!" The officer had squatted next to the body and had wedged a gloved hand under the torso, turning it face up. Bingham's stomached heaved, but he managed to turn his head quick enough to suppress the gag reflex.

The police officer was unfazed by the appalling sight. He stood, wiped his hands together and commenced a walking survey of the scene of battle, Bingham following just behind.

"Had a burn victim inside Everal Barn just a couple days ago. Looked like he'd been torched from the waist up sometime before. Had on a nice suit over some intensely fried skin, with bits a feathers imbedded here and there. Another weird thing: cause a death was lead poisoning. A couple .38's in the noggin. Wouldn't know nothin' 'bout that, would ya Mr. Harvard?"

"No, sir," Bingham responded. He realized that this body must have been the tar and feathering victim of the week before. Because he was running for dear life with Elmer, whilst being shot at repeatedly, Bingham could not know that the hapless bootlegger, Vincent, was shortly thereafter put out of his misery.

"Anyways, the callers said yer' little happy home here was the target a some powerfully rough Klan shenanigans."

Classifying a full-scale siege on a private residence with the attempted abduction and murder of his wife and servant as "shenanigans" seemed to Bingham to be a bit of an understatement. However, in light of the recent intense violence plaguing this normally quiet town, surely an ironic sense of humor was a necessary job requirement for a peace officer.

"So what's your offense, Mr. Harvard? Get caught attending mass? Join a labor union? Make a passing comment about Negros bein' the equals of the white man?" The law man stopped his tour and turned to face Bingham. Standing face-to-face, Bing noticed then that the officer was big—not quite as tall as Julius' six and a half feet—but immensely muscular and broad of chest and shoulder.

"Well, sir...uh, officer...?"

"...Hanshaw."

"Well, Officer Hanshaw...."

"Bein' technical, that's 'Chief' Hanshaw. But seein' as my

squad is made up a my cousin, Jeffrey, and my younger brother, Joseph, I try not to rub it in."

"Okay, chief...."

"Hell buddy I was just havin' ya again...I am the 'Chief,'" 'n all but you can call me by my first name...."

Bingham hesitated, anticipating another interruption, and unable to read the name badge on the officer's uniform in the darkness.

"...Jon." The law man supplied.

"Okay, Jon. My wife employs a servant...a guardian of sorts. He's been with her family since before she was born...in Kentucky. We kept him on after we wed a few years back. He's a black man."

"So, you have a black man livin' with ya?"

"Yes, that is correct."

"Well, sir, with all due respect I think it may be better for the time bein' if you'd set up a place for the Negro closer to his kin. There's a enclave just north a here, fleeing slaves took it over and some clever folk took to calling it 'Africa Road.' Someone there's sure to board your fella."

Bingham gave a noticeable grimace and gave careful thought before he spoke. "I don't disagree with you, Jon. You are not the first person to make that suggestion. However, my wife has some very...strong opinions on the matter. You are welcome to take it up with her."

"I'll do that. Look, I ain't got nothin' against the black folk. You'll find the people here in Westerville got an aversion to intoxicatin' spirits but not ta their fellow man; regardless of race, creed or color. Heck, Otterbein College here matriculates two or three Negros a year. But we're not dealing with locals. This pack a bedsheet bandits...." The officer swept his arm over the scene of prostrate Black Legionnaires, "...are from the area of Buckeye Lake, a county or so to the east. They're armed to the teeth and they outnumber our police force ten to one. All we seem to be accomplishin' so far is cleaning up the messes they leave.

"What I'm sayin,' Mr. Harvard, and don't read nothin' conspiracy-like into it, is that I can't guarantee your family's safety with a Klan magnet livin' with ya."

"I appreciate your candor." Bingham responded. "This combat zone seems to be all the proof anyone would need to confirm the wisdom of your words. But...tell me, Jon, are you married?"

"I fancy sayin' that marriage is love. Love is blind. Therefore, marriage is an institution for the blind." Jon smiled.

Bingham chuckled. "Well, it seems you are at least aware of the potential hazards in being wed. So you understand that a fellow has got to pick his battles with the missus?"

"Sure enough."

"Well then, debating the topic of sending Julius back home is a battle I do not want to fight."

"Suit yourself. But I'll take you up on lettin' me get a word in with Mrs. Harvard. If things take a nasty turn, I gotta least be able to tell myself I tried."

"I admire your good conscience, Jon...and your courage. You have my blessing. If there is nothing else you need from me? It looks like you have your work cut out for you."

"Yes, sir. We'll take it from here." As the police officer spoke, an REO ambulance pulled up at the curb. He turned to the disembarking medics to continue his duty of coordinating the "clean up."

* * * * * * *

"I'm going with father to Senator Harding's 'front porch' oration, Bing is coming with me, and that is final." Lady Kate stood glaring at her older brother, intimidating despite the foot difference in height.

"Be reasonable, Kitten! The two of you have stirred up hornets' nests and now you want to lead them right to the door-step of the Republican nominee for President of the United States?!" Roderick Maxwilton, agent of the United States Secret

Service, had arrived at his sister's residence upon Julius' wireless call roughly an hour after the local public safety personnel had left the scene of the house raid.

"We did not just 'stir them up,' Roderick, we dismantled them. There is no one left to lead anywhere. You heard Bingham. He said the highest head-count he made at the conclave was twenty people. As of this morning, one is dead and twelve more are in Federal custody. That leaves just nine terrified Black Guards who've likely run home in fear for their lives."

Roderick opened his mouth to speak, but his sister didn't give him a chance. "Mr. Drake asked us to get the vigilante attacks on the bootleggers and 'speakeasies' stopped. He was convinced the Black Legion was at the heart of it. 'Stop the attacks, and the mafia backs off,' he said. So there you have it. With the black knights gone, the arsons and the murders stop, the gangsters' mission is over, and so is ours." Katherine contentedly took a seat in her parlor and folded her arms in her lap. Her brother followed suit in a nearby stuffed chair. Bingham had remained present and seated the entire time. Julius and Fred could be heard laboring away at the damaged house.

"You deserve a gold medal for capturing thirteen Klansmen, just you and Julius. Truly, that is remarkable. But can you be certain their leader was among them?" Roderick rebutted.

Katherine gave a confident reply. "First of all, two of that number were Bingham's doing. He was assigned to make an assault from the back of the house with two others, but they had an unfortunate run-in with the brickwork, head first." Roderick looked at Bingham who gave a sheepish smile and shrugged his shoulders.

Kate continued. "Secondly, the chief of police has informed me that preliminary interrogations of the men in custody show that the black knight who burned to death was 'Thomas,' the name of the fellow Bingham knows to be the 'Grand Wraith,' or leader of the Black Legion.

"I must say that I am very impressed by that man—the police chief. I did not know how I would explain the window snares and trap floors to the police, but it turns out that Fred, the fellow I hired to build and install all of it, is father to two of the officers on the Westerville force. The third is his nephew. They knew their father's and uncle's handiwork on sight and didn't ask a single question."

Bingham recalled passing the chief of police in the doorway after he had tried to "get a word in with Kate" about Julius. The chief's flushed face and mumbled cursing suggested he had not made headway with his advice regarding Julius. As for identifying the dead Klansman, Bingham had seen the horribly disfigured remains and doubted immediate relatives would recognize him—let alone fellow black knights who knew only a first name and a rough estimate of size. But Bing kept his thoughts to himself, choosing to embrace his wife's rosy assessment.

"Very well, Kitten." Roderick sighed in defeat. "Surely you are not intending to bring Julius too?"

"I would not hesitate to do so Roderick except that he and Fred plan to spend the day fishing to-morrow."

"There is a young man of my acquaintance that Kate and I will be bringing along, Roderick." Bingham spoke from his chair nearby, referring to the former newspaper boy, Elmer. "I promised him a handshake and an autograph from Douglas Fairbanks—I hear he will be there to-morrow."

Bing recalled how he had sprung the invitation on little Elmer while the child was taking pot shots with his slingshot at a rat in the horse stable. He got so excited, he overshot and took out a window instead.

"Yes, Roderick," Katherine added. "He is only twelve years old. No obvious mafia connections, and I believe the only pajamas he wears have cowboys and Indians on them—no black robe and hood."

"You slay me, really," was Roderick's sarcastic response. "I guess I'll see both of you...and your guest tomorrow." The agent rose from his chair, gave his sister a hug, shook Bingham's hand and departed back for Marion, Ohio.

CHAPTER EIGHTEEN
THE MAN FOR US

Flash powder cameras popped in unison under the enormous maple tree just feet from Senator Warren Harding's face, forcing him to squint in mid-swing. The errant horseshoe narrowly missed a spectator, landing a yard or more from the pit.

Unfazed, the affable statesman quipped, "'Close' only counts in horseshoes and hand grenades. Seeing how off that throw was, it is fortunate for you boys that I'm pitching horseshoes."

The crowd of thirty or more reporters erupted with laughter. Hundreds of spectators and political supporters encircling the newsmen added their own polite mirth despite the fact that few could have actually heard the droll comment. Cameramen at either end of the horseshoe pit exploded another round of photos of the sportily clad Senator from Ohio as he launched another horseshoe.

The day was sunny with moderate temperature, unusual for an August day in Marion, Ohio. It was perfect for a game of horseshoes and Presidential campaign festivities at the home of Warren and Florence Harding.

The Senator's attire, albeit casual, was immaculate. A dark, conservative tie, crème colored slacks and like-shaded shoes and dress shirt. His sports coat was draped over a low hanging tree branch nearby. His thick, silver hair was coiffed such that not a hair moved despite his physical activity and was striking more so for its contrast to his neatly trimmed, heavy dark eyebrows.

"Can't say I've ever had more'n two or three folks observing my game playing. Never really thought of this diversion as a spectator sport."

A youthful-looking man chimed in, pencil and steno pad exposing him as yet another reporter, "Why, it isn't the horseshoes we're here for, Mr. Senator, it's you. Governor Cox and that Franklin Roosevelt fella ain't gotta chance. You're a 'shoe-in' to be the next President of the United States."

A few fellow reporters chuckled at the lame pun. A brief expression of befuddlement crossed Senator Warren G. Harding's face, replaced instantly by apparent understanding as he too gave a chuckle.

In the distance, the sound of a brass marching band could be heard. Building in volume, it was apparent that the procession was approaching the Harding residence.

A matronly, spectacled woman stood just inside the screened back door of the house and addressed her husband slinging horseshoes in the back yard. "Wurr'n? Wurr'n?! Mr. Jolson is on his way, dear. And I hear the band approaching."

Caught again in mid-swing and distracted by his wife's call, the Senator let fly another errant horseshoe. This one sailed deep among the bystanders, its impact accompanied by an anonymous, pained "Oww!" A tug-o-war instantly ensued over the horseshoe by souvenir hunters, like baseball fans swarming for a foul ball hit by "the Babe."

Oblivious to the commotion he caused, the statesman donned his dark sports jacket and addressed the ever-attentive reporters, "The Duchess calls, gentlemen. I must answer."

A chorus of laughter and flashing camera powder followed Senator Harding through the back door of his Queen Anne style house and out of sight.

* * * * * * *

"My Lord! The man can club them with horseshoes and still have a crowd eating from his hand!" Harry Daugherty let the curtain drop and turned from the window facing the Harding's backyard and horseshoe pit. He now noted the none-too-happy visage of the chairman of the Republican National Committee.

The dapper man was pacing with military stride back and forth along the width of the guest room at the Harding residence. For his title and achievement within the Republican Party he was unusually youthful in appearance: well-groomed, well-dressed, brown hair, sharp, chiseled facial features. His nose at profile looked as if it were one half of a razor-sharp arrowhead.

At formal campaign events he was "William Harrison Hays, Sr." His friends called him "Will."

With a commanding voice, he exclaimed, "Remember that little chat we had with Warren at the Blackstone Hotel in Chicago back in June, Harry? You know the one we had just before the Party nominated him as their candidate for President of the United States!? Do you recall the question I asked him—the one you had answered for me at least a dozen times before? I insisted on looking Warren in the eyes and asking it myself. 'Senator, are there any embarrassing episodes in your past that might be used against you?' Did you hear the same answer I did, Harry? It was very blunt, if I recall. 'No!' He said 'No!'

"Come to discover not two months later that the Honorable Senator from Ohio presumably doesn't find 'embarrassing' social drinking during national prohibition, a Catholic sister-in-law, and a grossly limited formal education?!!

"But we dealt with those bombshells, didn't we, Harry? The newlywed sister-in-law got an all expense-paid honeymoon in Europe - courtesy of the Republican Party.

"Now you've dragged me here to secure the silence of a private detective and his 'client' because he has evidence that the 'good Senator' fathered a child out of wedlock?!

"Before I go in there and hand over a small fortune of the Republican Party's money, answer me this; what are the odds this fellow is wrong—knowingly or otherwise?"

The chairman's goose-stepping had continued unabated during his entire rant. It was more than Harry could bear. He boldly stepped in the party leader's path, placing his hands on his shoulders: "I can't be certain, Will. The detective told me directly that he is not certain either. He's just trying to narrow down the suspects. I think if this was some kind of extortion racket, he wouldn't share with me that he's hedging his bets. But, you've seen the detective's file; you tell me. He has connected a lot of dots and those that have anything to do with Warren's comings and goings. Even if he is mistaken, the Democratic Party wouldn't care. There is evidence enough to make the case to the public and the truth of it won't matter come Election Day."

Resignedly, the chairman asked, "Have you spoken to Warren about this? Can't he shed some light?"

"That's exactly what the detective wants me to do. But I have stalled him for as long as I can. I told him it could take a week or so to look over his material, double check his sources. I was done in about half an hour. The less the Senator knows about this, the better. To be perfectly fair, Will, the way the P.I. tells it, Warren may be absolutely ignorant. The girl left the state without a word, early in pregnancy, probably didn't tell Warren a thing. If this situation does get messy, at least the Senator will have the benefit of being genuinely oblivious."

The chairman gave an audible sigh. "So who is this detective? Where does he come from? What's his name?"

"He was a lieutenant of the detective bureau, New York City Police Department. Then he hung out a shingle as a private detective in New York. Be warned, Will, this fellow has told me more than once that this particular investigation is more personal than professional. He's a good friend of his client. Although he won't give me a name, he says he owes his benefactor everything and means to pay it back with interest. I don't think he can be 'bought.'"

"Everyone has a price, Harry. But what's the name, the name!" the chairman insisted.

"It's Rodney Rushton. He's in the next room if you're ready?" the campaign manager inclined his head toward the door.

The chairman responded, "You do the introductions. I'll take care of the rest."

* * * * * * *

The exit doors of the Marion train station erupted with a flood of passengers disembarking from trains originating from all points on the compass. Like flotsam on a rough sea, groups of people traveling together were swept apart in the depot and forced to regroup outside the station. Not so with the Harvard party: Bingham, Kate, Kate's father, and Elmer Pfleager.

Bingham's size and physique drew little attention when alone, but amongst other people—particularly in the tightly knotted crowd—the contrast of his build to that of the average man was astounding. His unhesitating stride cut a swath through the throng much like Moses parting the Red Sea. Kate held the hand of her elderly father, both strolling unmolested in the peaceful wake of her husband's path. Elmer was sandwiched between husband and wife, but not for long.

"I can't see further ahead than the backs of folks in front of me. Elmer, we need a look-out." Bing spoke over the hubbub of the masses. He quickly turned around and grabbed the boy under the armpits and casually plopped him on his shoulders as if he were no more than a winter scarf.

Little suspecting that he would be drafted for crow's nest duty, Elmer had only a second to kick and complain. "Hogwash! Babies ride on shoulders!"

"Very well, Mr. Pfleager," Bing teased. "Just point in the direction of the highest concentration of people...likely the most decorated residence."

The ex-newsboy shot out his arm as instructed.

From behind Bingham, the elderly statesman glanced at Elmer's pointing finger and called, "Bingham, son, I am sure if we just follow the tide of this crowd we will arrive on Warren's doorstep."

Bing responded, "You are no doubt correct, sir. I fear my progress can only carry us along so far until we encounter the stationary crowd in front of the house. Your formal invitation should take us the rest of the way to the company of the good

Senator and his celebrity guests."

Bingham referred to the embossed card sent from the campaign offices of Senator Harding to his former congressional ally and close friend, the retired Senator Maxwilton from Kentucky; Katherine's father. He carried his years without frailty with only his wealth of snow-white hair belying his advanced age. Having mentored the junior Senator, Mr. Harding, during his freshman year in Congress, Senator Maxwilton had long since passed the torch to a younger generation of politicians. He returned with his wife, Kate's mother, to their stock farm in Lexington and was presently savoring his golden years immersed in his favorite task of raising thoroughbred horses. Where his wife had selected to remain at home, he felt it both necessary and honorable to respect his former protégé's invitation and "send him off" to the Oval Office.

Without the invitation, the quartet soon discovered that their chances of getting within one hundred yards of the Republican candidate for President of the United States and illustrious guests were absolutely nil.

The hundreds of people the Harvards had encountered upon arriving at the Marion train station were just one of the dozens of waves of humanity who had been amassing around the Harding residence throughout the early morning and afternoon.

Forced to halt at the densely packed mass of people still the length of a football field away from the center of attraction, Bingham's height and Elmer's post on his shoulders gave them an uncommon view of the scene ahead.

The sight for most of the distance was little more than the backs and tops of heads—male and female alike. A daring squirrel could have jumped from bonnet to bowler without touching earth for at least one city block. Along with a limitless number and variety of United States flags, a dozen or more handmade signs poked up from the sea of heads: "You Tell'em Harding," "The Harding Front Porch is a Friendly, Neighborly Front Porch," "Warren Harding Will Consult With The People. The White House Isolation Will End."

Watchers desperate for a better view climbed trees, boys and men alike, clinging from branches like well-dressed monkeys. A brass marching band, twenty or so strong, blared out tunes striding left, then right in front of the house, acting as a moat separating the masses from the object of their attention.

The focus of the crowd's attention was a 2½-story frame structure in the Queen Anne style, with a gabled roof, green clapboard siding, and cream colored trim. The large Colonial Revival porch, with one rounded end, dominated the front of the house. The base of the balustraded porch was fieldstone, as were the pedestals, which supported paired Ionic columns.

From second story trim to the base of the massive porch, red, white and blue bunting decorated the residence. Erect, fluttering flags cascaded down either side of the stone stairway leading from the front porch to the packed sidewalk.

That stairway was crowded with people—likely stars of the silver screen and national politics—however, Bingham recognized none of them. In his former, demanding capacity as a bank president, he had little time for the former and no interest whatsoever in the latter.

Seated up on his shoulders, Elmer excitedly enlightened Bing. "That's Al Jolson in the three piece with the boater hat front and center. Oh my gosh! That's Mary Pickford and Douglas Fairbanks. I bet you didn't know they got married just a few months ago."

Bingham thought, "It is not possible for me to care any less about the nuptials of celebrities." Instead he said, "I was not aware of that Elmer. You are certainly a living encyclopedia of Hollywood trivia."

Without the benefit of Elmer's narrative, Bingham heard the sounds of singing voices from the Harding porch:

> We need another Lincoln
> To do the country's thinkin'
> Mist-ter Harding
> You're the man for us!

As the crowd began to join in the chorus to the popular campaign song, Senator Maxwilton caught the attention of a couple of uniformed service men, raising his deep-toned voice to be heard over the cacophony.

He spoke as he displayed his invitation, "Gentlemen, I am a guest of the Honorable Senator from Ohio. I wonder if you are providing escort to the house?"

"Absolutely, Mr....." The foremost soldier took the extended paper, looked down at it and then back at the retired Senator for Kentucky. "...Senator Maxwilton. Are your daughter and son-in-law with you here today, sir?"

"Why, of course," the older man pointed to the man immediately in front of him and to the woman at his side. "Does that create a problem, officer?"

"Well, no sir. Not for you. I'll have you by Senator Harding's side in a moment. However, we have orders from the head of Secret Service that Mr. and Mrs. Harvard are to meet with the Director immediately. I'm happy to take you and the boy ahead, but the Harvards will have to go with Private Cook here."

Before Senator Maxwilton could protest, his daughter interrupted. "It is all right father. Roderick hinted yesterday that we should expect this. Would you mind terribly introducing Elmer to Mr. Fairbanks? From the moment our train left Westerville, he has talked of little else but shaking his hand and getting an autograph."

"Not a problem, dear, my pleasure."

Bingham lowered Elmer to the ground next to his father-in-law. "Please do not worry, Senator. We'll have an officer reunite us after the Director has spoken."

"Very well, Bingham. I will see you soon then?"

"Yes sir, I can only hope so."

The quartet parted ways—the retired Senator, hands on the shoulders of Elmer, following a soldier to the Harding front porch, and the Harvards walking behind another uniformed man striding quickly toward a neighboring house.

* * * * * * *

"That fat envelope you just slid across the table at me probably ain't filled with campaign literature?"

"No, Detective, it is not," said the chairman of the Republican National Committee. "I think we both know precisely what is in that envelope."

Rodney Rushton sighed, and slowly clenched his fists. The exhaling air caused a mini tempest amid the cloud of cigar smoke surrounding his head. He had spent the last hour with this smooth-talking politico on the naïve assumption that this was proper protocol in communicating with Senator Harding. Rushton hadn't kidded himself that he would get a personal audience with the Republican Party's nominee for President. All he had asked was that the man convey to the good Senator his own handwritten letter and Bingham's squashed toy soldier. It would then be up to the Senator how, or if he would respond.

What he was getting for his efforts was a gentleman's bum's rush.

The man Rushton knew only as "Will" had first tried flattery: "You are obviously a very competent investigator and a loyal friend to attempt to piece together your client's parentage back over thirty years of cold evidence."

But when blarney failed, the party operative had endeavored to convince the detective that his probe was futile or at best, misguided: "It is not entirely confidential that the good Senator is incapable of fathering children."

Rodney had nearly fallen for that line—he had read something in the press to that effect. But the personal physician's conclusion—saddled with enough disclaimers and caveats to make one's head spin—was based on a very recent physical. Surely a fifty-four-year-old man's physiology is not what it was during his college years.

Next, "Will" tried to put off Rushton: "You've said that there are two or three other persons—in addition to Senator Harding—who merit further investigation. Why don't you move on to them and spare the Senator this...distraction amidst this very...sensitive time of his career?"

Rodney barely let the man finish his sentence, "Spare me the sass, *now* is likely the *only* time I could hope to get even an instant of the Senator's attention. If the polls are to be believed, Warren Gamaliel Harding will be in the White House come springtime. The wall of political hacks and security personnel separating the then-President from the public—let alone a nosy private investigator—would multiply at least ten times, and you know it!"

Abandoning flattery, the politico dared to threaten the seasoned ex-New York City police lieutenant: "We know that you have spent some time in prison for a very serious crime... Detective...and that you were pardoned, under mysterious circumstances by the Governor of New York. Surely, you would not want that...experience...to come to light? In the event that the information you have regarding Senator Harding was leaked, your reputation would likewise be disclosed. You, and your 'evidence,' would be instantly discredited."

Hearing that threat a year or so ago might have caused Rushton to instinctively throttle the smarmy man, but in that time he had fought and defeated his twin demons of rage and humiliation.

He said simply, "Do your worst, Mr. Chairman."

And now, finally, the chairman was resorting to out-and-out bribery.

Rushton had had enough.

"I'm done beating my gums." Bing's close friend rose to his feet, stabbed the stuffed envelope with his index finger and slid it violently toward the seated chairman. Boarding passes from San Fransico to Siam and loose currency of high denomination slid from the loosely closed package and sprinkled like snow upon the man seated opposite.

Not giving the chairman the opportunity to say another word, Rushton spun on his heels to swing the door open and slam it behind him. The sole occupant of the room remained seated, not bothering to brush off the paper money clinging to his suit jacket, a look of fury on his face.

* * * * * * *

Rodney Rushton faced a wall of people outside. In his anger and frustration, he plowed through the mass with more aggression than he might have. Undaunted by the curses from ruffled spectators, the private detective made his way to the front of the Harding home.

Organizers had constructed a bit of order from the chaotic mob and coordinated a receiving line for guests and spectators alike to shake the hand of the Senator and Presidential candidate. Rushton tramped to the head of the line, making an unwavering path straight to the Senator. While doing so, he reached into his suit jacket for the letter and toy figurine, resorting, out of desperation, to convey his evidence directly to his target.

Of course, all that the detail of Secret Service agents observed was an angry looking man charging toward the man to whom they were entrusted to protect to their last breath. Furthermore, the suspect was skirting the orderly line and reaching into his suit jacket for what may very well have been a weapon.

Before Rushton could get within twenty feet of the Senator and pull his hand from his jacket, a phalanx of men in civilian garb planted themselves directly in his path, hands on exposed, holstered guns.

Rodney immediately grasped the situation, stopped cold and audibly cursed his utter stupidity in forging ahead half-cocked.

Mercifully, one of the Secret Service men was Roderick Maxwilton, Lady Kate's older brother and a friend of Rushton's. He immediately recognized the detective and spoke.

"By all that's holy, Rodney, what do you think you're doin'! Do you have a deathwish?!"

"Ahhh, Rod'rick, everything is Jake. I got a little hot under the collar and I'm bein' a sap. I just wanted to give the good Senator from Ohio this here note and toy." The detective began to pull his hand from his suit jacket pocket.

Instantly there sprang a chorus of snapping, unlocking holsters. "It's copacetic, men," Roderick ordered. "I know this man. Get back to your posts. I'll take it from here."

The Secret Service agent grasped Rushton's arm and hustled him away from the receiving line to a less populated space behind the Harding home. "This better be real good, Rushton."

"Ah, heck. I don't mean to cause you any headaches, Rod'rick. This is it: Your brother-in-law just wants to discover his own flesh and blood father, an' I agreed to do the leg work. Turns out his pa could be any number of folks—not suggestin' his ma was amoral—just that she's long buried an' I ain't got more than a list a'her college classmates to go on f'r evidence. I've spelled everything out in this here letter. I wanna give the Senator the opportunity to let me know if I'm barking up the wrong tree." Rushton placed the folded letter with the imprinted toy soldier in Roderick's open hands.

"So what's with the vandalized figurine, Rushton?" The agent asked.

"It's a longshot, but I'm hopin' maybe Bingham's unusual physical strength came to him through his father's family—no history of it from his mother's side. Maybe seein' evidence of his kid's muscle will turn on a light in the father's head. That bit of handiwork on the toy is Bingham's...when he was about a month old.

"All I want is to get that letter an' toy to the Senator's attention—if 'the shoe fits,' so to speak, wonderful. If not, I move on."

Roderick sighed, "So I'm either going to join the Senator's family tree, or be assigned security for a military outpost in northern Alaska for even suggesting the soon-to-be commander in chief fathered an illegitimate child!"

"This ain't for me, Rod'rick. I get to walk away when the job is done and my life won't alter one wit." Rushton shuffled his feet and hung his head, sure that his investigation had hit a wall. "It's f'r Bingham and yer sis, that's all."

Roderick shook his head like a wet dog. As much as he bluffed and blustered in her presence, his little sister was his pride and joy. She had been his loyal sidekick, even when his parents had lost faith. He owed her this.

"If I promise to put this in the Senator's hands, would you agree to go away...immediately?" Roderick offered.

"Absolutely! It's the berries, Rod'rick!"

"You are welcome. The fact is, Kate would surely scalp me if I did not get this information in the right hands for Bing."

"You can be sure about that." The detective retorted.

"Consider it done, then. Good day, Rodney."

CHAPTER NINETEEN
BAD TIDINGS

Daniel Drake, Director of the Secret Service, stood on the porch of a private residence immediately adjacent to the Harding home as Kate and Bingham, with military escort, ascended the steps and approached. He was listening intently to the speech being given by the Republican Party's nominee for President, Senator Harding:

> "...If we can prove a representative popular government under which the citizenship speaks what it may do for the government and country rather than what the country may do for individuals, we shall do more to make democracy safe for the world than all armed conflict ever recorded."

"Aaarrrhhhh!" The Director pounded the porch banister, cursing to no one in particular. "That man never fails to use one hundred words when a half dozen will do. Try this *Wurr 'n....*" The Director executed a dead-on impersonation of Florence Harding's pronunciation of her husband's name. "...ask not what your country can do for you—ask what you can do for your country."

"You should really try professional speech writing, Mr. Drake. You have a gift." Katherine quipped as she now stood with her husband, along with the soldier just next to the Director.

Drake was noticeably startled, absorbed in the moment.

He quickly restored his usual stoic demeanor and addressed his guests. "I hope the two of you have had a good morning, because your day will be going rapidly downhill from here."

"It is nice to see you again too, Mr. Drake." Kate responded sarcastically.

The Director gave an equally insincere smile, dismissed the soldier and waved the Harvards through a doorway into the house.

They entered what appeared to be quarters meant for a parlor and a dining room of a single family residence now efficiently converted to a makeshift command center. The area was bustling with harried agents, clicking teletype, and static feedback of at least three wireless radios. The Director led the couple past the busy workspace and through an open doorway to another room.

This room retained its domestic décor; a family room with comfortable upholstered furniture in abundance, shaded brass floor lamps, well stocked floor-to-ceiling bookshelves built into two of the four walls, and an enormous stone fireplace at the opposite corner. Only one of the three floor lamps was lit, casting barely enough light to encompass a sofa, settee and a beautifully carved oak coffee table. The two windows were shuttered, curtains drawn. Drake shut the heavy door and the three took their seats.

"If I did not think you would have too much difficulty disposing of our bodies amidst the mob, one would wonder if you planned to 'bump us off,'" quipped Katherine.

"Make no mistake Mrs. Harvard; I had my apoplectic tirade scripted just moments after your brother advised me of your stubborn refusal to keep clear of Marion. Antagonizing both the Black Legion and the mafia and then racing to the locale of the very individual, or event, you were sworn to safeguard from both seems to me to smack of a profound error of judgment."

Katherine jumped to her feet and pointed her finger at the Director's face in preparation for a righteous rebuttal. She never got the chance.

The Director stood to meet the verbal attack, "Don't get in a lather Mrs. Harvard! Please let me finish. I said I 'scripted' my discontent, and did not, and will not deliver it. On further reflection, I must concede that you and Mr. Harvard had every reason to think you had accomplished your mission."

"You have a very unusual way of expressing your appreciation, sir," Bingham commented dryly. He remained seated.

"My apologies for the less than enthusiastic reception. Disposing of more than half of the Black Legion in Westerville— possibly including their Grand Wraith was an amazing feat, and *should* have settled tensions, but...."

"But what?" Katherine interjected.

"...it didn't." Drake finished.

The Director went on, "Almost from the moment dawn struck after the raid on your residence, Mrs. Harvard, some rather disappointing intelligence has been relayed to me from undercover agents and informants in the field."

"Such as...?" Kate coaxed.

The Director turned to Bingham, still reclining comfortably on the settee. "Do you suffer this antagonism at home, Mr. Harvard?" he asked. "You have my sympathies."

Bingham made no response.

"Mr. Drake, do not avoid my question." Katherine continued.

"Very well. Proprietors of dozens of hotels and motels in and around central Ohio are reporting an unusual glut of check-ins and reservations. The guests are giving addresses of origin from all of the known Ku Klux Klan concentrations in Indiana, Ohio and Michigan. One hostelry with roughly one hundred rooms is entirely booked with just residents from the Buckeye Lake area, well east of Columbus, and the home base of the Black Legion.

"Failing some bedsheet convention that I'm unaware of, it looks as if the Ku Klux Klowns are massing 'troops' and preparing for war." The Director paused dramatically.

"Also, just in the last week, known mafia footsoldiers are disappearing by the dozens from New York City, Atlantic City and Chicago, and reappearing in Columbus and Westerville."

"So let me get this straight," Katherine, hands on hips,

responded. Drake sat and pushed himself back on the sofa, attempting to add an inch or two distance between him and the outraged Lady Kate.

"By your own measure, Bingham and I have accomplished our mission; we have done what we were told by you and your highly educated and experienced tacticians. But instead of running from the battlefield in defeat, the combatants have instead multiplied their forces and redoubled their efforts!

"Pardon me for saying so," continued Lady Kate, "but it would seem to me that the failure is not in the execution of the orders, but the orders themselves, and a fundamental misreading of how the 'enemy' would respond. And by extension, our decision to join my father for this Presidential campaign event in Marion was not at all 'a profound error of judgment,' but merely misplaced faith in the tactics of the Secret Service!"

The Director raised his head and sighed. "Yes, ma'am. You are correct...."

Not expecting a concession, Kate was struck silent, mouth open in preparation for continued argument. Instead, she returned to her seat, attentive to the Director's resigned response.

"...I underestimated the KKK's resolve, as well as the mafia. With the benefit of hindsight, a clash of biblical proportions between these two groups was pre-ordained. Consequently, I maintain that the actions and plans of the Service, as well as the fine display the two of you gave in Westerville did no harm. At worst, we have precipitated the confrontation by a few days; we did not cause it."

Chagrined by the Director's humbled posture and words, Lady Kate responded. "Speaking for Bingham, and myself, neither of us would suggest that you or the Service is to blame. We are both somewhat shocked by the information you have conveyed to us. Had you seen the destruction at my residence, you too would be startled to learn how quickly the Legion and the KKK have regrouped...even reinforced their numbers."

"I sincerely appreciate the vote of confidence Mrs. Harvard," continued a chastened Drake. "Despite the circumstantial evidence suggesting that 'Thomas,' the Grand Wraith, was killed in your skirmish, I'm beginning to have doubts. Leaderless Klan or Black Legionnaires would need a color-coded map and personnel escort to wipe their...noses, let alone give the clarion call for a mid-western conclave."

For only the second time during the trio's conversation, Bingham chimed in: "I too have my doubts about having beheaded the monster that is the Black Legion. I know that the Grand Wraith stood in the vicinity of where we found the charred Legionnaire identified as 'Thomas.' He was there anyway, when three of us got the order to go to the back of the house and commence an incursion. That is the last time I saw or heard the Grand Wraith. It wouldn't be surprising that there was more than one 'Thomas' among the twenty of us. It is possible that the captured black knights genuinely, even correctly identified *a* 'Thomas' just not *the* 'Thomas.'"

As her husband spoke, Katherine's thoughts raced. The compound blow of witnessing the violent death of the Anti-Saloon League's plant manager, followed instantly by the ferocious raid on her residence had blunted her otherwise razor sharp powers of reasoning. Even now, with the benefit of calm reflection, those events rattled Lady Kate so that she lacked her usual confidence to independently draw her own conclusion. Instead, Katherine thought out loud.

"Would it make sense to profile the Grand Wraith as a two-faced, vindictive, manipulative, homicidal hag?"

"Mrs. Harvard, you have just described my mother-in-law," the Director jested. "Seriously, do you have some reason to think our Grand Wraith is a woman?"

Bingham suddenly straightened his posture, as if his wife's expressed thought sparked his own cognition.

Katherine explained to her husband and the Director the details of her relationship with Eunice Parker, the dinner they had together, and the 'murder' of Jackson Knutson linking both to the assault on her residence and attempted lynching.

An excited Drake stood ramrod straight. Before he could

speak however, Bingham interrupted.

"I have heard 'Thomas' speak on several occasions—both excited and seemingly composed. When aroused, the Grand Wraith takes on an unusually feminine tenor...in fact, it is a shrill soprano voice uncharacteristic of any male voice I have heard."

Drake added, "Women have been known to join the ranks of KKK and Black Legion...usually along with their husbands. Having the missus taking a leadership role is something new to me, but Black Legion members never see each other in their civvies." Bingham nodded agreement. The Director continued: "Kate, where is the lovely Mrs. Parker now?"

CHAPTER TWENTY
LIGHTING THE FUSE

Eunice released the third and final gas-filled balloon, setting it on a sweeping arc just a foot from the littered basement floor and an inch above the flaming wick of a wax candle. For a person engaged in the wholesale destruction of private property, Mrs. Parker was remarkably composed, her actions smooth and deliberate.

Composure and skill had come with experience. This would be the eighth speakeasy she'd set aflame.

An enthusiastic amateur might have used a larger balloon filled with a greater volume of gasoline, which would have extinguished the candle as it rushed out, rather than be ignited by it. Eunice Parker was no amateur.

Even so, an accomplished fire bug would give pause before sneaking into a known business of organized crime, in the fading light of dusk within the pedestrian-heavy environs of down-town Columbus, Ohio. Not Eunice.

Multi-story buildings forced an early sunset to the narrow ally immediately behind the saloon. The *tinkle* of broken glass was inaudible over the rattle of horseshoes and car tires over cobblestone, the honks and backfiring of thick automobile traffic during this, Columbus' after-work rush.

Mrs. Parker's lumbering, graceless physique could not be made to be stealthy. Force of will alone overcame nature's handicap and she extruded her body through the street-level window, remarkably attracting no attention whatsoever.

The rest was just simple physics: making sure the gas-filled balloons were securely tied to the exposed wooden beam of the basement, that the strings were just the right length so that once the oscillations of the balloons died out they would come to rest directly over the candles.

Timing was very important, too. Eunice had to give the balloons a considerable swing to provide her the few minutes necessary to make her maladroit departure back through the basement window and from there to her waiting flivver just a block away.

All went according to plan.

* * * * * * *

"Is he dead?" the bemused patron asked the bartender as he straddled a stool, belly-up to the bar.

The target of his inquiry was a man immediately next to him atop his own stool, slumped face down on the rough hewn top of the oak bar.

"Nah. Ossified, sure enough. Smells funny too. But he ain't dead," the barkeep answered. He stood behind the bar and pounded a fist on the wooden surface just inches from the head of the unconscious form.

"Reggie!" he yelled, "Reggie!"

Reginald Parker lolled his head back and forth—presumably building up steam to raise it from the bar top. With a shudder he pulled his arms from their sprawled posture at either side of his head, and with bony, fumbling hands grasped the edge of the bar. He slowly lifted his head.

Reggie was not quite dead, though the curious patron could be forgiven for thinking so. The barely conscious man looked like a corpse. Shriveled from dehydration, yellow, taut skin barely covered his skull. His eyes were sunken and bloodshot, and black bags hung like marsupial pouches under each. His nose was bulbous and nearly purple with erupted capillaries. Chapped and bleeding lips failed to hide horrifically receding gums and grayish black teeth. In stark contrast to his withered limbs, Reggie's abdominal area was bloated.

Neither was Mr. Parker 'ossified,' or drunk. At his late stage of alcoholism, his hours of imbibing had barely sustained his addicted body. The days of drink-induced 'high' or euphoria were long, long gone. His apparent stupor was in fact physical exhaustion due to gross malnourishment and imminent renal failure.

"This ain't a flop house pal. Get a wiggle on!" No stranger to the ravages of advanced alcoholism, the barkeep did not need the added complication of disposing of a stiff. If he did his croaking outside, the public health folks would have to deal with it instead.

Even in his considerably diminished capacity, Reginald Parker knew the routine; first angry words, then physical ejection. He wished to avoid the latter at all costs. Lurching to his feet as if the newly animated undead, Reggie knocked over his own stool and shambled to the darkened, guarded exit. The bartender signaled to the man seated at the door to open up. Had the signal been delayed just one instant, Reggie would have no doubt plowed face first into the door. As it was, the door swept open just inches in front of his gaunt face and he staggered outside to the fading light of day, plowing instead into the back end of a Model-T parked oddly close to the front door of the speakeasy.

Senses as dulled as they were, a few events immediately ensued that registered in Reggie's addled brain.

The solid front door to the juice joint slammed shut, multiple locks audibly clicking into place from the inside. The driver's-side door of the car to which Reggie was pasted swung open, and a black human-shaped haze misted out, flowed to the gin mill door and wedged a two-by-four between doorknob and the solid asphalt stoop.

Rough solid hands grasped the alcoholic from the back at either forearm, nearly lifting Reggie off his feet in haste to push him into the back seat of the Model-T.

Terror brought Reggie further, unwanted elucidation.

The driver of the car turned her head to look behind in the act of putting the flivver in reverse, thereby exposing her face to the sole occupant of the back seat.

"Eunice!?" Reggie uttered with a dry, hoarse voice.

"Yes, Reggie, of course it is me! Did you entertain the idea that this was some overly aggressive cab service?" Eunice Parker was flushed with excitement, never once making eye contact with her husband in favor of focusing her complete attention on directing her car from the scene.

Seated ramrod straight in tension and fear, Reggie glanced in the rearview mirror. What he saw only terrified him more.

The front and side of the speakeasy was in full view. Enormous tendrils of flame shot up from the ground at the building's foundation, reaching to the first floor of the two-story structure. It appeared as if Satan was reaching an enormous hand up from the bowels of the earth to yank the saloon back to hell.

"In the name of all that is holy, Eunice, what have you done!!?" Reggie choked out.

"Now exactly what would you know about 'holiness,' you godless, boozing stooge!!? I set that abomination aflame and rescued your sorry soul from certain damnation...at least for a time," Eunice yelled, eyes remaining glued to the busy street.

"You knew? You knew I was there? And you set the place on fire...? How...? Why?"

"I've known for years, Reginald. You never had the moral fortitude to honor your promise to me to stop drinking. Sure, you stopped bringing alcohol to the house—instead you just went to the booze. I resolved that if I could not contain this vice in my own home—in my own husband—I would take my mission to the public; my mission to rid this land of alcoholic spirits, and you would be my unwitting accomplice. Like a hunting dog with the scent of game spoor in the air, you led me to the kill every time."

Ill health, shock and terror combined to keep Reggie in a befuddled state. However, he had just enough cognitive ability to know he was confused, and the will to inquire. "You...you followed me?"

"Yes, Reginald, I followed you." Eunice sighed to the windshield as she made repeated glances to the rearview mirror. "It did not dawn on you that the gin mills you patronized seemed to spontaneously combust less than twenty-four hours after you staggered away? Oh...I delayed two or three torchings in favor of rooting out suppliers, but I always got around to it within a few days."

The back seat of the car was silent. In the last year or two Reggie's short term memory vanished entirely. There was less and less activity for Reggie to recall because of the ever increasing, unpredictable blackouts. He did recall being bounced from more than one bar. Getting sick on the barkeep, an occasional violent rage all tended to make him persona non grata. Scurrying from a speakeasy with flames at his heals should have been memorable, but it wasn't.

Reggie caught sight of his wife's face in the rearview mirror. Her eyes were alive with excitement, her usually pursed, taut lips spread to a grin as she fixated upon the activity behind their car.

He turned to look out the back window to see what it was that had caused his wife's sudden animation.

A Model 38 Pierce-Arrow barreled along just a few hundred yards behind the Parkers' car, appearing to pick up speed. Immediately behind it, at turns and hills, Reggie could see another car; a Model-T by the looks of it.

As Mr. Parker looked, a passenger next to the driver of the nearest car reached his arm out the window and pointed in the direction of the Parkers' Model-T. Reggie glimpsed two successive flashes of light emitting from the passenger's hand, followed almost instantly by a metal-on-metal *ping ping* at the trunk of his car.

"My God, Eunice! We're being shot at!" Reggie rolled himself over in a sprawl to the floor of the back seat.

Mrs. Parker ignored her husband's cries, focusing instead on the road ahead. Also, she was counting the number of gunshots from the cars behind. Her little flivver was no match for a Pierce-Arrow in speed, and she knew it. All she had to do was remain slightly ahead for just a short time more....

Reggie's head arose from the back—in full view from both the front and behind. The look of surprise was apparent even through his haze.

"This stuff was lying on the floorboards in a heap. What are these, Eunice?" his voice quavered as he held up a black robe in one hand, a black pointed hood with crude holes for eyes and mouth in the other. Reggie's inquiry was at least in part rhetorical. He knew precisely the use to which these articles of clothing were put. His sightings of members of the Black Guard, or Black Legion pre-dated his advanced stages of alcoholism. He still held out slim hope that at least his wife was not the owner of these garments and that maybe they had found their way into the car by happenstance.

Annoyed at the distraction, Mrs. Parker tersely replied, "Well, that's my house dress Reginald. I was on my way to the cleaners to have it pressed when I happened to see you out on your daily stroll and thought I would give you lift. The hood is to cover my curlers should a guest come calling at our home."

Current circumstances notwithstanding, this had always been the tone and content of Mrs. Parker's communication with her husband: hostile, dismissive, belittling. Reggie accepted a certain level of responsibility for his condition; moral failing, weak impulse control, etc., etc. But a lifetime with a spouse who could not distinguish a sermon from a conversation, a single honest mistake from a sweeping criminal conspiracy; these and other intense elements of Eunice's character went far in making Mr. Parker what he was at this moment.

And so it was a vicious, self-defeating cycle of cause and effect in this relationship; a marriage only in name. Mrs. Parker attributed her zealous, public prohibition crusade to her husband's advanced alcoholism, while he in turn pointed the finger at his wife's zealotry for driving him to drink.

Disregarding her husband entirely, Eunice kept a close eye on their pursuers. The Pierce-Arrow had gained within a dozen yards and the Model-T behind it had moved into the on-coming line of traffic, giving it, too, a clear shot at the Parkers' fleeing flivver.

Ping, ping, ping, ping, tinkle, tinkle.

A torrent of seeming hailstones riddled the back of the Parkers' car, a couple bursting through the back window and spider-webbing the front windshield. Eunice had not noticed that Reginald had dropped like a stone in water behind her. She found the sudden cessation of slurred speech and witless observations relieving.

The three automobiles raced north on the Three-C Highway from Columbus to Westerville. Vehicles—gas-powered and horse-drawn—not involved in the melee dodged as best they could, leaving more than one tipped-over car and several spooked horses.

The Parkers' Model-T, only a few feet in the lead of the trio, careened in a sharp right-hand turn off the Highway and onto a graveled, country road. The three cars were forced to proceed single file. Woods, with thick underbrush, pressed in on the narrow road from either side making the already darkening day blacker still.

Just ahead, the forest gave way to acres of clear-cut fallow farm land. Only the lead car could see the scene ahead as Eunice's car served as sufficient block of the view for the two cars behind her.

Had the occupants of the chasing cars seen what Mrs. Parker was recognizing with relief, they might have had a better chance of escape.

Over six thousand gowned and hooded Ku Klux Klan swarmed upon the field, most on foot, many on horseback.

As the three autos cleared the access road and entered open ground, six enormous crucifixes lit up around them. The flames raced up the main posts and rushed along the cross-beams. Like a legion of fire ants upon unsuspecting prey, the Klansmen closed a circle around the cars and began to converge on their targets.

White-clad marksmen took careful aim at the engine blocks and tires of the two pursuing vehicles. Already frantic to brake their cars and attempt to make a quick reverse out of the ambush, the Pierce-Arrow and second Model-T had cut their speeds considerably just before the fusillade of gun fire crippled them. The lead Model-T was permitted to pass through the human barricade without a mark.

Eunice steered her flivver a few yards further from the encirclement, stopped the engine and pulled the emergency brake. A greeting party of a half dozen horse-mounted Klan trotted toward the car. Before they were close enough to distinguish her female facial features, Eunice had hurtled from the driver's seat and swung open the back passenger door to grab her hood. She had just yanked it over her head and adjusted the eye holes by the time three of the six Klan dismounted and approached her on foot.

All four stood at the open passenger door looking in on the corpse of Reginald Parker sprawled on the floorboards. A round from the gun of a pursuing car had drilled him from the back of the head leaving a disproportionately huge exit wound where his face had once been.

"Who is the stiff, Thomas?" One of the Klan inquired.

"Bait, brothers...bait. He has served his purpose. Although his carcass might serve as fertilizer for the farmer who has offered us up this meeting place. Please have a couple of the new initiates dispose of...this, will you?"

Eunice turned to face the inquirer. He was the "Grand Dragon," or formal leader of the KKK, distinguished from the rank and file by his red robe and hood, colorful insignia on the chest, and a completely exposed face.

"We have more immediate concerns, however," Eunice continued, having dispensed with her spouse of ten years. "The occupants of those two cars have two rounds of ammunition remaining...."

Pow, pow.

"...Forget it." Mrs. Parker, or Brother Thomas, pulled her blood spattered gown from her husband's cold, dead hand, raised her arms and slid the robe over her hooded head. Making the last fastenings, she faced her brethren again, pointing to the cars with their trapped occupants, and spoke, "If you are prepared, let us begin the festivities to cleanse this earth of four more pope-loving, rum-soaked, whiskey-swilled criminals."

"Very well," the Grand Dragon spoke. "If you will follow us, Thomas. I think you will be pleased with the arrangements." With a sweep of his arm, he led Eunice further into the clearing. A large cauldron of stewing tar stood over a raging fire, and burlap bags of goose down were piled high nearby. At the tree line, four strung nooses swayed in the evening breeze.

Under her hood, Thomas grinned, accepted an offered paintbrush, and without further word strode toward the execution site.

CHAPTER TWENTY-ONE
DEADSHOT

"It's a seriously twisted mind that comes up with this stuff. To say nothin' a actually perpetratin' it on another human bein'," said Mikey as he sawed at the fourth and final noose with his pocket-knife. Coming from a young mafia gangster who had fitted more than one man in a pair of cement slippers, the irony of that statement was lost on his erstwhile partner, Tony.

For his part, Tony had mercifully repressed any conscious thinking with the help of a pint of the highest proof bourbon he could lay hands on. He focused instead on the basic motor functions of completing the task at hand. His job was to catch and lower the bodies of his former gang members, as his smaller and more agile partner climbed the trees and cut the ropes that suspended them by their necks just a foot or two from the ground.

The four victims were unidentifiable for their head-to-toe coating of pitch and feathers. This came as a perverse comfort for Mikey and Tony because it was impossible to make the association between these smoking, grotesquely disfigured corpses and the four friends they had known from childhood.

With help of lantern light, two other men stepped in just as Tony lowered the last body to a waiting tarp on the ground and unceremoniously rolled it up. They bound it with hemp rope and lugged it to a waiting pick-up truck carrying the other three bodies.

Tony waited as his friend dropped to the ground from the

tree and walked to him. With uncharacteristic silence, the two men strode to the waiting Pierce-Arrow, its engine running.

A driver sat in front, and passengers occupied three of the five seats facing each other in the back. Tony and Mikey took up the remaining two seats. Despite its six occupants, not a sound interrupted the hush in the interior of the luxury car. The pick-up truck, converted now into an impromptu hearse, kicked into gear and drove from the scene to send the dead on their way in a more dignified manner.

Tony gave a discreet nod to Phil, seated opposite him, and mouthed the words "It's done." Phil nudged the man next to him at a window seat.

"Al...we're all done here."

Without turning from the car window, the gang leader spoke, "No mama should have to see their son lookin' like that. Ain't no dignity at all in what they done to those boys." Capone's normally even monotone carried an edge. Rage bubbled just below the surface and was evidenced by his beat-red complexion, grinding teeth and clenched fists.

Phil and Frank had known Capone as a young child, and had seen him vent his wrath on any number of unsuspecting victims. Still, they had never once seen him this angry. Some person or persons' fate was being decided in that head of his. They chose simply to remain quiet in anticipation of some cue from their boss.

Shortly, the crime boss turned from the window, leaned back in his seat and surveyed his four lieutenants: Phil, Frank, Tony and Mike. A single overhead interior light cast feeble illumination upon the solemn gathering.

"Was the bar a total loss?" Capone asked.

"Uh, yeah boss," Frank hesitantly responded. "Building's a pile a cinders. Before Stanley and Sid set off in pursuit of the fire-bug they radioed that the doors had been wedged shut from the outside. Nobody got out. But we'd been keepin' most a the hooch in a warehouse next door...as ya ordered...saved about three grand a stock."

"And what about that 'fire-bug,' Phil?" Capone turned an intense glare at the man seated immediately next to him.

"The 'bug' is a 'bird,' boss. Or a fella with a hurt back. Moves like she's gotta corset on a few notches too tight, hips and bust are all wrong for a guy...by the wireless call we got from the look-outs. Assuming she's the pyro what's done all eight of the torchings, she's operatin' in the same exact territory as the Black Legion. That is, all the tracks lead back to Westerville... including this last caper. Also, she ain't a dumb dora...if'n these burnings and ambushes are any example. The dudes in dresses generally ain't got the market cornered in cogitating, so she's likely the big cheese among 'im."

"Hey, boss?" Tony interrupted, letting the bourbon do the talking, whereas reasoned sobriety would have dictated continued silence. "We ain't gonna chase'im into Westerville... are we? Got thousands a footprints out there...way more'n thousand. There's 'bout twenty a us."

Suddenly regretting the decision to sit so close to Tony, Mikey edged away a few inches for fear of collateral damage. All were surprised at what they heard.

"Yer right Tony. Absolutely right. Man-to-man odds ain't in our favor. Martin?" Capone said as he slid open a window dividing the front from the passenger compartment of the car.

Reaching through the window, Capone grasped something and pulled it through. It appeared to be a very unusual looking gun; over two feet long, with a hand grip at the front and the rear, no buttstock or sights, but a big, disc-like magazine the diameter of an averaged-sized man's head.

Mikey was convinced that Capone would shoot Tony right then and there. His concerns were misplaced. Al had other targets in mind.

"Gentlemen," Capone announced like a proud father. "This is the Model 1919 Thompson Submachine Gun. It blows out about 700 .45 caliber rounds a minute with a range of about nine rods. And...how many a these do we got, Martin?" Capone spoke over his shoulder to the unseen driver.

"Ten, boss. Right off a the production line," came the reply.

"So that's 7000 members of the pajama posse a minute getting aerated. Even things up a bit for ya...Tony?" Capone added.

"Uh, sure boss." mumbled Tony.

Mikey's sigh of relief was audible.

"Seems they've got a pow-wow of sorts goin' on in the center of the 'Dry Capital of the World,'" Capone looked at Phil as he spoke. The lieutenant nodded slowly.

Al continued. "No doubt the pyro-dame will be there. We're gonna mow down as many of those damn goons as we got ammo for. I especially want the fire-bug. Once I have her head on a pike, we make tracks to Chicago. Got it?"

Asking the same question Mikey and Tony had on their minds, Frank inquired, "So what about the bullet-proof strong man that's running around in scarlet and gray when he ain't torpedoing for the Black Legion? Didn't we want 'im out of the way?"

By response, Capone glanced at Phil. With his boss' nod, Phil answered Frank's question for the group.

"He's dead. Russell spotted him comin' outta his house all dolled up in Black Legion robes just a couple days ago. Sat tight waiting for a shot until early this evening. Probably round the time Stan, Sid and the other guys started chasin' the pyro-dame, Russell radioed in that he'd caught the joker walking outta his house, this time with the scarlet and gray duds on. No mistakin' 'im. Used the porch light to line 'im up in the sights and took 'im out. One shot."

Frank wasn't entirely convinced. "That's bully Phil, but you 'n I each hit that guy square in the back while he was bustin' that kid free. All it seemed to do was give 'im a tail wind."

Phil seemed prepared for doubt, "An that's exactly what I told Russell before he set up, Frank. So he got'im in the head, with a .30 aught six and watched 'im drop. Ya know Russell was a sniper in the Great War. Sent plenty a them spiky helmeted Huns straight to hell under worse conditions than this. Ain't no doubt, he's a deadshot."

CHAPTER TWENTY-TWO
WALLS COME DOWN

"It's customary when fishin' to use a pole, Julius," Fred said jokingly. "I brought a spare thinkin' you might not have a rod and reel amongst your valet supplies."

The gangly manservant languidly strode through the wet undergrowth toward the creek bank where Fred Hanshaw stood waiting, bait and tackle at his feet. He extended a walking stick in front of him to part a nest of nettles and loped through.

"I's preciate you's thoughtfulnis' in bringin' uh pole fo' me Fred, but I's come fully prepared." Facing his new friend at creek side, Julius fetched up his walking stick and pointed it toward the slow moving water. With a slight click and then a series of successive clicks the end of the cane telescoped outward. Narrowing segments of alternating hollow and solid shafts of ash wood sprung from the base. Ceramic line guides popped out from the rod at either side of the nickel-silver joints. From a gunny sack under his arm Julius plucked a brass-cased bait-casting reel. In doing so, he dislodged a heavy bound book. The unnoticed tome made a quiet landing on wet foliage at the manservant's feet. With a satisfying snap Julius attached the reel to the rod just above the "cane's" grip.

"You're uppity for a black man...you know that don't ya." Fred quipped.

"Yes suh, I s'pose I am that." The valet responded solemnly.

The handyman was thrown by Julius' sudden somber turn and hastened to lighten the mood.

"Well, looks like you thought of everything, Julius. You got some toilet paper!" Fred pointed to the dropped book while kneeling to pick it up. Julius made a quick grab for it, but not before the handyman read the cover.

"Paradise Lost!?" Fred thundered. The bellow scared two turtles off a passing log.

"Heard of it?" Julius responded, hopefully.

"Well, I suppose. Saw a copy lying about the house. One of my kids attends Otterbein and got saddled with that for a class. I can promise you he wouldn't have read it by choice. You have any children?"

"Well suh, gotta chillen' name of Rosabel. She goin' ta college too, Tuskegee. Gonna graduate soon...with honors."

"It's a nice feelin' seeing your offspring betterin' themselves, isn't it. How old is your kid?"

Julius made an incomprehensible utterance amidst feigned throat clearing.

"Try that again, Julius."

Head down, as if talking to the fishing tackle, the valet mumbled, "Twelve, suh."

Fred was uncharacteristically quiet. He stared at the discomfited manservant with a quizzical expression. Julius refused to look him in the face.

Finally, the handyman spoke, "So your plantation slave language is bullshit, right?! I'm not Thomas Edison, Julius, but don't insult what little wit I got. No one I know reads epic poetry, fathers a child prodigy, and talks like an imbecile. Also, I'm from Kentucky, born and raised, just like you. I never once met a man nor woman, black nor white, educated or otherwise sound like you."

Concern etched on his ebony face, Julius looked up at Fred. "My father was a house slave, Fred. When I was just a sprout, he taught me that a man of his considerable size and deep voice would damn near scare the knickers off of a master and his family. If I wanted to stay out of the fields, be a house slave, with a light workload, and a chance to have a family I had to play at being an idiot. A stupid man, no matter how imposing, isn't a threat to the master of the house. Now my father was set free, and I grew up a free man. But I couldn't get past introductions for a job as domestic help...until I resorted to the idiot talk. And here I am. Right or wrong, degrading or not, it's my reality. I've got a good thing now and I don't want to upset the apple cart. You'll have to suffer the façade."

"Well...okay...," Fred stuttered. He hadn't expected such a sweeping confession. It would take him some time to iron out the rationale and implications of Julius' choice to live the paradox of a genius and a dimwit. For now, the handyman thought, he would respect his friend's decision and brush the matter aside.

"Hey, does that thing actually cast or is it just a fancy whipping switch." Fred said, nodding to Julius' retractable rod.

With a sigh, and a quick look over his shoulder, Julius responded, "Well, I have only used it once or twice, but I think I could thread a needle with a baited hook at twenty paces."

"Oh, is that so?!" Fred flung his lucky fishing hat back up the shallow bank. The various lures dotting the exterior gave the cap enough weight for a modest pitch fifteen yards away from the men. "Land a hook inside that hat and I'll be scaling today's catch." Fred scoffed.

* * * * * * *

Fred was scaling the last of the fish on the back porch of the residence shared by Julius and Lady Kate.

The popping and sparkling of the dynamite fuse first caught his eye as the lit explosive traced an arc in the air through the black night and bounced onto the porch floorboards. Roughly thirty white-garbed Klansmen formed a tight mob several yards from the house. The thrower had stepped ahead of the crowd to make his toss and was now making haste to return to his pack.

Fred barely heard the racist obscenities that were spewed in his direction as he focused all of his energy and concentration on saving himself and Julius.

Julius, just inside at the kitchen window looking out upon the back porch, did not require Fred's warning. Glancing up from his task of cleaning greens at the sink just below the window, Julius had a better view of the amassing army of Klan. Where Fred's frantic assessment took in about thirty, Julius' elevated line of sight gave him a clear view of hundreds of ghost-like apparitions making a semi-circle around the house.

The two men hurled themselves through the kitchen and into the hallway leading to the front of the house when the back of the residence erupted in a fiery conflagration. Jagged planks of wood, ceramic tiles and broken piping exploded from one side of the kitchen, making mincemeat of the entire area.

Fred pushed Julius ahead of him in the narrow hallway, and as a consequence took the full force of a dislodged cabinet door to his upper left shoulder. Had Fred charged ahead, leaving Julius behind, that same wooden shrapnel would have lanced one of the valet's lungs en route to spearing his heart.

Both men landed in a heap just within the parlor at the end of the hallway. Whirlwinds of dirt and dust poured through the decimated kitchen and over their prostrate bodies.

Without a word, Julius rose to his knees and clawed at a throw rug, absently whipping it forward and off the floor. He clasped a sunken handle amongst the exposed hardwood and threw open a three-by-four-foot trap door. Inside sat a veritable arsenal of weaponry and supplies.

The cache was no surprise to Fred. He had helped Julius build and install the secret storage place. He was no stranger to the contents either. Two of the three Browning Auto-5s were his own—part payment for his labor in designing and installing many of the fantastic traps and snares in this house.

Among the stores were hundreds of rounds of shotgun ammunition, four gas masks, two loaded revolvers and Julius' whip.

With barely a pause, Julius grabbed one of the Auto-5s and spun back around to face the shattered kitchen and hallway from which the two men had barely escaped. Ears ringing and useless for now, neither man heard the clatter and rustle of the four-man raiding party.

Uninjured and more inured to the violence of a siege than Fred, Julius anticipated a lightening raid to follow the bombing. He met the lead raider head-on with a full blast of buck shot from five feet. The close range gunshot instantly stained the white robe to a speckled red. The force of the discharge blew the man backward into the rest of the rushing horde.

The second Klansman in line did not have a chance to regain his feet before two rounds peppered and then separated his head from his shoulders. Julius let the two remaining raiders gain their feet, turn and run from the inside of the house.

Like an exasperated character in a silent movie, Julius' mouth moved as if he were trying to communicate something. At mid-sentence, Fred's inner ear ringing began to fade and the servitor's enunciations became audible. "...won't be no trappin' folk in window snares and trap doors this time around. They's on to us from the last time. But it still seems like they want us alive, less'n that raiding party jes came in looking for souvenirs."

As he spoke, Julius bundled as much ammo as he could under his arms, affixed his whip to a belt loop, hung a gas mask around his neck and grabbed a shotgun in each hand. He directed Fred to do the same.

The sudden rush of adrenaline acting as a temporary analgesic, Fred's injury barely slowed his pace. He followed Julius to a small niche behind a solid-looking couch and the center load-bearing wall at the middle of the first floor.

The two hunted men dug in for their final stand.

A second, terrific explosion rocked the back of the house—this time detonating the corner where the dining room sat next to the kitchen. Now the wall at the back of the first floor, including two corners, was nearly gone. With nothing to support the back of the second story, two upper story bedrooms and a wash-room came crashing down into the backyard.

Just half of the house remained standing.

Then came the voice outside over the bullhorn.

"Y' come on outa there now or we comin' in after ya'. I ain't givin' no conditions of surrender."

* * * * * * *

Even over the noisy car engine, the first explosion of TNT sounded like a distant train derailment. At about 9:00 p.m. on a weekend, Westerville had long since rolled up its sidewalks, so there were no other sounds of industry to compete with the detonation.

Drake put his hand on Roderick's shoulder to get his attention and pointed to the side of the road. Roderick immediately pulled over. The unexpected thunder clap on an otherwise cloudless, star-filled night brought Katherine Harvard to attention in the back seat.

The three were in one of the government issue Model-Ts puttering south on State Street toward Katherine's residence. They had just departed from Bingham's home on Plum Street, dropping him off to gather at least one of his two scarlet and gray uniforms with instructions to meet them at Kate's place immediately.

With much complaint from Kate and Bingham, the Director of the Secret Service ordered that it was time to pull up stakes in Westerville and retreat to Marion until the presidential campaign was over. The task of capturing and arresting Eunice Parker was best left to undercover, regular agents of the Secret Service, and not for the two "lightening rods" that the Harvards had become.

To Daniel Drake, the urgency of the mandate was such that the Harvards were ordered to retrieve only critical effects from their Westerville abodes and to return to the Secret Service post in Marion that same night. Katherine and Bingham were not afforded an opportunity to meet the Republican candidate for President of the United States.

In an act that reeked of hostage-taking to Lady Kate, Senator Maxwilton and young Elmer Pfleager were ordered to stay in Marion until the Harvards returned. Drake had insisted that he was merely protecting the elderly statesman and the boy from possible harm in being in proximity to targets of both the mafia and the Ku Klux Klan. As evidence of his concern, the Director of the Secret Service had insisted that he and Lady Kate's brother, Roderick Maxwilton personally escort the husband and wife on their urgent errand.

A second distinct *boom* caused Katherine to jump in her seat. "That sound came from the vicinity of my house," she cried, with rising panic.

And would that thickening haze blotting out the moon happen to be smoke coming from the same location?" Drake inquired as he pointed just above a line of trees.

"Oh, dear Lord, yes...." Lady Kate's response was cut off by the wail of a siren.

With no other traffic to obstruct their view, Drake, Roderick and Kate could see the Westerville police squad car, followed close behind by a single REO Speed Wagon, pull from a garage along State Street. They picked up speed as they proceeded south in their direction.

Drake got out of the parked car and stood in the middle of the road, facing the on-coming emergency vehicles and waving his arms. Both automobiles stopped in the road and the front passenger of the lead car jumped out and approached Mr. Drake.

Showing his Secret Service badge, the Director detailed their observations thus far to Jon Hanshaw, the chief of police. He quickly extended an offer of assistance.

Clearly anxious to get to the scene of the explosions, but grateful for the offer of professional help, the chief shared the very little he knew to the group.

"...It is your house, Mrs. Harvard. Would have been out here sooner, but had to make sense of the hysterical phone calls we were gettin' from your neighbors 'bout what's goin' on. Gotta be baloney, but the callers are saying the neighborhood's been invaded by thousands of KKK with a few black-clad Black Legion folks mixed in. Seems they took it personal you an' the black fellow rejectin' 'em a few days ago. They're blowin' the hell out of yer house and hollerin' over a bullhorn for somebody to surrender."

"According to my mom," continued Jon, "our dad made a full day of his fishing trip with your servant fella...he hasn't come home, anyway. I'm guessin' we'll have ta save his bacon too."

A continuous stream of muffled gunfire punctuated the chief's explanation. "Sounds like whoever it is, they're putting up a hell of a fight. You all wanna get in behind us, we're gonna get as close as we can; see fer ourselves what's goin' on."

CHAPTER TWENTY-THREE
BEHEADING THE DRAGON

"We must keep this a White Man's country...," shouted the red-clad "Grand Dragon" from his bullhorn. He stood aloft a small stage of bare wood, flanked on one side by three Black Guards, and on the other by three more white-robed Klansmen. A thirty-foot, flaming cross served as a backdrop. The flags of the United States of America and the Confederacy fluttered on posts jammed into the earth at either side of the wooden platform.

"...Only by doing this can we be faithful to the foundations laid by our forefathers. The republic was established by White Men. It was established for White Men. Our forefathers never intended that it should fall into the hands of an inferior race...." An army of hooded, robed Ku Klux Klan surrounded the makeshift podium where stood their leaders and officers three to four feet above their pointed heads.

"...Every effort to wrest from White Men the management of its affairs in order to transfer it to the control of blacks or any other color, or to permit them to share in its control, is an invasion of our sacred Constitutional prerogatives and a violation of divinely established laws...." The orator stood in the center of an open, treeless field just behind the bombed-out wreckage that was once the residence of Katherine Harvard and her servitor, Julius. The speaker seemed oblivious to the continued gunfire coming from the ruins. He was confident in his safety. That confidence was not misplaced. Roughly eight thousand KKK brethren surrounded the Grand Dragon, his guards and lieutenants on the stage.

Ignorant of the white robed bodies piling up at the two or three points of entry into the rubble, the rhetoric continued "...We would not rob the colored population of their rights, but we demand that they respect the rights of the White Race in whose country they are permitted to reside...."

The gunfire abated, soon to be followed by masculine shouting, the muffled crack of a whip, and then cheers from the Klansmen immediately surrounding the dynamited house.

"...When it comes to the point that they cannot and will not recognize and respect those rights, they must be reminded that this is a White Man's country!" Upon this last sentence the entire crowd of torch-bearing thousands erupted in cheering, whistling and shouts of "Amen!!"

As if choreographed to coincide with the rousing conclusion of the Grand Dragon's speech, two men, one tall and black-skinned, and the other short and Caucasian—both bloodied and beaten—were dragged feet first into the open night air from the wreckage of the house.

Bound at the wrists, and pulled to their feet, the two condemned men were pushed and kicked by outraged Klansmen toward a small clearing amongst the enormous mob.

The prisoners, Julius and Fred, stumbled through a gauntlet of spittle, rocks and vile obscenities en route to a steaming cauldron of pitch and two hastily erected gallows.

* * * * * * *

Chief Hanshaw drew the bolt of his Springfield Model 1917 service rifle up and back with an audible *click, clack*. He chambered one round, and then slammed in a five-round clip just in front of the trigger mechanism.

At the window next to him, his brother, Joseph, and his cousin, Jeffrey secured a heavy tripod on a low-sitting coffee table and mounted the Browning Model 1917 machine gun on top. A fully loaded 250-round fabric belt hung from the side.

Both weapons were .30 caliber, both used .30-06 cartridges. Likewise, all three of the handlers were well-trained and experienced in their use.

In calm rebuttal to the Secret Service Director's exasperation regarding their plan of attack, Jon quickly recited the family members' credentials.

The three had signed up and shipped off together to the French Western Front as members of the American Expeditionary Forces under command of American General Pershing in early spring 1918. They had distinguished themselves in offensives at Aisne, Meuse-Argonne and the Battle of Saint-Mihiel. In addition to the medals from grateful European nations, all three were heavily decorated by the United States military and given their "tools of trade" to take home to Westerville as gifts from Uncle Sam.

"Joseph's got a better relationship with his M1917 than his wife. I get kinda uncomfortable being in the same room with those two," the chief quipped.

"...says the guy who shoots German officers on the toilet," the younger Hanshaw retorted, never once taking his eyes from his own weapon.

The chief turned his head with a clenched jaw to respond when Drake stepped between the policemen and lifted his hand, palm open to diffuse the building sibling spat.

"I don't even want to know the story behind that comment. Just tell me you can hit that costumed hate-monger with the bullhorn?"

Jon was incredulous, "You mean the fellow standing on the four foot stage, dressed head to toe in a bright red gown, back-lit by a flaming cross and yelling bloody hell just a hundred yards away? Yeah, I think I might nick him! You and your sidekick do your job and Westerville PD will do theirs," the chief finished, pointing to Roderick Maxwilton.

Satisfied, Drake stepped back. His "job," along with Roderick, was to take off at a full sprint through the crowd of Klansmen to

Julius and Fred the moment the chief brought down the Grand Dragon with sniper fire. As additional cover for their race to the Klan prisoners, Joseph and his cousin were assigned to create more chaos by firing their massive machine gun into the crowd.

Their makeshift launching point was a single family residence just at the edge of the open field where the thousands of Klansmen had gathered. The house, along with dozens of others, had been hastily vacated by the terrified occupants during the assault on Kate's property.

"Is it absolutely necessary to fire 'into' the crowd, chief?" Lady Kate inquired. "The Grand Dragon, his guard and lieutenants may be incurable madmen, but many of those men are merely misguided dolts."

Joseph tore his attention from preparing his weapon to respond to Katherine. "Look, Mrs. Harvard, assuming I was inclined to spare the life of even one of these pinheads in ponchos—which I'm not—this ain't the sort of gun you can 'aim.' I'm either gonna prune some trees, or aerate that field, and I doubt falling branches will scare off that mob."

"Besides," Roderick interrupted, "You are not the one running into the conclave to pull out Julius and Fred, Kate. I, for one, appreciate any distractions these officers can serve up."

"Indeed, I was rather rudely vetoed when I offered to join you Roderick! Instead, I was assigned 'sewing duty.'" Katherine pouted.

Pillow cases with crude eye holes and hastily threaded bedsheets worn more like a Greek toga were necessary to help Drake and Roderick blend in as well as possible during their incursion. Kate hastily finished the last hood/pillow case.

"Here you are then," Kate announced as she stood and handed the Director and her brother their improvised disguises.

"Attagirl!" Maxwilton stood to receive his "uniform," but his expression turned to puzzlement as he inspected his garment. "Now just a minute! What are you trying to pull, Kitten!"

Even by the faint light of the single oil lamp on the floor in the room, fist-sized, red and pink hand-stitched flowers were evident on Roderick's white robe and hood.

After quickly ensuring that his disguise did not bear similar decoration, Drake quipped, "Well, Roderick, you will look very...pretty. You should thank your little sister. Those Klan fellows are more likely to pinch your fanny than shoot you."

With a smirk of triumph on her face, Kate added, "If that doesn't suit you, I am happy to make alterations to the children's bedding...that is, if you prefer hand-sewn ponies and kittens to a rose theme?"

"Humph!" was Roderick's only reply as he yanked on his embroidered gown.

The team of would-be rescuers came to agreement on other details of their plan. Once Fred and Julius' release was secured, Drake and Maxwilton were to get their charges into the American Issue printing plant. It was a much shorter run to the plant from where Fred and Julius stood. Also, Kate was reasonably certain that the Klan would not destroy the building for fear of doing harm to their own sacred social initiative: prohibition. Kate and the Westerville police force would join the four men as soon as they were safely inside the plant.

Her only reservation was that Bingham's last instruction before setting off to retrieve his uniforms was that he was to meet the Service and his wife at her residence. However, the men in the group convinced her that Bing was a "big boy," and would easily discover the change of plans once he saw the ruins that Lady Kate's house had become. Not entirely convinced, Kate nonetheless gave the appearance of going along with the plan.

"Take your places," the chief commanded, "they've got 'em out and are herdin' 'em to the gallows."

Joseph chambered the first round from the belt with a loud *crack* of metal on metal. Jon unbuttoned the cuffs of his dress uniform and quickly pulled up his sleeves exposing black and blue ink stains from wrists to shoulder. The dull lighting prohibited a clear view of the design or pattern of the tattoos, but it was evident that this former soldier had been decorated with more than medals.

Jon gently lifted the bottom pane of his window, rested the barrel of his rifle on the sill and crouched to look down the barrel sites.

Drake and Roderick descended the stairs to the first floor. Drake stood ready, braced to open the front door of the house opening directly into the crowded conclave.

Intent on their own tasks, no one noticed that Lady Kate, too had tiptoed down the steps, remaining in the shadows of the staircase. She clutched her own makeshift hood and robe.

For an excruciating twenty seconds, the interior of the house was utterly silent.

* * * * * *

Kneeling, shirtless and roped to the ground like vicious dogs just before they are euthanized, Fred and Julius had already suffered grievously at the hands of the KKK. One eye swollen and blackened, Fred's upper left shoulder was an open, bleeding wound, threaded with wooden splinters from the first explosion. Sadistic Klansmen made a point of targeting the shoulder with savage punches and clubbings.

As deep as his suffering was, Fred was the model of health and vitality in comparison to Julius.

Lady Kate's servitor looked like Jack Johnson in the 26th round of the Heavyweight Championship boxing match with Jess Willard—just as the "Galveston Giant" was K.O.'d.

Julius could hardly see for the blood running from his scalp into his eyes. His nose was broken and he was deaf in one ear. His neck and throat were raw and bruised from a Klansman's attempted strangling. The suffocation was cut short within a gasp of his life for no other reason but to preserve him for the barbaric torture and hanging to follow.

Though little consolation to them now, the handyman and the servitor had given back more than they had received.

While cornered in the wreckage of Lady Kate's house, the

two men had discharged every one of the shotgun shells from the enormous cache. Bodies of dead Klansmen piled seven deep in a semi-circle around them—eventually serving as a gruesome barricade to the endless flood of "white knights."

When their ammo was spent, Fred used one of his Auto-5s as a club, as Julius exacted crippling lashings with his whip.

But their desperate resistance could not last.

So here they were. Two white-clad Klansmen were just three or four feet away, walking toward them. Each gripped a broadhead paintbrush, dripping and steaming.

Their time was short, and so were Julius' words to his friend, "You're a good an' brave man to the core, Fred. I'm glad I knew ya." The last words came out choked and wavering, partly from injury, mostly from emotion.

Fred glanced up at the tar covered paintbrush just over his head, tightened his jaw and fixed a stern, absent gaze straight ahead. Without turning his head to look at Julius, he said, "I'll see ya in Heaven, Julius."

These were the handyman's last words before the warm liquid touched his head.

Fred had expected screaming pain and for a brief instant assumed that the nerve endings in his scalp had burnt out. But then, curiously, he began to hear the distant, repeated *cracking* sound of gunfire, and the grisly almost rhythmic sound of puncturing meat.

And then a body fell on him.

Broken from the paralysis caused by the anticipation of imminent death, Fred's eyes and brain slowly began to absorb and process all that was going on around him.

The first thing he registered was that he was alive, with no additional injury and that the ropes restraining him to the ground were disconnected and hanging loose.

His next observation was the Klansman who had been seconds from scalding his head was thrashing on top of him in an effort to extricate yet another individual sprawled on him. It was this pile-up that yanked away Fred's restraints.

The person at the top of the heap was clad in red robes and might have had a red, pointed hat except that a section of his head, from the ears up, was entirely missing.

Two other bodies lay nearby, one in white, the other in black robes. They were both dead of obvious bullet wounds to the head.

Dispirited, if not simply terrified, Fred's would-be executioner finally rolled the corpse of the Grand Dragon off and hastily fled the scene.

Sweat and blood had loosened the bindings at the handyman's wrists. Heedless of his throbbing shoulder, Fred gave a desperate pull. The ropes gave, as did already-frayed ligaments, and Fred cried out in pain.

Liberated of bindings and bodies, the handyman put a hand to the top of his head to rub away what he assumed to be congealed tar.

Instead, his hand came away dampened, clutching two walnut-sized masses, both oddly slick and pliant. By the firelight cast by the nearby cross, Fred could see the dark red blood smeared on his fingers. He realized with horror that the masses were brain matter that had splattered freely upon him in the midst of the carnage. Gagging, he frantically wiped at his head with both hands to rid himself of any more gruesome remains.

Fred then turned his attention to his friend. He was surprised to see Julius free and miraculously on the brink of giving renewed battle.

The servitor's tormentor, unlike Fred's, would not be put off from his murderous task. Undaunted by the bullets and falling men around him, this "white knight" was intent on inflicting his credo upon the bound and helpless black man.

Unbeknownst to him, Julius had been straining to break his bonds from the moment his hands were tied, and the distraction of the mayhem allowed him to succeed. Release could not have come at a better time than when the "white knight" attempted to make a brush stroke on the servitor's head. Julius stopped the thrust entirely; grabbing his assailant's swinging arm with an iron clutch of his left hand. His right arm shot out in a lightening under-cut, slamming deep into the Klansman's stomach.

Like the high-striker, carnival midway game, the concealing white hood and the pitch-covered paint brush in the Klansman's hand shot into the air as the servitor's fist made impact. With practiced skill, Julius grabbed the top heavy brush from the air.

As the Klansman's mouth sprang open by the force of air expelled by his flattened stomach, Julius jammed the brush inside, dripping bristles first.

The man in the white robe collapsed to the ground. With the little air left in his lungs he emitted a primal, though muffled, scream.

Fred did not even flinch at the ferociousness of the act. The seemingly endless demonstrations of inhumanity he had experienced in just the last few hours had hardened him to man-on-man violence.

Other, more pressing events demanded the former captives' attention.

The impromptu conclave was in complete chaos. Klansmen scrambled in desperate retreat, in every direction. Swarms of tracer fire tore through the crowd like rabid lightening bugs, slapping robed figures to the ground moaning or silent and unmoving.

The enormous, flaming cross just behind the two men shuddered twice, slowly tipped to the left and then plummeted to the earth. At the wrong place at the wrong time, three Klansmen were caught by the falling crucifix, and their robes burst into flame. They flailed about in panicked torment until they were shot down or burned to death.

Fred and Julius stood back to back, surging with adrenaline, but entirely uncertain as to what to do other than stand in place until an opportunity for escape presented itself.

In contrast to the distant *ratta-tat-tat* of machine gun fire, the *clap*, *clap* of measured revolver discharge gained in volume. The former captives tensed as the mass of scurrying white-robed people parted and two of their number burst through, abruptly halting just feet from the restive duo. One was shorn of his concealing hood. Both were armed with smoking revolvers in each hand.

Frantically scanning the littered turf for something with which to arm himself against the two assailing Klan, Fred started at the deep, baritone laughter of the servitor. He turned to see Julius giving one of the Klansmen a full-armed bear hug, lifting the shrouded man off his feet.

He was convinced now that Julius had taken many more blows to the head than he had, until he spoke.

"Ohh Mr. Roddy, sir. I's sure glad to see you. I see's your sister done dressed you this mornin'." Julius chuckled as he stared at Maxwilton's floral gown.

"I's guessin' this here's another agent of the Secret Service." The big man said, indicating the second white-garbed person.

As Drake lifted his pillow-case cover to disclose his face, Roderick spoke, "Actually this is my boss, Julius, Mr. Drake. Are you two in any condition to make a run for the printing plant over there?" Roderick pointed to the squat, saw-toothed building in the distance.

Not recognizing either man, but satisfied that Julius seemed to know them, Fred responded. "Hand over one o'them bean-shooters and I think we'll be okay."

Close together, the four armed men made a rapid jog to the printing plant. The ceaseless machine gun fire continued to cause havoc among the massed KKK, preoccupying them to a man with the preservation of their own lives.

Roderick aimed carefully and shot out the stubborn dead-bolt of a side entrance. The team crept carefully into relative safety of the building. Drake slammed the door shut behind them and he and Maxwilton dragged and pushed a heavy printing appliance against it as a barricade.

As if on cue, the machine gun fire outside came to a sudden stop. The members of the Westerville police force had ceased their cover fire and were making haste to the printing plant before the KKK could regroup.

* * * * * * *

Lady Kate proceeded unseen and unmolested through the pandemonium, running in the wake of the path blazed by her brother and the Director.

Her vision was impaired by the limp pillow-case-turned-hood repeatedly collapsing on its own weight, pinching closed the crude eye holes. Even under ideal circumstances the small apertures eliminated all peripheral vision. Also, in the dark of late night, with the blazing crucifix now leveled, she could only barely make out the hurtling white forms of darting Klansmen running for their lives. Tiny yellow trails of light, like blazing miniature meteors zipped from behind her to the left and right, felling "white knights" like wheat by a scythe.

Even so, with Roderick's and Drake's white togas as a focal point, she was able to observe the rescue of her servitor and handyman and their collective successful retreat to the printing plant.

She was now free to pursue her own objectives.

Lady Kate made a swift path to the ruins of her residence. Bingham had had plenty of time to retrieve his suit of armor from his abode and make it to her house for the planned rendezvous. Even if he were delayed a few minutes, Katherine thought she could put that time to good use attempting to retrieve her most treasured possession from the half of the house that remained standing: "The Warhorse."

Neither Drake, nor her brother could fathom permitting Kate to expose herself to mortal injury for pursuit of the Webley. Katherine didn't hesitate to take the risk.

Pulling her hood off for a clearer survey of the interior of the house, Katherine was horrified to see the mounds of dead and dying Klansmen piled around her parlor couch like a haphazard wall of sandbags. With the cessation of machine-gun fire outside, she could hear the moans and wheezing of wounded men.

She called her husband's name, seeing no sign of him anywhere. Katherine ascended the rickety staircase to what was left of the second story—her bedroom and a guest room at the front of the house. The devastation was such that half of Kate's climb was exposed to the open air, and she had to leap a small chasm from the end of the shattered top steps to the entryway of her room.

Continued calls to Bingham went unanswered. However, Lady Kate located her massive revolver from the floor of a tumbled wardrobe. Gun in hand, she made a careful descent, intending to crouch amongst the rubble at the ground level until her husband arrived.

An armed squad of Ku Klux Klansmen met her at the bottom of the staircase.

Caught off guard and outgunned ten to one, Kate wisely dropped her Webley and raised her arms.

The lead Klansman wore the regalia of the Black Legion. Purposefully pulling up the hood at the face so that only Kate could see, Eunice Parker glared at her former co-worker. Exposing herself only long enough for Lady Kate to identify her assailant and catch a menacing wink of an eye, Eunice quickly dropped the mask back in place.

"Brothers, here stands the silver-lining of the otherwise dark cloud we have experienced this evening," Eunice announced to the score of white-clad men immediately at her back.

"A Jewish banker's wife with a predilection for co-habiting with Negro men. Committing her soul to hell will be some solace for the tragic death of our Grand Dragon."

The now inflamed assembly converged on their helpless prey.

CHAPTER TWENTY-FOUR
LIKE FATHER, LIKE SON

The warm spatter of tear drops on his face brought Bingham to consciousness. Bleary eyed, but vaguely aware, he was surprised to see that the face looking down at him and leaking tears was his mirror reflection, more advanced in age. This Doppelganger shared Harvard's high forehead, heavy square jaw, big gray eyes, even the large nose albeit in proportion to the rest of his face. Although similarly straight, the twin's hair was silver to Harvard's brown. He had Bingham's identical heavy eyebrows, yet a bit darker and streaked with white.

In the instant Harvard lifted his eyelids and took in the face above him, the observer's eyes glanced away, and disappeared from view. Head aching, Bingham did not even turn to follow the path of the retreating form.

To the accompaniment of sniffling and a cough, he heard, "Mr. Rushton, I think our patient has revived."

Detective Rodney Rushton hurriedly entered the room, a trail of cigar smoke attempting to keep up. He looked down at his friend lying on his back in bed. "Well, whadda you know? Senator, I think we have missed our calling. Bringing this fellow back from the brink is makin' me think I should uh taken up medicine."

Rodney smiled with joy and relief at the groggy man. He bent and placed his open hand to the side of Bingham's head. "Ya got a knot the size of a golfball on the noggin, but if that's the only souvenir ya get outa the experience, yer damn lucky.

Can ya talk? How d'ya feel just now?"

Like the accompaniment of the house orchestra out of synchronicity with the scenes of a moving picture, Bingham was having trouble absorbing, let alone responding to all that was going on around him.

His last recollection was having emerged from the side door to his residence in the dark, wearing his "suit of armor." There had been a sudden sharp impact to the side of his head. Now he was waking up with this weeping, older version of himself gazing down upon him.

To everyone's relief, Bingham spoke, first quietly and then growing in volume to a normal, conversational tone. "Uuuh. I guess I am verbal." He lifted his head slightly to look down at his torso and limbs, lifted each appendage in turn experimentally, and bent at the elbows, wrists, knees and ankles. Lastly, he turned his head from side to side, catching a brief glimpse of the older him seated upon a wooden chair next to his bed. Satisfied, Bing spoke again, "Everything is attached and reasonably functional. What is going on Rodney? Where am I? Who is our... guest?"

Still standing over his prone patient, Rushton replied, "To make it short, Bingham, someone shot you in the head." The Detective reached in his jacket pocket and opened his clenched palm just to the side of Bing's face so that he could see its contents.

It was a crumpled pellet of grayish metal, about the diameter of a quarter coin and four times as thick.

"This here slid off your armored headpiece when Senator Harding lifted you from your stoop. If I had to guess, I would say it was a 30.06."

Squelching a wave of nausea, Bingham pulled himself to a seated posture, his back against the head board of what he now recognized as his own bed at his residence in Westerville.

"Looks like I made at least one very passionate enemy during my short time here," Bingham said, while absently rubbing the back of his head.

The wooden chair next to his bed creaked in protest as the unknown guest stood next to Rushton at Bing's bedside and spoke, placing a hand on Rodney's shoulder, "Your loyal friend and I had a nice long chat, Mr. Harvard. He knew the few facts you could tell him about this 'mission' before the two of you parted ways. After I interrogated one of my own Secret Service agents at the house, we got the whole story; the KKK, the mafia, the Anti-Saloon League, and then we...that is Detective Rushton and I...agreed that a polite social call to your residence was in order. If my wife and campaign manager knew I had snuck out and where I was headed, they'd be fit to be tied."

"Anyway," Rushton interrupted, "we came here first an' found you sprawled out on your own porch, down f'r the count, sportin' that spiffy football uniform. But f'r that armored head-piece ya had on, I am certain ya would be running f'r touch-downs in Heaven right now."

"How did I get up here?" Bingham inquired, curious how both of them, let alone just one, had transported his roughly two hundred and thirty pounds of body and armor up his steep, narrow staircase.

"Well, aaa...that's a interestin' story Bing...." Rodney stalled.

"I carried you." The stranger said in a matter-of-fact tone.

Bingham noticed that his unknown guest, now standing, was at least six feet tall, probably 200 pounds or more. Even so, few people can lift their own body weight, especially up a flight of stairs. And this man looked to be in his mid-fifties, not in his physical prime.

"Actually, Bing," Rushton chimed in again, "before I could even get outta the car, Senator Harding had ya cradled like a babe in one arm, tore open the door with his free hand, an' *ran* with ya up the stairs. I didn't know whether to be awed at the show uh strength 'r terrified that the two of ya would end up crashing through the staircase with all the weight."

Now Bing was dazed *and* bewildered. The Senator recognized the expression on his face and turned his head to the Detective and whispered quietly, "Give him the whole story,

Rodney. I do not think the shocking nature of it could be any worse than the confusion he's feeling right now."

The older man seated himself again. He leaned forward, placing his elbows on his lap, his open hands on his face.

In his characteristically succinct manner, Detective Rushton shrugged his shoulders, pointed to one man and then the other. "Bingham Harvard, this is Senator Warren Gamaliel Harding, frontrunner f'r the Presidency uh the United States of America an'...your father."

With a look of disbelief, Bingham slowly turned his head to look at each of his house guests. As a final experiment to ensure his lucidity, he methodically clenched one fist and gave a slight rap to the side of his injured head. The sharp flare of pain reminded him that he was indeed in the land of the living.

Filling the awkward void, Rushton added, pointing casually to the Senator, "It took me almost two years, Bing, but it's a lead-pipe cinch. The Senator agrees."

The statesman silently nodded his head in acknowledgement.

Rodney continued, "It was yer fantastic strength that broke the case, Bing. I had resorted to huntin' down an' interviewin' yer mom's college classmates...."

In response to Bingham's raised, single eyebrow, the Detective paused, "Yeah, yer mom. She went to Ohio Central College to be a school teacher. Anyway, there ain't no blood test in existence that could guarantee a match. That's assumin' I could've got anyone to submit to 'em. So I was left with just talkin' to those alumni that would agree to talk to me; hopin' to see some family resemblance, maybe get a tearful admission. Honestly, I didn't know what to expect.

"After gettin' told off more'n twice by folk not appreciatin' bein' accused a fatherin' a child outta wedlock, I tried a different tact. I composed a letter. Got it delivered to the person I wanted to talk to by some neutral, third person. The idea was to give the reader the option uh meeting me at a designated place an' time, or just tossin' it away an' forgettin' about it like they had the past thirty 'r so years.

"I detailed all that I knew about yer mom, her schoolin', her family, yer birth. On a lark, I mentioned the squeezed toy soldier ya mashed as a babe. On the off chance your super strength was inherited, I thought that might spark somethin' f'r the reader. Even sent the toy along with the letter a time 'r two as evidence. That was a dicey prospect—knowin' I might never again see the little soldier, but it worked out.

"Just this mornin' I finally made it to the Senator," Rushton motioned toward the attentive statesman. "Your brother-in-law, Rod'rick, delivered the letter f'r me. I had at least twenty disappointin' dead ends 'r no responses by then, so I didn't hold out much hope. Was I wrong!

"'Fore I got in to my room at the Marion Hotel after eatin' dinner, the Honorable Senator had already talked himself into my suite an' was waitin', letter an' toy soldier in hand. He just said one thing, 'May I meet my son?' Then he grabbed the brass lamp on a table, twisted it into a pretzel without breakin' a sweat, an' sat down.

"I'm not too proud to say, Bing, I nearly upchucked my two dollar steak dinner."

Fearing that perhaps the Detective was straying from the topic, the Senator finally spoke. "Your mother was a lovely, intelligent woman, Mr. Harvard. On my honor, I swear to you that I had not the foggiest idea that I was, or could be a father."

From the corner of his eye, Bingham could see Rushton nodding his head in concurrence.

"Yours was not an immaculate birth...if you follow me...," the Senator hesitated.

Bing understood the elder Senator's discomfort in making explicit reference to his "relations" with his mother. He nodded his head in acknowledgement.

The Senator continued, "...it was simply that in the midst of what we both agreed was a very beautiful relationship, she left... disappeared. I had no idea she was pregnant. I never saw her again. I tried. Her crazy father threatened to shoot me on sight, and only confirmed that she was alive and well...and rid of me."

It was evident by the Senator's listless posture and miserable expression that the thirty years past felt as if it were only a day.

"With the maturity born from aging, I came to understand what happened. Your Detective friend verified it in a meeting with your grandma, Mr. Harvard. Turns out now that the crazy one is six feet under and your granny is in an asylum. Wonders never cease. She had a few keepsakes from her kids, and measured up with the things you gave your Detective friend here, it finished the puzzle that was our mutual history.

"I did not have the emotional fortitude, even at age twenty, to be a responsible adult, let alone a husband or a father. I guess it's clear now that your momma had that epiphany well before me. She never mentioned being with child. Not once.

"I did not know what I wanted to 'be' at that age. Like you, I was born with incredible, physical strength. I fantasized well into my twenties about becoming a super-detective, like Nick Carter from the dime novels."

A big smile appeared on the Senator's face, as he recounted his untamed youth. "I would actually prowl around the town of Iberia in the evenings during my college years. I wore a black domino mask and set out on 'missions to right wrongs.' I caught a fellow slapping a woman once. Stripped him down to his long-johns and hung him high on a flag pole in the public square by the waistline of his skivvies.

"Then once I thought I could help an old woman get her cat out of a tree. The thing was too narrow to climb, so I just grabbed the highest branch I could reach and bent the tree nearly in half to get the cat within my grasp. The rotten feline clawed the hand I was using to hold the tree. I let go in pain, and catapulted the critter over to the next block. As angry as that old woman was at me, I was sure glad to be wearing the mask."

All three men laughed out loud at the story. It was clear that Bingham was fully recovered.

Harding went on, "I discovered too late that short of being the 'strong man' in the freak shows at the carnival, even astounding physical strength could not put bread on the table.

"Plain and simple, your mother was convinced she and her family could care for you better than this man-child." The Senator pointed to himself.

"Surely, Rodney will give you the details later, but suffice to say that Eve...that was your momma's name...may have been right in her assessment of me at the time, but she grossly over-estimated her family's willingness, or ability to take in their unwed, pregnant daughter."

Mistaking the reference to him as a cue to speak, Rushton interrupted, "But you discovered eventually that workin' in a 'freak show' *could* pay the bills. Right...? Politics?'"

The Senator gave a sharp look at the Detective. Clear that he had spoken out of turn, Rushton wasn't certain the glare was for the interruption or the disparaging metaphor. In any case, he refrained from further comment.

Senator Harding continued, "I did eventually mature. I hid my physical abilities with the exception of an occasional parlor trick to liven up a party. I bought a share in a failing news-paper in Marion, married a woman who knew how to run a business and it thrived. And, yes, I did gain public office, even ran for governor of Ohio once, and lost. Ended up a Senator in Washington, D.C. representing Ohio.

"And now, resolved that a career of righting wrongs was just a silly, childish dream, I discover you, Bingham. From what Rushton has told me, and what I squeezed out of that unsus-pecting Secret Service agent detailed to me, you solved the puzzle I abandoned in my youth. You made your money *first*, married and then commenced the Sir Galahad odyssey.

"I do apologize for that bout of weeping you caught me at when you awoke. It was unseemly. It's just that when I looked at you I saw not just a son I didn't know I had, but the embodiment of all of my dreams realized. Seeing you lying there insensible made me feel sad for you and cheated myself for the fact that you might die before we even had a chance to meet."

At a loss for words, Bingham Harvard looked with tear-filled eyes at Senator Harding. His father lowered his head silently.

Bing had dreamed of meeting his biological parents for as long as he could remember. He imagined how they would look, dress, and talk; where they would live and work. In his mind he scripted every word of the warm and loving hours-long conversation that he knew they would have.

But yet he lay here stumped, within arms reach of the man he must call Father. As much of a physical trauma Bingham had suffered from the gunshot to his head, he was experiencing as much emotional trauma.

A raucous *boom* shattered the somber tableau.

Grateful for the distraction, Rushton marched to a bedroom window. He moved a curtain and looked out. "That's the second thunderclap I've heard in less than five minutes an' there ain't a drop uh rain on the ground 'r a cloud in the sky."

Rodney turned to face the inside of the room again. He was surprised to see Bingham launch out of his bed and race to the bureau for his helmet. The sudden movement jolted the Senator from his reverie and he stared with a bemused, tear-stained face at his son's actions.

Bing spoke as he shoved the helmet on his head and began to secure the straps under his chin. He had remained clad in the rest of the outfit. "The Director of Secret Service, Roderick and Kate dropped me off here for the quick errand of retrieving one of my uniforms. You found me just as I was attempting to leave my house to meet them at our agreed rendezvous, Kate's house. Director Drake was entirely convinced that Kate and I had not only made ourselves targets of the mafia and the KKK, but that we had sparked an imminent, all-out war between the two. He ordered us and gave us personal escort to come back to Westerville, grab our essentials and return to Marion for the duration of the presidential campaign."

"I'm havin' trouble connectin' the dots, Bingham. What does that have to do with the cloud bursts we've heard?" Rushton queried.

Bing obliged, "The Service confirmed that thousands upon thousands of Klan were converging on this area as of very early this morning. It is likely Capone and his ilk were the ones responsible for whacking me in the head this evening. That means both groups are precisely in the same place."

To Rushton's continued look of perplexity, Bingham finished in frustration. "Those sounds weren't from weather activity Rodney, those were man-made explosions, and close by too. I would bet the farm that Kate and the Service are right in the middle of it."

Turning to his now composed new-found father, Bingham added, "Sir, I am so glad to have met you and sincerely look forward to the moment when we may continue our conversation, however, you might understand how present circumstances must cut short our reunion."

As he spoke, Bing stepped quickly to his bedroom door. The Senator shot from his chair and blocked his son's path. "So you, alone, are going to fight off thousands of KKK and Mafioso, and rescue your wife and the United States Secret Service?" He asked incredulously.

"Yes." Bing replied simply as he placed his hand on the Senator's forearm to gently nudge him aside.

Catching his hand in his, the Senator spoke, "Let's at least double your odds. Where's that extra suit Rushton told me about?"

Bingham and Rushton gasped in surprised chorus. Rushton spoke first, "Senator Harding I can't help feelin' a little responsible f'r your safety havin' sprung this fatherhood news on ya an' draggin' ya here to Westerville to meet Bing. I just can't let ya do what ya got in mind to do."

A flame of anger flashed in the Senator's eyes as he stood his ground in front of Bing and spoke to them both. "I have suffered the petty dictates of political 'handlers' for my entire career. The publishing business I own and started is very obviously run by my wife, not me, and I have squelched my God-given gift of super strength in pursuit of both of these endeavors. Do not mistake my words as some sort of resolution to abandon politics or my newspaper. But I damn well know an opportunity—albeit a brief one—to flex my physical muscle. And I will not have a private *dick* tell me otherwise."

Embarrassed by his outburst, the Senator tried to tamp down his obvious passion, "Look fellows, just humor my mid-life dilemma. Okay? Inside every older person is a younger person wondering what happened."

"Okay." Both men said in resigned unison.

Bing quickly brushed his face with the sleeve of his uniform to clear his father's spittle and then stepped to his chest of drawers. He lifted the various articles from the drawer and hurriedly tossed them one by one on his bed: the long sleeve, deep gray, scarlet stripped shirt, a gray leather helmet, scarlet 'pants,' and a pair of scarlet gloves each with protruding ridges across the knuckles.

"There is a pair of steel toed boots in the closet—you can kick down a door and not feel it. I know; I've done it." Resolved to Harding's demand, and fast becoming appreciative of the man's insistence, Bingham smiled at the Senator's already beaming face as he finished the presentation of his battle togs.

"My wife, Katherine, commissioned these and had them tailored for my measurements. I think it might be a...tight fit." Bing attempted to avoid making direct reference to Harding's superior "stoutness," since the two men were otherwise identical in height, even shoe size: 14.

"It is true Bingham; I've got you by twenty years and at least twenty pounds," the Senator responded jovially. "I'll be fine." He added, "So your wife makes you suits of armor and my wife handles the press for me. It sounds as if the ladies in our lives have much in common. I cannot wait until they meet."

Uncertain if he heard fear or anticipation in the Senator's voice, Bing did not respond. Instead he ushered Rushton from the room and closed the door so that Harding could dress in privacy.

Just as the Senator began to lace his boots—the final article of the scarlet and gray ensemble—a firestorm of machine gun fire commenced outside.

CHAPTER TWENTY-FIVE
A SHOW OF STRENGTH

"Your wife's house servants need to be replaced...immediately." The Senator quipped.

In his shock, the Night Wind did not hear his newfound father's attempt at levity. At the moment, he tried to comprehend the level of sheer devastation and where amidst the rubble his dear wife's body must lie.

The lower back portion of Lady Kate's residence was blasted away; the upper back section tumbled down to fill the void.

And then there were the bodies; dozens upon dozens of human arms, legs, and some heads poking out of white-and-black-robed forms lying prostrate all over the front parlor floor. At a semi-circle around a bullet-riddled, overturned sofa, the bodies were piled seven deep. Even in the full darkness of night, with what remained of a ceiling blocking the moonlight, the violent death these persons met was evident in the contrast of deep red splotches upon white shrouds.

"This explains all those white masses dotting the field just past Lady Kate's house." Rushton's voice was uncharacteristically hushed as he, too carefully shuffled along the parlor floor looking for signs of Lady Kate while attempting to avoid slipping in puddled blood or stepping on a sprawled cadaver.

The Night Wind hastened his stride to the staircase leading to the second story. He bent and retrieved a large handgun.

"This is Kate's Webley. Only she would have known where to find it in the house, and it is not likely she would have left it behind unless forced to do so."

"Even then, I ain't so sure she'd give it up," Rushton added as he and the Senator carefully stepped over rubble and bodies to get a closer look at Bingham's discovery.

The Night Wind permitted some of the tension in his arms to slacken as this small bit of evidence gave him hope for his wife's survival.

"So she was abducted?" Senator Harding inquired. A distant *toot, toot* of a steam locomotive echoed in the distance.

"That's a fair guess; but where to?" Bing responded.

Rushton chimed in, still in hushed tones, "She didn't do this...not with a Webley." He swept his arms to encompass the carnage. "These Klansmen were taken out with lead shot...20 gauge, at least. The spread uh the impact is huge—a lot bigger than single bullets."

Rushton rolled over a body using his loafer as a wedge and pointed to the robed figure's unblemished back. "An' no exit wound at all."

The Night Wind cracked open his wife's prized weapon, and the extractor emptied the 6-round cylinder into his hand. Making a quick count, he announced, "All six shots are accounted for, and the barrel's cold. No one has shot this revolver recently."

"So we have a lot more questions than answers." Harding said. "All the shooting stopped the moment we stepped outside of your residence, Bingham. The only folks we've seen are dead. We haven't checked that field next door. Maybe we can snag ourselves a live Klansmen—make him talk...even a wounded one would do. Your wife couldn't be too far away."

"He's gotta point Bing," Rushton intoned. "We gotta find us a witness, Klansmen 'r otherwise, 'r we're gonna end up wanderin' around aimlessly while who-knows-what's goin' on with Kate."

"What are we waiting for then? Let's have a look outside." Bing handed the now reloaded revolver to Rushton. "This outfit doesn't have any pockets, Rodney. Put this in your trench coat, will you."

All three men made their way out the trampled front door.

As they began the task of checking for signs of life among dozens of bodies lying about, Rushton attempted conversation to distract himself from the morbid labor.

"R'member reading somewhere ya bein' a member uh the Klan, Senator...not that I believe much I read in the papers, 'specially 'round election time. Yer invitation to this conclave get lost in the mail?"

Also grateful for any distraction, yet keeping his eyes on the work at hand, the Senator responded, "You are a very plain-spoken man, Mr. Rushton. It's good you have no aspirations to politics; your candor would be your downfall. As for your question, I'll answer as bluntly as you have asked: No. I am not, nor have I ever been a member of the KKK. Indeed, you make a good point. Had I any association whatsoever with these hate-mongers, surely I would have been notified of this conclave if not given formal invitation.

"Truth be told, the only 'fiery summons' I've gotten came from the Duchess calling me away from my Saturday evening poker game."

Rushton's toothy smile was evident even in the dark of night. He was finding "the senior Mr. Harvard" to be a fairly affable fellow, if only occasionally victim to bouts of passion.

"Even so," the elder statesman continued, "you may have heard or read about my 'taint' of colored blood? Seems the rumor mill tries to get me one way or another. Fact is, how do I know, Rodney? One of my ancestors may have jumped the fence."

As the older man spoke he placed a booted foot on a prostrate body and shook it. Seeing no sign of life, he picked his way to the next one.

Observing the Senator's technique, Rushton offered a critique. "Senator, sir, I'm no physician, but just 'cause a guy doesn't respond to a shakin' doesn't mean he's croaked."

"Sure enough Detective," Warren responded, "checking for a pulse—even if we find one, will only get us an unconscious witness. What good could he be if he can't talk, or wasn't even lucid during the action?

"Besides, if I have to bend down to check for a pulse one more time in this undersized uniform I'm going to rupture something. *Fitting* into an outfit and being able to *function* in it are two vastly different affairs. Especially when the garment is threaded with strips of nickel plated steel. It's not like I could ever 'break it in.' I should be grateful at least my head didn't get as fat as the rest of me. Otherwise this helmet would be odious too."

The hushed conversation was interrupted first by the distant sound of pressurized steam bursting from a smokestack, followed by a double *toot* of a train's horn.

Then a woman's piercing scream ripped across the battlefield, muting the horn by decibels.

To Rushton's ears, the source of the desperate cry was close. It seemed to come from just past a nearby line of trees, just over an embankment—likely the train rails themselves.

Having been conducting his search for a conscious witness closest to the apparent source of the yell, Bingham led the charge toward the person he knew very certainly to be his wife, Lady Kate.

Albeit somewhat stiff-legged, the Senator, too launched into action like a rodeo bull at the opening gate. Despite the Senator's too-tight uniform, Rushton, running as fast as he could, was left to take up the rear.

The Night Wind stormed into the treeline at the bottom of the embankment. His plan was to steamroll through the underbrush.

He barely noticed the thick vine slung horizontally between a pair of trees just at his chest. The Night Wind was clothes-lined backward, crashing to the ground on his back.

Panting with the effort to catch up with Bingham, the Senator looked down upon his felled offspring. "Now you weren't planning to just race out into the open like some crazed bull, were you?"

Given a moment to restore his wind, Bing might have quickly responded in the affirmative. He wasn't given the time.

"You think those sadistic goons in gowns aren't close enough to spit on? We need a plan, son."

Just then Rushton sprang into the underbrush. The Senator's outstretched arm and open hand were the only thing keeping the Detective from tripping over the prostrate Night Wind.

"Now listen here, men," the Senator spoke hurriedly, "seeing as how the Klan did not fare too well in that field we just skedaddled from, they likely sought refuge out of firing range, just on the opposite side of this embankment. We go hurtling ourselves up there, with the moon and stars to back-light us, the missus Harvard is not going to be any better off." The Senator pointed to the top of the embankment wherein there appeared a struggling silhouette flailing upon the railroad tracks.

"Rodney, do you have some implement to cut stout cord?"

A jack knife shot from the sleeve of Rushton's trenchcoat as if by some unseen ejection mechanism. With reflexes born from much practice, the ex-police detective grasped the deadly utensil as it slid up his open palm, simultaneously depressing a button and springing forth a six inch blade. "Back on the NYC police force I used to have armed back-up. Since then, this here is my new 'partner.'"

Too hurried, and somewhat disturbed by Rodney's acumen with such a crude weapon, the Senator merely pointed to the bound shadow at the top of the embankment and gave terse instruction.

"Keep her between you and the Klan and just cut her bindings—don't pull her free or let her move until it's time."

"And what 'time' is it that I'm waiting for?" Rushton asked.

"Oh, you will know, all right. The important thing is that you not alert the Klan that something is amiss until Bingham and I complete our tasks."

"Aaaaa...okay. Bing, you gonna take this bet?" Rushton asked dubiously.

"Yes, Rodney...I don't yet know my role in this caper, but I'll go with the Senator's plan."

"Well enough," said Harding, "now come along with me." With a grunt of exertion from the constricting jersey, the Senator bent down and grasped his son's extended arm, jerking him vertical, and then nearly on to his face. "Sorry about that. It would seem that the excitement has imbued me with excess adrenaline."

The scarlet-and-gray-clad duo ran off together in the direction of the on-coming locomotive. Rushton watched as the two appeared to exchange brief dialogue and then separate. The Senator lurched up the embankment, dropped fully to the ground as if hugging the inclined earth and then crawled over the closest rail and disappeared from Rushton's view, between the two rails.

The Night Wind ran as fast as Rushton had ever seen him move. He kept to the base of the embankment, well out of sight of anyone on the opposite side. Bing's shadowy form soon disappeared around a gradual curve in the rail line.

Rushton heard the whistle of the locomotive blow again, but could not see it for the curve Bingham had just traversed.

Stumped as to what his friends were up to, Rodney had clear instruction at least on his task. Another shrill scream from Lady Kate sped him to his destination.

"Take a breath, Kate." Rushton whispered as his head came level with hers just over the closest rail. "The cavalry has arrived."

The ex-police detective began to saw at the inch-thick hemp rope pinning the woman under her arms and fixing her shoulder blades to the top of one of the rails.

"Oh...Rodney it's you. Thank you. Oh, please be careful." Kate whispered. "I can barely lift my head to see, but I'm certain the Klan did not wander far from here."

Ignoring Harding's specific instruction, Rushton lifted his head to see the other side of the embankment.

As the Senator had assessed, the surviving Klansmen had constructed a sprawling encampment just at the base of the embankment opposite the battlefield. Dozens of white tents were staked out just at the base of the incline, and continued on twelve deep away from the tracks.

Bobbing his head up like a skittish prairie dog, Rushton didn't have the luxury of time to make a precise head count. However, his guess of "several hundred," as he whispered it to Kate, was a near-enough approximation.

The train came into view clearing the bend in the tracks. Its powerful electric carbon arc light showed first upon the side of the tracks wherein the Klan were encamped, and then began its sweep to the rails and the straightaway ahead. Rushton and Kate would have surely been spotlighted, their attempted escape exposed to watching Klansmen; except that the blazing light suddenly and unaccountably snapped off. Darkened, but still visible for the moonlit night, the locomotive gained speed as it approached its intended victim and rescuer.

Rushton glimpsed the silhouette of three flying, human figures—one carrying the other two under each arm—launch from the engine's cabin through the billowing white smoke. The three forms proceeded to tumble together down the twenty-foot embankment opposite the Klan outpost. Later, the Night Wind would confirm that it was he who had smashed the carbon arc light, and rescued the engineer and fire man from what turned out to be a freight and not a passenger locomotive.

As the last of the bindings fell away, Kate began to lift her shoulders from the rail in anticipation of rising—only to be held fast by Rushton's restraining hand. In a harsh, whispered tone she challenged her would-be rescuer. "What seems to be the problem Rodney!" Kate hissed.

"Look here, Lady Kate, I've got specific instruction to keep ya here until it's 'time,' y'understand?" Rushton had to raise his voice to be heard over the approaching train. "Bingham and his father are up to somethin' and they said they couldn't afford the Klan seein' ya slinkin' away, gettin' suspicious and findin' 'em out."

"Bingham's 'father,' Rodney?" Kate was incredulous.

"Chester has died...."

"...and left a few clues to discover Bing's biological kin, and I found 'em. His dad is Senator Warren Harding and he's what's come up with this caper to rescue ya while not gettin' ourselves strung up by that army of KKK," Rushton finished.

In the light of the reflecting moon Rushton could see the astonished look on Lady Kate's face. He could only suspect at that moment she was struggling with the possibility that her liberator was insane.

Katherine Harvard was experiencing many distressing emotions. Presently, her senses were being bombarded by stimuli, any one of which would have caused a weaker soul to unhinge. The rails at the back of her neck and legs were vibrating like the surface of a church bell rung by an increasingly overenthusiastic alter boy. And then the shuddering stopped.

She turned her head toward the on-rushing freight train and immediately regretted the action. It was less than 200 yards away and from her prone posture appeared more monstrous and colossal. Her observations of trains from any perspective other than as a passenger were limited, but it appeared this locomotive was moving at an unusually accelerated speed.

Desperate to save herself from danger but being prevented from doing so by Rushton's unrelenting weight on her shoulders, Kate snapped.

"Dammit Rodney, if you don't let me up right this instant that cow catcher is going to paste us both along these tracks like warm butter on bread!"

Rushton's face, so close she could feel his breath on her cheek, took on a shocked expression.

"Now you've gone and done it, Kate." Resigned to the fact that he had been spotted, Rushton bobbed his head up over the tracks and took a long look at the opposite side.

Roughly a baker's dozen Klansmen were violently gesturing in the direction of their victim upon the train tracks. Although he couldn't hear a word for the roar of the train, Rushton had little doubt what was transpiring. The platoon of Klansmen were armed and were making quick time up their side of the embankment en masse.

Rushton looked toward the approaching train frantic for some sign that it was time to retreat with Lady Kate. His unspoken prayer was answered.

"By all that's sizzlin' will you look at that!" Rushton yelled to Kate as he moved his head out of her line of sight down the tracks.

Both stared in awe—entirely careless that a dozen armed murderers were just yards away and closing fast.

Outlined by the face of the train engine and its billowing steam, the figure of a man knelt in the center of the tracks. Like a gardener pulling weeds he yanked and tossed away at least six railroad spikes from their mounts. Then he grasped the partially unfettered rail and bent it in half.

The vibrations from the rail at Kate's neck instantly ceased, just as the rail at the back of her knees had gone quiet moments before.

With the ease of a baker molding dough, the figure on the tracks clasped the bent portion of the rail and gave it a twist. Turning to Kate and Rushton, the silhouette raised his arm and in a sweeping gesture, pointed away from the rails.

It was "Time!"

Rushton hooked his hands under Kate's armpits as she lay on her back across the rails. Anticipating an imminent fusillade of gunfire from his front, and the impact of the locomotive bearing down just a few yards to his right, Rushton's only thought was to throw both Kate and himself clear of the tracks and behind the embankment as swiftly as possible.

As Rushton rose, he pulled Mrs. Harvard vertical too, dragging her body up and along the length of his. The few Klansmen who had been alerted to the attempted rescue were just visible a few feet from the tracks. The lead shroud was leveling a mean-looking sidearm, while a second tucked the stock of a rifle to his shoulder.

The hiss, clack and roar of the multi-ton locomotive smothered all other sound. The front tip of the cow catcher was a mere twenty feet from Lady Kate and Rushton.

As Rushton leapt to his feet he used his momentum to launch both of them in a backward, tandem dive.

The air went silent as the locomotive went airborn.

In their plunge from the tracks Kate saw the underside of the train engine just feet from her upturned face; a tangle of jointed coupling and piston rods like the metallic legs of a giant grass-hopper, pneumatic drums, and hollow piping. The crushing wheels spun impotently; free of the friction of the rails.

The freight train turned in a slow barrel-roll. It had not merely fallen, but flew upon the densely populated KKK encampment as it corkscrewed up and off the upturned rail at one side and tipped to the earth on the other.

Rushton crashed to the slanting embankment on his back, using himself as a cushion for Lady Kate's weight. The back of her head collided smartly against his mouth, and he tasted a metallic tang of blood. Other than chaffing from the tightly bound rope, Katherine was unscathed.

Sprinting side by side, Harding and Bingham rushed to the base of the embankment. Bing dropped next to his wife, rapidly patting her about in a frantic search for injury. In an instant he fixed upon her face, anticipating the pallid complexion born from a feint heart under intense stress.

Instead he met a piercing glare from a face rose-red with anger.

"Did you concur with the plan to hold me to the tracks until I nearly died of fear!" Kate screamed.

"Well, dear...I did agree...but...." Bingham stuttered but was interrupted by a swat from his wife's open hand to the side of his head.

"Ouch!" the cry was Kate's, not Bing's, for her palm had collided with the broad, nickel-plated chin-strap of her husband's football cap.

Undaunted, she continued, "You will have me chauffeured for the whole of my life Bingham Harvard! Thanks to your little 'plan,' I will surely faint should I get within a mile of another locomotive."

Deciding that the better part of valor is discretion, Bing remained silent. So too did Rodney Rushton knowing that as the fellow who actually held Lady Kate to the tracks, his assault was imminent.

Bing's newfound father was also wordless; his head held at a tilt, eyes looking off at nothing in particular, he spoke to no one in particular. "Now this is curious. The engine's smokestack was mashed eliminating any venting, and surely the impact ruptured the...."

The ground shuddered and a wash of furnace heat rushed over the embankment.

"...boiler!"

The quartet looked skyward as erupting shrapnel swarmed over their heads shredding the tops of trees unfortunate enough to exceed the height of earthen bank. Amidst the bits of dirt, metal and splintered wood a blazing, hooded torso soared into a scorched pine tree; impaling itself on a shattered branch.

"Now that is just gratuitous!" The Senator moaned. "I think that little encore to our creative use of the locomotive may merely have bought us a few minutes' time. From where I stood upon the rails I could see at least one other significant encampment—a large village of military surplus tents complete with stabled horses. Surely as we speak, swarms of Klansmen are sweeping in our direction. We need to get out of here, quickly."

Sufficiently distracted from her outburst, Mrs. Harvard stood. While brushing grime from her casual gown, she added, "The rest of our group has retreated to the American Issue printing plant. Indeed, I was to be with them, but for my insistence that I find you first, Bing, to share the changed location of our rendezvous."

"Why the printing plant?" Rushton asked.

Lady Kate explained, "It is no secret that the KKK is supportive of national prohibition. I have discovered that an even more violent sect of the Klan, a group called the Black

Legion, is presided over by a very well-thought-of and highly published employee of the American Issue publishing company. She is a true zealot and I am convinced she would sacrifice all—including pursuing us—to avoid causing damage to prohibition's propaganda headquarters."

"To the printing plant then...," Harding announced.

"Wait a second," Rushton interrupted. "Bingham, what became of the train's engineer and fire man?"

"A curious thing, that," Bing answered. "I was certain I'd made life-long enemies for hurtling those two from a moving engine and causing the destruction of their train. Instead, they both took a good long look at my outfit and started chanting 'Go Bucks,' 'Go Bucks.' They added that if I moved like that on the football field 'Ohio'd take the national title for sure this year.'

"Then they each gave my hand a hearty shake and sauntered back along the rails the way their train had come whistling what sounded to me like a college 'fight song.'"

"That is very strange." The detective added.

"Indeed. In any case, they must be well out of harm's way by now."

"...we should be so wise," the Senator interjected and then quickly turned to Lady Kate as the quartet began to move toward the stand of trees that separated the rail embankment from the open, body-strewn field.

"Dear Lady, we have never met, and I regret that we must do so under these circumstances, but I have come to learn that we have a mutual loved-one."

"...Dear sir...Senator...until you spoke, I'd thought my friend, detective Rushton mentally unbalanced. He gave me this joyous news at the same time he announced that I was prohibited from escaping the path of that steam engine. Although I am just now beginning to gather my wits about me, I must say that I am truly pleased to welcome you to the family." Kate and Harding clasped hands as they walked. She continued, "I see that my husband has lost no time establishing a father-son tradition of lending you some portion of his wardrobe?"

"Ah, yes...you refer to the football uniform." The Senator added. "It seems the final straw in detective Rushton's investigation into Mr. Harvard's heritage was our matching...physiology.

"I was merely taking advantage of the fantastic enhancements provided by this wonderful garment as it seemed you could use some assistance this night. You have discovered a truly unique tailor."

"Thank you for noticing. It is true. On another note, I must add that I believe we share a relationship with yet another person dear to us—that is my father, retired Senator Maxwilton, from Kentucky."

"You are the daughter of the Honorable Ernest Maxwilton! Dear me, it is a small world, is it not...?"

Rushton interrupted, "I hate to break up the 'tea party' ladies, but we've been spotted."

Like the horsemen of the apocalypse, four mounted Klansmen cleared the hedgerow. One held the trademark flaming cross.

Just above the heads of the riders, an unbroken phalanx of white robes crested the vacant peak of the train embankment. Several shrouds held aloft flaming torches. The force appeared to be spread hundreds of yards wide and hundreds of persons deep.

The random flash of gun powder lit up patches of the enormous mob, followed shortly by *pops* and *cracks*. The path was entirely clear between the legion of Klan and their four targets. While presently out of range of revolver or shotgun fire, the angry horde was eagerly closing the distance.

Without a word, Bingham and the Senator acted.

Putting himself between the impending swarm and his wife, Bing swept Kate off her feet. One arm at the back of her knees, the other at her back, the Night Wind seemed barely burdened as he doubled his stride and accelerated his speed in a mad dash to the printing plant.

At the same time, Senator Harding grabbed the private detective in an identical hold, although meeting with some resistance.

"This is entirely unmanly!" Rushton protested, "Let me the hell down!"

Tightening his grip, without breaking stride, the Senator retorted, "You are neither fast enough nor bullet-proof my good man—and rest assured, given the choice, I would have preferred the embrace of the lovely Lady Kate to yours."

The fleeing four could not run fast enough as the mounted Klansmen brutally spurred their horses, breaking from the foot-soldiers in an all-out charge.

With a pained grunt, the Senator sprawled to the earth, mashing his burden beneath him. One of the horsemen had scored a lucky pistol shot. The bullet could not penetrate the suit of armor; but was enough to throw the older man off his feet.

Just thirty feet from the entrance to the printing plant, capture was imminent.

The Night Wind dug in his booted feet to break his momentum and attempt rescue of his father and friend.

Peeking over her husband's shoulder toward the charging horsemen, Kate was the first to observe a dramatic reversal of fortune.

First one, and then a second of the four Klansmen jerked backward off of their mounts. Each spasmodic lurch was precipitated by a gruesome spray of blood from their upper bodies.

The two remaining cavalry did not appear armed—or at least had not drawn their weapons for their burdens of flaming cross and confederate flag. The two survivors desperately pulled on the reins of their chargers, broke in opposite directions and attempted to flee. Before they had fully turned, the cross-bearer was swatted from his saddle, dead before he hit the earth.

Unfazed, or entirely ignorant of the fate of their cavalry, the legion of Klansmen on foot continued their charge toward the plant.

Before Bingham, with Kate in his arms, could reach the Senator and Rushton, two figures had charged out of the printing plant and dashed to their sides. By the flickering light of the burning cross on the ground, Katherine could identify her brother, Roderick Maxwilton and Dan Drake, Director of the Secret Service.

As the burdened Night Wind kept pace nearby, the two men from the plant quickly helped the Senator and detective to their feet and pulled them toward the sanctuary of the plant's single door. The Director shouted to Bingham and Kate over his shoulder, "We thought we'd lost you Mrs. Harvard, and were just about to search your wrecked home when we heard a horrible crash, then an explosion and saw the four of you appear out of nowhere."

As the Director spoke, the Night Wind cleared the building's threshold and the chief slammed the door shut behind him. All were now relatively safe inside the American Issue printing plant.

The Secret Service Director continued, "Under protest, we sent off Julius and Mr. Hanshaw with two of the local constabulary as escort to a hospital for their wounds. It's just Roderick, me and the Westerville Chief of Police holding up in the plant. It was the chief who snipered those Klansmen off their horses."

With a loud sigh of relief, the Senator unfastened his football helmet at his chin, exposed his crop of silvered hair and commenced an attempt to restore some order to his person.

Until that moment, the Director of the Secret Service had no idea of the identity of this second Night Wind. At the sight of the Senator, Drake let out a fearsome string of expletives so intense as to put a blush to the cheeks of longshoremen or construction workers.

"...that is just bully! Now we have the presidential nominee taking bullets and under siege by an army of enraged KKK. Is it even possible to make this mission more of a farce?!"

CHAPTER TWENTY-SIX
THE ENEMY OF MY ENEMY...

Katherine Harvard was having doubts about her theory on the sanctuary of the American Issue printing plant.

Bricks, torn from the cobbled streets, erupted two and three at a time through the multi-paned windows at all four sides of the building. High-caliber bullets and swarms of shotgun pellets *pinged* and *cracked* from every surface: interior brick walls, presses, and light fixtures. The latter were exploding like fireworks. Jagged shards of glass and shattered bits of tin light covers showered upon the seven huddled human forms at the floor.

Rodney Rushton put to words everyone's unexpressed doubts, "That Black Legion harpie either ain't callin' the shots or she's changed her priorities about preservin' the source of prohibition's propaganda."

As if to reinforce the statement, the main entrance door caved in with a crack of fractured wood.

Kate, now reunited with her beloved Webley, and Jon, the Westerville Chief of police, had previously positioned themselves behind two presses just a few feet away from either side of the main entrance.

By means of sturdy hemp rope and a dislodged railroad tie, the Klan had constructed a makeshift battering ram. For the last five minutes they had pummeled the sturdy oak door.

White-clad Klansmen stormed through the entryway two at a time even before the dust had settled.

Two at a time, they died upon that same threshold as Lady Kate and Jon, with his Springfield Model 1917 service rifle, took deliberate aim, needing no more than one bullet for each hapless intruder.

Seeing their comrades drop at the door and piled three deep in seconds, the rest of the raiding party were forced to take pause outside to reconsider their strategy.

The defenders used that brief respite to reinforce their bulwark. By use of their superhuman strength, the Night Wind and Senator Harding each took hold of printing machinery ten times their weight and shoved them into the opened doorway.

Meanwhile, Roderick and Drake were going through the final checklist to set up the Browning Model 1917 machine gun. In response to Roderick's final "check," Drake gave the thumbs-up sign and jammed the written instructions into his jacket pocket. This cursory instruction manual was the last gesture of police officer Joe Hanshaw as he reluctantly handed over his "Great War" service weapon in favor of transporting his father and Julius to the hospital.

Just as the onslaught resumed with another volley of bricks, a piercing voice, aided by a bullhorn, brought the siege to a halt:

"Stop this vandalism immediately or suffer the consequences!

"This building is the voice of national prohibition! We cannot be fool enough to silence this sacred social accomplishment just to rid ourselves of the cancers within!"

Eunice Parker stood atop the hood of a Model-T, head to toe in her Black Legion regalia, now somewhat wrinkled and disheveled from the events of the last couple of hours. Lifting her hood just enough to place the megaphone to her mouth, she hardly noticed the thick patch of dark blood smearing the instrument at its widest expanse; a gruesome memento from its prior owner, the Grand Dragon.

It had taken Eunice just a few minutes to assert herself as the new Grand Dragon, pro-tem. The elected Grand Dragon and his two immediate lieutenants had perished within seconds of one another at the podium during the Klan's attempted lynching of Julius and Fred. Their bodies had been shamefully abandoned in the resulting mob panic.

Never before had there been a necessity to consider the line of succession beyond the Grand Dragon. However, as Eunice was quick to remind challengers, the KKK Charter and By-Laws had in fact provided for the succession of the Grand Wraith—the leader of the Black Legion—under these circumstances.

Mrs. Parker had no need to fear any challenge to her claim of authority. Surviving officers secretly breathed a sigh of relief that the Charter and By-Laws had provided them a dignified excuse to avoid the possibility of being a sniper's target.

Fanatical but not incautious, Eunice was careful to keep the massive trunk of an enormous maple tree between her and any possible line of fire from the printing plant.

Her first command as the new Grand Dragon was to hurl a volley of smoke bombs through the plant's saw-toothed, windowed roof. In theory, assured that the building was entirely fire-proofed, smoking-out unwanted occupants was not a bad strategy. Unfortunately, Eunice had not surveyed the extent of the damage done to the structure immediately prior to her command.

Not one pane of glass of the many hundreds remained intact by the time the Klan had retreated from its initial assault. Bricks, bullets and buckshot had left the printing plant entirely window-less at the four sides.

Nearly a dozen arcing trails of smoke made hissing tracks through the night sky from all angles around and above the printing plant. The muted sound of tinkling glass was evidence that at least some of the projectiles had crashed through the ceiling and entered the plant interior.

Those that had been off target spewed their smoke from the roof, which in turn wafted down the sides of the exterior walls and upon the Klansmen themselves. Additionally, because the printing plant was little more than a brick shell stripped of windows, much of the smoke produced from those few bombs that landed inside blew back out.

In the end, the besieged occupants of the building fared no worse than their attackers.

Just outside the growing cloud of smoke, a convoy of six automobiles—two Model 38 Pierce-Arrows and a foursome of black Model-Ts—raced north on 3-C Highway and came to a tire-peeling halt at the curb just in front of the printing plant.

Klansmen within the smoke cloud could make out little more than the fuzzy silhouettes of multiple vehicles and the repetitive sound of slamming car doors.

Without an ultimatum or even a warning, there suddenly ensued a hail of gunfire emitted from the newly arriving cars into the hordes of KKK surrounding the printing plant.

Confused and terrified Klansmen hopelessly scrambled for shelter, but there was none to be found. White shrouded men flopped to the ground six to twelve at a time. Those who had made it around the sides of the plant and to the back were met by further storms of lead from gunmen who had left the main firing squad and surrounded the building.

Inside the plant, the formerly besieged were likewise confused. Ignorant of the newly arrived automobiles outside, it appeared to them that, contrary to the Grand Dragon's instruction, the Klan had resumed their barrage of gunfire upon them while attempting to infiltrate the plant. Ku Klux Klan frenziedly fleeing the gunfire outside threw themselves into the plant through the vacant windows. Mistaking their actions as a suicidal tactic to exhaust the defender's ammunition, the seven adults inside the plant were willing to oblige.

Retreating to the relative safety of the windowless power plant, the defenders prepared for what they feared was their last stand. Jon and Rushton crouched at either side of the doorway. Kate and Drake stood alongside them. Together, with their revolvers and rifles, they had a panoramic view of all possible entryways to the plant's interior—even through the heavy smoke and darkness.

At the start of this apparent second wave of the siege,

Roderick had immediately taken a bullet. Harvard and Harding tended to his wound at the very back of the power plant, away from the smoke and gunfire.

"This just isn't right," the Director shouted over the chattering gunfire.

"Mr. Drake, are you having a moral dilemma on the taking of human life?" Kate responded sarcastically.

"Hardly, Mrs. Harvard. If this isn't Darwin's 'natural selection' in action, I do not understand the term." As he spoke, the Director plugged a Klansmen off a window ledge.

"It's that gunfire," he continued, "I vaguely remember a demonstration at Camp Perry by Brigadier General Thompson just weeks ago. I was there representing the Service, but the Treasury and the City of New York Police Department had folks there too. The General was showing off a hand held machine gun...not like that monstrous Browning we have. It was a relatively little thing; no stock, no sights, and a big circular magazine that held at least one hundred rounds. Its purpose was to 'sweep' enemy trenches in the War, but he was putting it to mass production for civilian public safety."

As the Director spoke, Jon took two more shots into the smoky plant floor, dropping two more Klansmen upon a window ledge.

"The arrogant son of a gun named it the 'Thompson Submachine Gun.' He got indignant when one of the NYC flatfoots dubbed it the 'Tommy Gun.'"

Rushton fired his .38, missing his target by a country mile. Kate followed up with a lethal shot before the shroud could find cover behind a press.

Frustrated, the private detective vented on the Director, "So does your little trip down memory lane have some point?!"

"Don't lose your temper at me, Mr. Rushton just because you can't hit the broad side of barn. And, yes, there is a point. Those guns outside sound just like Tommy guns...a lot of Tommy guns. But that can't be right because there couldn't be more than 40 units available. The Service's order hasn't even been filled.

"Also, whoever is firing those weapons isn't trying to get us."

"How do you figure that, Director?" Jon demanded.

"The first assault sent bullets rebounding all over the place in here. Except for that stray shot that hit Roderick, there haven't been more than two or three ricochets this time around. Unless of course the shooters have Rushton's sense of aim, it just doesn't make sense that so few bullets are making it inside, let alone near to us."

Less interested in contemplating some explanation to Drake's observations than defending his marksmanship, Rushton opened his mouth to return the Secret Service Director's insult.

He didn't get a chance to speak.

The sound of a revving, approaching engine, followed instantly by the reverberation of rending metal upon unyielding brick echoed within the printing plant.

As the smoke began to thin inside, Kate and Rushton could see the source of the crash.

A Model-T had been driven straight into the plant's brick wall, just at a four-foot-high brick window ledge facing the power plant's interior doorway. Neither driver nor passengers could be seen for the smoke. Either in desperation to flush out the seven occupants of the plant, or panicked for the apparent firestorm outside, the Klan had added yet another article to the list of property damage caused by their activities this night.

Fearlessly, Bingham and Harding raced from the shelter of the power plant toward the accordioned car, prepared to diffuse this assault and to fend-off any future attempts at using automobiles as battering rams.

The Model-T's engine roared and choked out black exhaust despite the immovable brick bulwark.

The ceaseless *ratta-tat-tat* of the machine guns came to an abrupt halt.

Thinking only of backing up her husband's charge and careless of her own exposure, Lady Kate bolted from the shelter at the power plant doorway. Webley drawn and aiming at the wreaked car, Kate focused all of her attention on the possibility of disembarking Klansmen, ignoring for the moment all other possible means of ingress to the plant.

She watched closely as Harding and the Night Wind hurtled over the window ledge at either side of the Model-T.

"The car is empty," the Night Wind said as he yanked the key from the ignition.

In a louder voice, the Senator announced, "Someone just jammed a piece of a two by four between the steering column and the gas pedal. We've been had..."

"Well said."

The voice came from Lady Kate's back. She felt the warm pressure of the snout of a gun barrel at the back of her neck.

Too startled to turn her head to glimpse her persecutor, Kate sensed the presence of Eunice Parker.

"No matter the fate of my brethren, or myself, you will die here and now, Katherine Harvard. I do not know how you managed to survive the locomotive and cause this carnage but you have dodged your destiny with hell for the last time. You will not take the presses of prohibition with you!"

"Put a sock in it, you pyro teetotaler!" An entirely new voice interrupted the scene, this one marked by a Brooklyn accent.

"I don't give a rat's ass if you blast the broad—*you* are gettin' your ticket punched in any case. And after I'm done here, I gotta make a visit to Atlantic City 'cause my luck is hot. Me and the boys came here expectin' some clue to run you down and ya' done us the favor of sendin' up smoke signals and a chorus a' gun-fire. Hell! We could a' found ya' even if we'd been blind-folded an' hog-tied!"

Harding and the Night Wind stood helpless—gazing from the outside through the vacant window at the double draw. Two Tommy gun toting gangsters had gotten the drop on them.

Bing immediately recognized his wife's assailant, although not her proper name. The black gown, even bereft of pointed hood gave the woman away as a member of the Black Legion.

He had no clue of the identity of the cherub-faced, dapperly-dressed man whose formidable handgun was drawn to the head of the same Black Legionnaire who held his wife at gunpoint.

That mystery was solved momentarily as the voice of the Secret Service Director burst forth.

"Drop it, Capone!" Came the Director's almost gleeful order, "and tell your thugs to toss the Tommy guns too! And be sure to slide one of them my direction—I've wanted one of my own for some time now."

If it weren't for his wife's imminent peril, the Night Wind would have laughed at the absurd tableau that presented itself before him.

Lady Kate was frozen at gunpoint by a female Black Legion member, who was herself held at point-blank range by "Capone"...who stood at the receiving end of a gun barrel held by the Director of Secret Service.

"Not that I am complaining, Alphonsus, but this is not your modus operandi at all." Drake chortled.

The crime boss noticeably cringed at the familiar use of his first name.

The Director continued, enjoying his bully pulpit, "A typical Capone murder is made up of men renting a place across the street from the victim's residence and gunning him down when he steps outside. It's quick, complete and you always have an alibi."

The similarity between the Director's description and his own, recent experience with a sharpshooter at his doorstep was not lost on the Night Wind.

"So what gives this time, huh, Alphonsus?" Drake went on, "You are drawing your very own weapon on a woman, not just in public view, but right in front of the Director of the United States Secret Service?!! You're losing your touch...and so early in your violent career too. What a pity."

Perspiration was rapidly beading on the crime boss's pronounced forehead. He had wisely familiarized himself with the various heads of national law enforcement. In his line of business such foresight was an occupational requirement. He knew almost as much about Daniel Drake as the Director knew of him. However, he had absolutely no idea that the head of the Secret Service had taken a personal interest in his vendetta against the KKK, let alone that he was present at this siege.

Capone had to think, fast.

"It would seem to me, Mr. Director, that I am defending the life of this here young lady," Capone announced, twitching his drawn weapon toward Kate Harvard. "You can see the get-up of the dame who got the drop on her as well as me. This here is a Black Legion member; a known instigator and mastermind behind a score of arsons, murders and tortures...some of which only coincidently happen to have been perpetrated against persons of my acquaintance.

"If I lower this gun of mine the lady here is sure to meet her maker.

"So you choose, G-Man! You can take down a guy whom by your own admission you ain't got nothin' on, thereby causin' the death of an innocent woman. Or you can let me do my civic duty saving the woman's life and ending the scourge of the Black Legion!!"

It was the Director's turn to sweat.

Drake quickly glanced at his injured agent, Roderick Maxwilton, as he leaned against the power plant doorway nursing a bloodied arm. The agent quietly whispered to his boss, "Truth be told, Director, at this stage that Black Legion person has a rap sheet as long as my leg. We haven't pinned a thing on Capone...yet."

"Hell's bells!" the Director grumbled, "Mrs. Harvard?" he shouted, "This wouldn't happen to be your bosom buddy Eunice Parker, now would it?"

"The very one, sir." Katherine stuttered, as Eunice drew back the hammer of her gun with an audible *click*.

The Night Wind could no longer restrain his urge to speak. "Director, in this instance, 'the enemy of our enemy is our friend.' Drop your weapon and spare my wife...please."

Teeth gritted so tight his jaw would surely snap, the Director made a fateful decision.

He lowered his pistol and released his grip, letting it drop with a *thud* to the hard floor. As he did so he nodded to the chief as a signal to do the same.

Unbeknownst to all, Jon had remained in his prone position on the floor, rifle pinpointed on the forehead of the crime boss. He understood the cue, and lifted his head.

The Director spoke quietly to Rodney Rushton, poised just to his left, revolver likewise leveled on Capone. "Let it go Rushton. You wouldn't have hit him anyway."

The private detective audibly hissed, and glared at the Director. Drake was unmoved.

Breaking eye contact with Eunice just long enough to observe the various men disarm themselves, a terrible grin spread across Capone's face. He returned his gaze to his target.

All present flinched at the sound of a gunshot, Eunice Parker particularly so.

The black-gowned woman flew off her feet, bouncing off the broadside of a press and rolled to the floor, face up, eyes closed.

"You don't deserve to die so fast you lunatic bird!" the mobster shouted as he strode toward the downed woman.

Kate's knees collapsed under her weight as she finally turned to face her intended assassin for the first time. She knelt on the floor, leaning heavily for support on the press to her right. She still clutched her Webley in a white knuckle grasp.

The crime boss stepped between her and the sprawled body, also kneeling to inspect his handiwork.

Bingham and the Senator remained at the point of submachine guns. Drake, Roderick, Jon and Rushton, all stepped forward to pull Lady Kate from the fray.

They had barely moved before an ear piercing scream exploded from Eunice's mouth, momentarily paralyzing all in mid-stride.

Rising from her seeming death sprawl, whipping her arms up, she snared Capone's head in both of her hands.

Before he could inhale in shock, the frantic woman had gouged a vertical trench down the side of the crime boss's face with her bare hand. Her other hand had taken hold of the back of his head in a vice grip so that the taloned fingers of her free hand could do their bloody work.

Yet another explosion burst forth, silencing the screams of both Eunice and the agonized Capone.

The Grand Wraith's body slammed to the floor again. Faint wisps of smoke rose from an hole at her chest. The gaping exit wound at her back unleashed a surge of blood that instantly haloed her torso upon the floor.

Distracted from his torn face by the discharging weapon fired so near his head, Capone turned and looked through his own bloody fingers to see Lady Kate collapse onto the floor; a smoking Webley in her hand.

Grunts of pain and cursing broke the momentary silence. Harding and the Night Wind had each seized their assailants in the instant they had been distracted by their boss' struggle. The Senator kicked his opponent into the jury-rigged Model-T and held him there with his booted foot. In the blink of an eye, Harding had lifted the Tommy gun from the floor, slid either half above and below the mobster's arms and twisted the two ends of the machine gun together, tightly encircling the gunman's arms above the elbows.

In the meantime, the Night Wind had pushed his foe face down on the asphalt, and stomped the Tommy gun to pieces. Thereupon he hefted his helpless charge to his feet and commenced a thorough frisk. Every out-of-place bulge was ripped away from the man's body by main strength—weapon, holster, concealing clothing and the occasional patch of skin. In seconds, the mobster was slumped on the ground, his snapped chest holster binding his hands.

"Gentlemen!" the Director shouted as he walked to the blown-out window and observed the restrained henchmen, "Why did you have to go and spoil those perfectly good Tommy guns!?"

"Don't fret too much, Director. You'll get yours."

Drake spun on his heels as Capone approached. His white dress shirt was streaked with his own blood, his right hand, likewise bloodied, clutched the ruined right side of his face.

"That wasn't a threat," the mob boss continued through teeth clenched in agony, "Consider it a token of my appreciation for deep-sixing that wench."

Taken aback at the mobster's temerity, Drake responded, "What makes you think you are going to walk out of here, Capone, let alone with any hardware?"

"You G-Men are a laugh riot, really." Capone answered. "What makes me think I'm gonna walk?!

"For starters, I didn't entrust my safety to just two palookas with Tommy guns...I had ten of 'im. The other eight are gonna get a little antsy if'n I don't show up at our cars at the curb soon...not that I'm threatin' you or nothin'.'"

"I would have never thought such a thing." The Director retorted.

Ignoring the crack, Capone continued, "Second, ain't no reason I can't 'walk,' bein' an honest, up-standin' citizen what hasn't done nothin' but stumble into this mob scene.

"I just saved a woman's life by plugging her intended murderer and a known fugitive of the law. Besides, I think we can all agree it wasn't me what gave the killin' shot in any case.

"Finally," the mobster paused to spit blood on the floor, "For some assurances from you, I may refrain from announcing to the press that the Republican nominee for President of the United States fancies himself a football player with a penchant for running around in the wee hours of the night twistin' up machine guns like they was licorice."

With a smile, the mobster pointed to the red-faced Senator sporting a sheepish grin.

"Not that I vote or anythin'. Personally I think all politicians are crooks," Capone finished.

"This just keeps getting better and better." The Director said, more to himself than anyone else.

Feigning a cough, Harding looked sharply at the Secret Service Director and raised a single eyebrow.

The signal was clear. "Fine, Alphonsus, what 'assurances' are we talking about exactly?" The Director grumbled.

"Well, off the bat, quit callin' me Alphonsus! Capone yelled. "More to the point, I want your word that you won't come after me; ever. Rest assured, I'll stay the hell out of Ohio, even D.C. and New York; just leave me be. I got honest businesses and all I want is to run'im."

Bug-eyed and slack-jawed, the Director was quickly flipping through his mental dictionary to find just the right words to tell the mobster to go to hell.

Before he could speak, the Senator gave another 'cough.'

Dan Drake shook his head in frustration, looked the mobster in the eye and said exactly what he was supposed to say, "Fine, you have a deal...you fat-headed little troll!"

Cringing from the insult as much from his tortured face, Capone glared back at the Director. "I'll take that as a 'yes.'"

"Victor?" the mobster yelled through the vacant plant window.

"Yeah, boss?" A well-dressed man strode through the clearing smoke toward the gathering at the plant window. He cradled a Tommy gun in his arms.

"Hand over the submachine gun, Victor," the mob boss instructed as the gunman stopped and stood near his employer.

The Tommy gun was handed from the thug's hands to Capone's to the Director's.

"This seals the deal, agreed?" The mobster said to the Director.

With pleading eyes, Drake gave one last look at the Senator. His response was a brief nod of the head, a stern facial expression and another raised eyebrow.

"Agreed." The Director nearly whispered.

"Well then, the sun sets even in paradise," the mobster announced with a sigh. He turned to look at Harding. "Senator, if you wouldn't mind too terribly, I can't begin to guess how we would get that gun off of around Phil's arms?"

As if he was unfolding a table napkin, the Senator parted the twisted machine gun and let it drop to the ground with a clatter. He didn't say a word.

Turning to slowly survey the entire scene of battle with his free eye, Al Capone gave a grunt, and a quick smirk. He awkwardly straddled the window ledge to the outside and walked away with his henchmen in tow.

Just as the sounds of the mob boss's convoy were fading in the distance, the wail of sirens and rumble of dozens of police cruisers approached. En masse, the public service department of nearby Columbus had answered the many fevered calls for help from Westerville residents thinking their town was being invaded.

The Night Wind leapt through the low window into the plant floor and attended to his wife. Trembling but conscious, Lady Kate was enfolded in her husband's loving arms and lifted like a babe from the floor.

"We need to get ourselves, and the Senator out of sight, Director," The Night Wind announced.

"Absolutely," Drake responded, "Roderick, the chief, Rushton and I will stay put and see that...a...story is told."

With a smile and a casual military salute, the Senator turned from the shambles of the printing plant and its occupants and followed his son and daughter-in-law away from the scene.

The first rays of morning sunlight reflected off of the bits of shattered window glass, giving the setting of such tension and horror an ironic, glittering glow.

As they quickly trotted toward Bing's residence, Harding turned to speak to his son, "Mr. Rushton tells me that your first career was as a banker." Giving his and Bing's uniforms a quick once-over, the Senator continued, "This must be quite a change for you...that is, bean-counter to Galahad? After what we just experienced, are you having any regrets?"

"No sir. I'm just getting started."

CHAPTER TWENTY-SEVEN
AFTERWARD

Referred to by the locals as the "War in Westerville," the dramatic events as related here were never reported to the general public. Had one taken to piecing together the sum total of published obituaries and inexplicable hospitalizations of out-of-towners, the loss of life amounted to 446.

Notwithstanding, within a generation or two the entire story faded from collective memory. Both nominees for President of the United States in 1920 were publishers of prominent newspapers in the state of Ohio. Governor James M. Cox was the publisher for the *Dayton Daily News*. Senator Warren G. Harding was owner and publisher of the *Marion Star*. Governor Cox feared that such violence and social strife in the State he governed would reflect poorly upon his skills as a leader. In the end, the story was buried in both his and all Democratic Party controlled newspapers.

The Republican Party saw no benefit in exposing these events for fear of disclosure of their candidate's involvement. Consequently, Harding's *Marion Star* newspaper, in league with all other party controlled presses, remained silent.

Warren G. Harding won the 1920 Presidential election by a landslide and became the twenty-ninth President of the United States. During the several months between the election and his oath of office, the President-elect vacationed in Texas and Panamá with his wife, a Mr. and Mrs. Bingham Harvard, and Julius.

Late in 1933, the Eighteenth Amendment to the United States Constitution—familiarly called Prohibition—was repealed. Westerville, Ohio remained "The Dry Capitol of the World" until 2006. In that year, residents voted in favor of letting commercial establishments serve alcohol.

On December 5, 1920, the silent motion picture, *The Mark of Zorro*, was released nationwide. The film starred Douglas Fairbanks and featured twelve-year-old Elmer Pfleager in an uncredited role as a 'Boy' befriending the swashbuckling hero in a time of need.

Alphonsus Capone kept his promise to cease all business in the state of Ohio and retreated to Chicago, Illinois. The facial scars given him by Eunice Parker earned him the moniker "Scarface." He went on to become America's most notorious gangster and the single greatest symbol of the collapse of law and order in the United States during the 1920s Prohibition era.

On the recommendation of a grateful President, all three members of the Westerville Police Department were appointed by Congress to become United States Marshals for the State of Ohio. Within one year of the appointment, there began a string of unsolved assassinations of any Ku Klux Klan member wearing any symbol of rank or leadership. Membership plummeted and conclaves were no longer held within the borders of the State. Recruitment and membership of Ohioans all but disappeared. Also, for lack of leadership or organization, the Black Legion relocated entirely to Michigan.

True to the letter of his promise, Daniel Drake personally never pursued Al Capone. Instead, he actively recruited a young investigator for the Retail Credit Co., Eliot P. Ness. On the recommendation of the Director of the Secret Service, Ness was hired by the Treasury Department, Bureau of Prohibition, and quickly seized Capone's breweries worth millions of dollars, and disrupted his bootlegging supply routes.

The Ohio State Buckeyes football team was undefeated during regular season play in the fall of 1920 and went on to compete in the Rose Bowl, the equivalent of the collegiate national championship, for the first time in the team's history. At every game, the Buckeyes were cheered on by an unusually enthusiastic contingency of Westerville residents and railroad employees.

Quickly recovering from his injuries and with a monetary gift of gratitude from the Harvards, Fred Hanshaw and his wife opened and operated a bait and gun shop off the banks of Alum Creek. In the back of the store, off limits to customers, Fred kept busy in a workshop designing and building contraptions to Lady Kate's specifications.

ABOUT THE AUTHOR

Christopher Robert Yates holds a B.A. in English Literature and a Juris Doctorate. Chris has several identities, none of them secret however: Nancy's Husband, Ben & Audrey's Dad, and Assistant United States Attorney.

In 2001 he authored *The Web* for a reprint of the *Master of the Flaming Horde*, the fiftieth installment of *The Spider Magazine* originally published in 1937 (Bold Venture Press, 2001). He was a fan of hero pulps years before, but actually seeing his name in print snapped Chris' tenuous link to reality, propelling him into the ranks of "disturbingly obsessive fans of hero pulps."

He is the editor of all four re-releases of the original novels of the Night Wind series: *Alias "The Night Wind," The Return of the Night Wind, The Night Wind's Promise*, and *The Lady of the Night Wind* (Wildside Press, 2007, 2008). He contributed the Foreword to *Alias "The Night Wind,"* and *The Night Wind's Promise*.

Behold "The Night Wind" is his first novel.

ABOUT THE ARTIST

Mark Maddox was born in Panama City, Florida in 1961. The child of a military family, he spent his early years in Germany, South Dakota, Maryland, and North Carolina.

Mark began drawing at an early age, inspired by artists like Jack Kirby, James Bama and many others. He felt he could not get enough of the art he admired so he created his own to fill the gap.

As a child he knew he would be an artist in his professional career. His family moved to Tallahassee, Florida in 1975 and upon graduating high school, he received education in commercial art from Lively Vocational Technical Center and fine art from Florida State University.

Highlights of Mark's recent illustration work include the covers for the books *Captain Hazzard: Curse of the Red Maggot* (Wild Cat Books, Feb. 2007), *Thrilling Tales*, Winter 2008, Issue One (Adamant Entertainment, Feb. 2008), *Captain Hazzard: Cavemen of New York* (Cornerstone Book Publishers, June 2008), *Black Bat Mystery* (Cornerstone Book Publishers, June 2010) and, *Crossovers: A Secret Chronology of the World*, Volumes 1 & 2 (Black Coat Press, Apr. & June 2010).

In 2010 he was the recipient of the first annual *Pulp Factory Award* for best cover art for *Sherlock Holmes—Consulting Detective* Vol. One (Cornerstone Book Publishers, June 2009).

Mark's desire is to create the most memorable illustrations possible and he approaches every project with that goal in mind. He now resides in Athens, Georgia with his lovely wife, Carlyn, and two beautiful children. Discover more about Mark Maddox and his artwork at

MaddoxPlanet.com.

www.ingramcontent.com/pod-product-compliance
Lightning Source LLC
Chambersburg PA
CBHW050359260626
47156CB00003B/800

* 9 781479 400270 *